"KINDRED MUST NOT FIGHT KINDRED!

"That is the law," Milo the Undying High Lord of the Horseclan said. "If Skaht kills Linsee, or Linsee, Skaht, both your clans will be driven forth, without weapons, food, horses, or prairie-cats, your names will be stricken from all Kindred records, and every warrior of the Horseclans shall become your blood enemy.

"If you do not believe my words, then you must look to the dark times, many years past, and learn for yourselves the truth of what I say. Would you see for yourselves? Then come . . ."

HORSES OF THE NORTH

HORSECLANS #13

ROBERT ADAMS

HORSES OF THE NORTH

A SIGNET BOOK

NEW AMERICAN LIBRARY

SIGNET TRADEMARK REG. U.S.PAT. OFF. AND FOREIGN COUNTRIES
REGISTERED TRADEMARK—MARCA REGISTRADA
HECHO EN CHICAGO, U.S.A.

SIGNET, SIGNET CLASSIC, MENTOR, PLUME, MERIDIAN AND NAL BOOKS
are published by New American Library,
1633 Broadway, New York, New York 10019

First Printing, June, 1985

1 2 3 4 5 6 7 8 9

PRINTED IN THE UNITED STATES OF AMERICA

For José E. Seco, M.D., gentleman-cardiologist and friend;

For Pam, who is well-come and most welcome;

For Keesh, Candy, Achmed, Pinktoes, Melanie and Tortie;

For all of the fan-friends and the fellow writers who wrote and phoned to wish me well;

For my mother, who celebrated her eightieth birthday this year;

For all the fine folk who presented CoastCon, Tally-Con and OrCon;

For Harriet McDougal, Jim and the ChattaCon Streaker;

And for Little Mother II, the pregnant hobbit.

Prologue

The prairies and high plains, huge and vast and always awe-inspiring they lie. To the untrained or inexperienced eye, they seem mostly empty, devoid of the life with which they really, truly teem. The grasses—grama grass, blue grama grass, side oats grass, screw grass, tickle grass, buffalo grass and hundreds of other grasses—seem to roll like the waves of some endless sea with the gusts of the untrammeled, ever-blowing winds. These hardy, long-acclimated wild grasses quickly choke out tender grasses loved by man as well as the frail, alien grain crops he was wont to cultivate when still his kind ruled this land.

Moving slowly across these grasslands, following water, graze and the dictates of the changing seasons, as did the bison before them, roam scattered herds of wild cattle. Each succeeding generation of these descendants of feral beef and milch stock is become longer of leg and horns, less bulky and more muscular. In a few areas, they have interbred with surviving bison. Privation has rendered both strains rangy and more hirsute than their domesticated ancestors, while constant predation has favored the survival and breeding of the quicker-tempered, incipiently deadly bovines.

Foremost among the predators preying upon these

7

herds—as well as upon the herds of wild sheep on the high plains—are the packs of wild dogs that are metamorphosing into wolves a little more with each new litter of pups, being shaped by the demands of survival in a savage, merciless environment. Already become big, strong, fleet of foot and as adept at killing as any pureblood lupine, these packs follow the herds of wild cattle and bison hybrids in the long migrations from north to south, just as the long-extinct prairie wolves followed the huge bison herds that once roamed these same lands. The packs do the new herds the same service that the prairie wolves did the bison. They weed the herds of the old, the injured or maimed, the spindly or sickly, taking too the occasional calf.

Of course, the cattle are not the only prey of the packs. The dogs feed on any beast they can individually or collectively run down and dispatch—deer, antelope, wild swine, horses, goats, elk, hares and rabbits or rodents of any size and kind, nonpoisonous reptiles and amphibians, other predators and, in an extreme case of hunger, each other.

For long and long, the packs had been the largest predators upon the plains and prairies, but now their hegemony was ending. Monstrous grizzly bears were descending from the mountains and emerging from the remote areas in which their species had survived the brief reign of firearm-bearing man. There were southerly-straying wolverines, too, and another race of outsize, exceedingly voracious mustelid, big as the very largest bear, though long-drawn-out and lighter in weight. Moreover, moving onto the prairies from the east were small prides of lions, as well as the occasional specimen of other big cats—all or most descendants of zoological garden or theme-park animals, as, too, were the tiny to large ruminants that had been breeding here and there and sometimes moving with the cattle herds in the warmer, more southerly reaches of the range.

In the wake of mankind, the grasslands had expanded apace and were still so doing. The roots of grasses and weeds and brush were helping water, sun, freezes and lack of maintenance to crack and sunder and bury macadam and concrete roads and streets, while rust, corrosion and decay ate away at railroad tracks. Spring floods first weakened, then tore away the bridges not destroyed by man in his terminal madness, and they also scoured the vulnerable floodplains of the deserted, ghost-haunted ruins that once had been thriving cities and towns.

Of the trees loved by man—peach, apple, cherry, walnut, pear, pecan and other crop trees and oaks, elms, maples, poplars, pines, firs and spruces—precious few have survived in the dearth of man's incessant care. Now, once more, as it was before man strove to bend the land and all upon it to his will, hickories, burr oaks, scrubby hazels, chokecherries, wild plums and dogwoods, cottonwoods, basswoods and red elms are swiftly proliferating to fill their rightful niches.

Only circling hawk and soaring eagle now can see the lines that once delineated the grainfields, gardens, orchards and pastures of the reasoning, but arrogant and unwise, primate who so briefly ruled over this rich land.

Here and there lie tumbled, overgrown ruins—large and small, vast to almost nonexistent—most still showing the blackened traces of ancient fires, others only aggregations of weather-washed stones, broken bricks, rotted wood and pitted, red-rusty iron. In the long absence of those who built them, the ruins now provide home or lair or shelter to the multitudinous rodentia of the land, to the gaunt, rangy, feral cats, to snakes, lizards, toads, bats, nesting birds and hosts of insects and arachnids and worms.

Even in those places that hold no ruins more substantial can be found the windmill towers, all sagging and rust-pitted or gray-weathered and leaning a little farther from off their rotting footings with each season, like the few sorely wounded survivors on some vast battlefield.

But wait!

Speak not too soon of the utter extirpation of man. His kind is not entirely missing from prairie and plains, although nowhere can he be found in his formerly huge numbers.

See, there, as the prairie sky begins to darken toward the encroaching night, one, two, three, many fires are becoming visible along the banks of a small, rushing stream. One could not see them earlier because, fueled by squawwood and sun-dried dung, they are all but smokeless. Bipedal figures move to and fro about these fires. Some are tending a small herd of whickering horses, while others prepare carcasses of deer and hare and other beasts for cooking, pick through baskets of gathered edible roots and plants or bring out saddle querns from the tents and begin to husk and winnow and then grind the painfully garnered wild grains.

Still others are laving their bodies in a sheltered backwater of the stream or washing their clothes on its banks.

Chapter I

Karee Skaht, her bath done, squatted on a flat, sun-warmed rock at the riverside, letting the ever-constant wind dry her bare, sun-browned body. She wrung out her long red-gold hair, then set about laving the sweat and dirt from her shirt and breeches —alternately soaking them with river water, then pounding them against the smooth surface of the rock with the calloused palms of her hard little hands.

In the wide, deep pool that spring floodwaters had excavated, others of the boys, girls and some of the leavening of slightly older warriors who went to make up this autumn hunting party bathed and swam, frolicked and rough-housed, while an equal number worked along the banks and awaited their own turn at the cooling, cleansing, soul-satisfying comfort of the water.

After a few moments, Karee was joined on the rock by Gy Linsee. At fourteen summers, he was only some half-year her elder, but he already overtopped her by nearly two full hands, and a wealth of round muscles rippled beneath his nut-brown skin. It was these round muscles, the big bones beneath, along with his almost black hair and dark-brown eyes that attested to the fact that one or more of his ancestors had not been born of Horseclans stock, but rather

had been adopted into Clan Linsee—one of the
original clans descended of the Sacred Ancestors.

Noticing the two on the rock, another boy swam to
where he had left his clothing, then came over to
squat on Karee's other side . . . a good bit closer than
Gy had presumed to squat. This one was a much
more typical Horseclansman—small-boned, flat-
muscled, with hair the hue of wheatstraw and pale-
blue eyes, his weather-darkened skin stippled with
freckles.

Although not really closely related, this boy was of
Karee's own clan and, at sixteen summers, was
already a proven, blooded warrior. On the second
raid he had ridden in the summer just past, he had
slain a foeman with spear and saber in single
combat, capturing his victim's horse and most of his
weapons and gear. The Skaht clan bard, old Gaib
Skaht, had even added a new couplet about the
exploits of Rahjuh Vawn of Skaht to the Song of
Skaht.

Karee only glanced briefly at Rahjuh, however,
then turned the gaze of her blue-green eyes back to
the Linsee boy, who had finished wringing out his
own long, thick hair and now was sending up sprays
of water each time his broad palm slammed down on
his sopping shirt and breeches and the thick-woven
squares of woolen cloth which the Linsees, the
Morguhns, the Danyuhlzes, the Esmiths and some
few other clans had of recent years taken to lapping
over and around their feet and ankles before donning
their boots.

For an absent moment, Karee wondered to herself
just how and why so strange a custom had commenced and persisted, wondered too how it would
feel to wear a set of the outré items of apparel. But
these were only fleeting thoughts, and her mind and
gaze quickly returned to the main object of her atten-
tions and present interest.

No one of her own clansfolk had hair so darkly

lustrous as that of this Linsee boy. The rays of the
westering Sacred Sun now were bringing out dark-
red highlights from wherever they touched upon that
so-dark hair. She also found somehow satisfying the
rippling of the muscles of his back and his thick
shoulders as he slapped dry his wetted and rewetted
clothing.

The Skaht girl caught the fringes of a narrow-
beam, personal-level mindspeak communication—
the telepathy practiced every day by the roughly
three out of five Horseclansfolk so talented—this
directed to the big Linsee boy.

"Gy, the stag is now all skinncd and butchered.
Since it was your kill, the heart, liver and kidneys are
yours by right, and the tenderloin, too, if you want it.
Do you want them raw or cooked?"

Still pounding away at his sopping clothing, the
boy replied silently, "Stuff the heart with some of
those little wild carrots and some sprigs of mint; I'll
cook it myself, later on. I'll have the liver raw . . .
shortly. But let the kidneys go to Crooktail, for her it
was first scented the stag and flushed him out of
heavy cover that I might arrow him, then ride him
down."

Behind Karee, Gy and Rahjuh, a prairiecat—larger
than the biggest puma, with the sharp, white-glinting
points of fangs near a full handspan long depending
below the lower jaw and with the long, sinewy,
slender legs of a coursing beast—clambered up from
out of the pool, claws scraping on the rock. At some
time in her life, the cat's tail had been broken a third
of the way between tip and body and, in healing, had
left the final third canting at a permanent angle from
the rest of the thick, furry appendage.

When at last fully upon the rock, the big cat shook
herself thoroughly, showering Karee and both boys
impartially with myriad droplets of cold river water.

"You half-dog eater of dung! Walking flea
factory!" Rahjuh shouted and broadbeamed all at

once, turning and shaking a clenched fist in the prairiecat's direction. "I was almost dry, too, you coupler with swine!"

Serenely ignoring the outburst of insults and the shaken fist of the angered boy, Crooktail paced with dignity over to where Gy Linsee squatted. Her big head swept down and then up, running her wide, coarse, red-pink tongue the full length of his spine. Then she seated herself beside him, her crooked tail lapped over her forepaws, mindspeaking the while.

"Twoleg-called-Gy, you remembered how much this cat loves kidneys. You will be as good a friend of cats as is your sire. You will be as good a hunter, too, and as good a warrior. You will be a mighty warrior and long remembered by your get and by theirs as the bards sing of you."

The big, dark-haired boy gripped his clothing with one hand that the currents of the pool might not bear them away. His other brawny arm he threw about the cat, squeezing her damp body firmly but with the self-control of one who knows well his considerable strength.

A few yards upstream from this tableau, on a higher, moss-fringed rock, three adult warriors sat abreast, sending up into the clear skies clouds of blue-gray smoke from their pipes. Even as they observed the cavortings in and about the pool below, they chatted, both aloud and silently.

Farthest upstream sat Hwahltuh Linsee, youngest full brother of the present chief of that Kindred clan, a permanent subchief in status and a subchief of this hunt, as well. He had seen more than thirty summers come and go; beast-killing and man-slaying were both old stories to him. It had been a knife—near on fifteen years agone, when he had been but a younker —that had deeply gashed and left a crooked scar across his blond-stubbled cheek. The hard-swung sword of a Dirtman—one of the farmers who worked the lands fringing the prairie, despised by and regularly preyed upon by the Horseclansmen, themselves fearing the always costly raids and intensely hating the nomads who attacked them—had cost him the most of his left ear, while his canted nose had been smashed flat in a long-ago running battle with non-Kindred plains rovers when his opponent—his last dart cast, his swordblade broken—had bashed him in the face with the nicked and dented iron boss of his targe.

Spouting blood, blind with agony and barely able to breathe, Hwahltuh had closed with the rider, dragged him from out of his saddle and throttled him with his bare hands. But the nose and the damaged jaw below had not healed properly, and as his speech was sometimes difficult of understanding, he had for years communicated principally by mindspeak, where possible.

Farthest downstream on the mossy-grown rock sat Tchuk Skaht, five or six summers Hwahltuh's senior. He was but a middling warrier; however, he was known far and wide as a true master hunter and tracker, so since this was a hunt and not a raid, he was chief of it. Not that he was not a brave and strong man; at the age of twenty-odd, on the high plains, he had fought and slain a wounded bear armed with only his dirk—a rare feat of skill and daring of which the bards of many a clan still sang on winter nights around the lodge fires.

The black-haired man who sat between them was taller and heavier of build—though not with fat, of which there was none upon his body. His name was Milo Morai, but his two present human companions, like all the Horseclansfolk—male and female, young and old—called him Uncle Milo. No one knew his age or just how long he had ridden with and among the Kindred and their forebears. He would live a year or two with a clan, then ride on of a day to the camp of another . . . and still another; possibly, he would return a score of years later, unmarked, unchanged, with no slightest sign of aging.

And there existed nowhere any Clan Morai, only the one man, Uncle Milo, peer of any chief. The most ancient of the bardsongs mentioned him, the rhymed genealogies of almost every clan told of his exploits in war and the chase; indeed, if some few of the oldest bard songs were to be believed in entirety, he it was had succored the Sacred Ancestors after the Great Dyings and truly set what were to become the Kindred on their path to their present near mastery of plains and prairie.

But there was no denying, for believers and non-believers alike, that Uncle Milo or someone exactly like him had been present in one clan camp or another, had ridden with the Kindred on hunts and raids and treks, for tenscore summers and more, for such a presence was mentioned in the songs—history-genealogies—of clan after clan, and clan songs of this sort never contained aught save bald truth.

Yet no man or woman, no boy or girl, no prairiecat of any sex or age, thought of Uncle Milo as being in any way unnatural or supernatural, for he lived, slept, ate and played among them. He sweated when they sweated, made love no differently than any other clansman, and bled when injured, though he healed very fast. His bladder and bowels required periodic emptying, too, like those of any other living creature. He only differed from them in that he neither aged nor died . . . or so it seemed.

The respect the Kindred afforded this man they all called Uncle Milo contained no awe and was in no way worship. Rather was it but an amplification of the natural respect granted to the old and the proven-wise of the clans, the deference due any chief —for, as the one and only member of his ''clan,'' Milo was automatically ''chief'' or Morai—plus the admiration of a warrior and hunter of consummate skills.

Up there on the high, moss-fringed rock, between Tchuk Skaht and Uncle Milo, lay another prairiecat. This one was a good deal bigger than Crooktail, he was a male and his furry pelt enclosed nearly three hundred pounds of muscle and sinew and bone. His name was Snowbelly, and he, too, was a subchief of this autumn hunt. He had had his swim and now lay white belly up, thick, powerful hind legs splayed widely and taloned forelegs bent at the wrists that the cool, evening wind might dry him more readily.

Despite his lolling head and closed eyes, however, the big cat lay fully awake and as alert as always, his razor-keen senses missing neither sound nor any windborne scent, most of his mind engaged, though, in listening to and occasionally contributing to the conversation of the men. Of course, his "speech" was perforce all telepathic—the "mindspeak" of the Horseclans—since his kind had never developed the vocal apparatus necessary for true, oral speech. But he emitted a constant, rumbling, contrabasso purr of appreciation for the thorough scratching that Milo and Tchuk were giving his exposed chest, belly, legs and throat.

Hwahltuh Linsee made a peculiar clucking sound and shook his head, silently beaming, "Crooktail should have given that impudent Skaht boy's damned rump a good sharp nip or two, in return for his insults. He had but just climbed out of the damned pool. So how were a few more drops of water going to do him harm or injury, hey?"

While Tchuk Skaht glowered at the subchief from under bushy brows, Snowbelly mindspoke, "No, not so. This cat laid down the law to all the rest when first we assembled for this hunt: if fight the cats must, they are to fight other cats—opponents who, like them, have fangs and claws and tough skins. Brothers and sisters of cats though you Kindred are, you are all just too thin of skin, too easily injured. So the wise and prudent Crooktail comported herself entirely properly, you see."

The big cat abruptly rolled over onto his belly and began to lick down the chest hairs rumpled by the scratching fingers of the two men, continuing his "speaking" all the while.

"Nonetheless, I do agree with Subchief Hwahltuh that that young Skaht should learn and show more respect for Crooktail, for she is both a fine hunter and a savage warrior, in addition to throwing consistently strong, healthy kittens."

Painfully striving to master his righteous anger at this outrage—unsolicited, completely unwarranted criticism of a Skaht by a mere Linsee!—Tchuk spoke aloud and as calmly as he could manage, shrugging. "Well, young Rahjuh *is* a bit higher-strung than are many . . . but then, so too is his sire. And no doubt the shaking of our esteemed cat sister startled him, eh?"

Milo Morai chuckled. "Before that boy learns anything else, he'd be wise to learn to keep his thoughts shielded from those who can sense such in the minds of the untrained or unwary. He may well have been a bit startled by his sudden, unexpected shower, but his outburst was the spawn of something else entirely.

"Be warned. He means to couple with the girl, Karee Skaht, during this hunt and intends that no one and nothing shall impede that purpose. Just now, her very obvious admiration of the big, straight-shooting Linsee boy has set him aflame with jealousy and jealous rage. You'd best have a word or three with him, Chief Tchuk, else he means to goad Gy Linsee into a death match; his thoughts are just that vicious at this moment."

Tchuk Skaht but shrugged once again. "Rahjuh is free to think whatsoever he likes, but he and every other Skaht in this camp knows full well that they'll surely answer to me if even anything so serious as a bloodmatch is fought, much less a death match between a proven warrior and a boy still undergoing his weapons training.

"As regards Karee Skaht, I have known her all her life and I'm here to tell you all that she's as smart as any and a bit smarter than many. She'll know better than to engage in anything more than lighthearted sport with a man of alien blood, no matter how big his muscles, how true his eye or how heavy a bow he can draw.

"Besides"—although his teeth showed in a supposed grin, the hard, malicious glint in his eyes gave the lie to the humor of lips and bantering tone—"the seed of something like a mere Linsee could no more quicken a true-born Horseclanswoman than could that of a Dirtman, a boar hog or any other beast . . ."

A low, inarticulate growl was Subchief Hwahltuh Linsee's only reply. He came to his feet as if powered by springs of tempered steel, his scar-furrowed face all twisted and quivering with the intensity of his deadly fury; his eyes were slitted, his knees flexed and his right hand clamped about the worn hilt of the heavy saber he had already half drawn from its scabbard.

And in an eyeblink, Chief Tchuk Skaht was facing him, bared steel at low guard, ready for slash or thrust or parry, his body crouched for combat, his lips peeled back from off his teeth in a grin of pure bloodlusting anticipation and joy.

But before either man could strike or even make to do so, Milo Morai was suddenly between them, sneering, his voice dripping scorn, disgust and disapprobation.

"Now, by Sun and Wind! I asked your clan chiefs for grown men of sound mind to head this hunt, and I'd assumed that that was what they'd given. But what have we here? A brace of drooling, bloodthirsty idiots, the bodies of warriors in which reside the minds of ill-disciplined children. No less than twice, now, have Skahts and Linsees ridden the raid against each other. *Kindred shedding the blood of their Kins-folk!* Do you two impetuous fools mean to make it three times? Mean to upgrade it to the status of a clan feud, a vendetta? You both know what that would mean.

"Have either of you two hotheads ever *seen* a clan dispersed after a Council of Kindred Chiefs had revoked their kinship? Of course you haven't. Neither of you were born the last time it had to be done. But I saw it, forty-six summers ago, it was.

"Of a time, there were two Kindred clans, Lehvee and Braizhoor. Their mutual raiding and stock stealing and murdering of each other had progressed to the point where their warriors did battle in the ten-year tribe camp. Around and about and even within the very pavilion of the Chiefs' Council did these lawless, arrogant men hack at and slash and stab one at the other, nor did they, any of them, even hesitate to let flow the lifeblood of those brave Kindred who made to mediate and put a stop to so grave a profanation of that Council Camp. In the end, warriors of other clans had to be called and gathered to disarm these miscreants by force of arms.

"For many days and nights did the Council ponder the matter, questioning the chiefs of the two clans and exploring any avenue that might solve the matter on a more or less permanent basis. But the warriors, subchiefs and chiefs of Lehvee and Braizhoor foiled the well-meant plans and schemes of the Council at each and every turn. They all thirsted for the blood of each other and meant to allow nothing and no one —Council, custom, Sacred Kinship, even the very Law itself—to stand between them and the slaking of that unnatural thirst.

"When one of the older, wiser chiefs of the Council made the suggestion that one of the two warring clans be sent far to the southeast and the other far to the northwest, there to stay until time and newborn leaders had smoothed over their differences, the chiefs of both Lehvee and Braizhoor stated that such a plan would only work for as long as it took the two clans to force-march to proximity again.

"In the end, after much exceedingly painful soul-searching the Council decided on the necessary course. An example was to be made of the lawless clans, an example clear for all to see. They were to be disowned by the Tribe, have their Kinship revoked and be driven out to live or to die upon the pitiless prairie."

Both Hunt Chief Tchuk Skaht and Subchief Hwahltuh Linsee had paled beneath their tans, horrified by the images of Morai's mindspeak. Slowly, Milo reached forth and took the sabers easily from grasps suddenly gone weak and nerveless before he went on with his sorry tale.

"Chief Djeen of Morguhn, who headed that Council, ordered first that all boys and girls who were not yet proven warriors be dispersed amongst the other clans there present in the camp, to be adopted into these clans when and if they proved their worth and loyalty. Women and older girls of the two miscreant clans were given the choice of slavery or an honorable marriage into another clan, and, naturally, most chose the latter.

"The horses and the herds of Lehvee and Braizhoor, the tents and yurts, the wagons and carts, clothing, tools and weapons, indeed, every last thing that any of them owned, all were divided amongst the gathered clans. All that done, the still-unrepentent chiefs and subchiefs and warriors of those onetime Kindred clans were driven before the Council and the assembled folk and cats of all the clans.

"A right pitiful-looking lot they were too, as I recall. They went clothed in such poor rags as they had been able to find discarded, mostly barefoot and all weaponless. Their hair had been shorn to the very scalps and their faces all were drawn with pain, for the bowstring thumb of each had but just been broken, smashed with a smith's sledge, that they might never again draw the hornbow of the Kindred.

"Before all of the folk and cats assembled there, the crimes of Lehvee and Braizhoor were recited and the just punishments decided upon by the Council were pronounced. Gravely, Chief Djeen of Morguhn stated that there no longer existed amongst the true Kindred, the descendants of the Sacred Ancestors, any such clans as Lehvee and Braizhoor, that the gaggle of men owned no protection under Horse-clans Law or customs and that if ever, after this day, they should dare to enter any camp of the Kindred, they might be done to death or enslaved just like any other alien.

"Each of the men then were given a knife, a pouch of jerky and a waterskin. So supplied, they were chivvied through the camps and onto the open prairie at lance points by mounted clansmen, then kept moving farther and farther for days by relent-less relays of warriors and cats. All of the bards were ordered by the Council to forget the very names of Lehvee and Braizhoor."

With the skill born of long practice, Milo Morai's mindspeak had not so much painted a picture as actually put his audience *there*, at the very scenes of that long-ago happening. The experience had left the men visibly shaken . . . as he had intended them to be.

Sternly, Milo said, "Now, gentlemen, now, Tchuk and Hwahltuh, is that what you two want for your own futures, eh? Your wives all wedded to men of other clans? Your children reared into those clans? The very names of Linsee and Skaht forgot of all the Kindred for all future time, while you lie naked and helpless and starving upon some faraway piece of prairie, there to die miserably and without honor, your bodies rent to shreds by wild beasts? If that *is* what you both want, gentlemen, here are your sabers —have at it!"

But the two clansmen recoiled from the familiar proffered hilts as if the weapons were suddenly become coiled vipers.

Milo nodded brusquely. "Very well, then. Now at long last the two of you are showing some of the intelligence that the Sacred Ancestors bequeathed you and your forebears.

"Hear me and heed you well my words. As you know, I am here among you at the express behest of the present Tribal Council. The chiefs of that Council are most disturbed at your ongoing mutual hostilities. They—and I, their surrogate—do not care a pinch of moldy turkey dung about what may or may not have begun these hostilities. They simply want them stopped for good and all . . . lest it become necessary to revoke the kinship of your two clans as warning to others.

"Kindred clans do not war upon Kindred clans, that is all there is to it! Haven't we Kindred enough enemies—Dirtmen to east, west, north and south, non-Kindred savages, predaceous beasts? So Linsee and Skaht must cease the feud, must give over tearing at each other . . . either that, or cease to be Kindred.

"I put together this hunt as a means to forge bonds of new friendship and kinship between the younger generation of Skahts and Linsees—those who will be the next generation of warriors. You two men are in charge of the hunt and of your respective clansfolk who are on the hunt. As such, you both must set an example. Therefore, you will henceforth cease badgering and slyly insulting each other *and* you will prevent any extension of this senseless feud amongst the younger folk by whatever means it takes to do it. Otherwise, I will send you both back to your clan camps and Snowbelly and I will take over your erstwhile functions. Do you both understand me?"

"Oh, prairie, broad prairie, the place of our birth,

We are the Horseclansmen, the bravest on earth."

Gy Linsee's singing voice was a very adult-sounding baritone, the envy of those boys and young men whose voices still were in process of changing and so sometimes cracked into embarrassingly childish trebles. A bard's son—though not the eldest—the big, dark-haired boy handled his harp expertly.

He was a quick-study, too, was this Gy Linsee, Milo Morai reflected to himself. Only once had Milo had to play the tune for the boy—a Clan Pahrkuh song, truth to tell, but with the words identifying clan of origin changed by Milo to encompass all of Kindred descent. Moreover, Gy Linsee had managed to come up with several extemporaneously composed verses that had to do with events of this hunt. He would be a young man to watch, thought Milo.

All well stuffed with venison and rabbit, fish, wild tubers, nuts and a few late berries, the threescore youngsters and the dozen or so adult warriors lazed about the cluster of firepits, which now were paved with ashes and glowing coals. But few hands were idle.

There were blades to be honed—knives of various types, dirks, light axes, hatchets, spear- and arrowheads and, for those of sufficient years and experience to carry them, sabers. The skins and hides of slain beasts must be cared for, along with other usable portions of the carcasses—and Horseclansfolk made some use of nearly every scrap of most game animals. Horse gear required constant maintenance. Under flashing blades of knife, hatchet and drawknife, seasoned wood from a tree uprooted and felled and borne this far downstream by some seasonal flood was fast being transformed into tool and weapon handles, axe hafts, shafts for arrows and darts and even spears.

Around one firepit, this one still being fed with chips and twigs and branches of squaw wood for the light, squatted a dozen Skahts. As fast as half of them could split the tough wood and smooth it into shafts of the proper thickness and length, Karee Skaht would affix a nock carved of bone or antler with a dollop of evil-smelling fish glue from the little pot that bubbled malodorously before her. Then she would pass the shaft on to her brother, Ahrthuh Skaht, for the fletching. Following this, using threads of sinew and more fish glue, Rahjuh Vawn of Skaht would complete the arrows, tipping them with prepared points of bone or flint or antler, for these were intended to be common hunting arrows and only war shafts received points of the rare and costly steel or iron.

Gy Linsee had again taken up his harp. He still sang of the plains and prairies, but this was a different song. The tune was soft and haunting, and it took Milo a while to recall where he last had heard it and what it then had been—a love song from far off Mexico.

"Oh, my lovely plains, you are my mother and my father," went Gy Linsee's song, rising above the sounds of water chuckling over the rocks of the streambed, the callings of the nightbirds and the soft whickerings of the horses grazing on the grassy bank above the camp.

"Kissed each day by Sacred Sun, endlessly caressed by your lover, Wind; the grasses in which you lie clad are as sweet to smell as summer honey, oh, my plains . . ."

The boy sang with his head thrown back, his eyes closed, his face mirroring the rapture and love that his fine voice projected. Simultaneously, his powerful mindspeak also cast out a soothing broadbeam sending which reached every man, boy, girl and cat to a greater or lesser degree.

Milo Morai, seated nearby and carving a new stirrup from a chunk of the seasoned wood, remarked, "That boy has the true gift, you know—

his fine voice and his abilities with that harp are only parts of it."

Hwahltuh Linsee smiled and nodded, looking up from honing the blade of his wolf spear. "Our Gy sings and plays songs mostly of his own composition, Uncle Milo, but he never forgets one of them, either. His voice and his harping are even now every bit as good as his sire's—which is why I am certain that my brother the chief will insist that Gy, rather than his elder brother, Rik, be named as heir to the office of tribal bard. Poor Rik, alas, could not carry a tune in a wooden bucket."

He sighed and shook his head sadly, adding, "And then the sparks will surely fly, fly for fair. For Bard Djimi is a man of exceeding strong will, and he truly dotes on his son, Rik."

Tchuk Skaht's brows rose upward, further crinkling a forehead already lined and scarred. Slowly, incredulously, he spoke.

"But, man, the matter be simple, on the face of it: the one son is far better qualified for office than the other, their ages or the precedent of birth be damned. And yet you seem to feel that your bard would openly defy his *chief*? Why, a bard is the third most powerful subchief in a clan, subordinate only to the chief himself, and the tanist."

Hwawhltuh shook his head. "Not so in Clan Linsee, Hunt Chief. We have no tanist, practicing as we do descent through the father rather than the mother. Our next chief will be the eldest son of my brother still living, whole of body and sound of mind . . . and approved by the council of warriors, at the time of my brother's demise."

Tchuk snorted derisively. "What a stupid way to pass on a chieftaincy! And I had thought that only Dirtmen and other such dim-witted, non-Kindred folk practiced primogeniture."

Milo's fingers ceased to move, and he gritted his teeth in anticipation of an explosive, probably extremely insulting retort and a probable repetition of the near-bloodletting of earlier this evening. But it did not occur, none of it; apparently, Gy Linsee's lulling broadbeam had done its purpose well, for although Subchief Hwahltuh frowned and his lips thinned a bit, he continued tightening the wetted sinews about the haft of his wolf spear. When they were to his satisfaction, he set the weapon aside, shrugged and bespoke the hunt chief.

"Some Kindred clans practice descent the one way, some the other way . . . as you should well know. Nowhere in the Couplets of the Law is any one method for choosing a new chief spelled out."

"But what," demanded Tchuk, "if all of your chief's sons die or be crippled before he himself goes to Wind, eh? What then?"

Hwahltuh again shrugged. "In so unlikely an event, Hunt Chief, I or my eldest son would be chosen chief . . . unless one of the chief's sons had left a son old enough to lead the clan in war. Simple, eh?"

"Simple, right enough!" Tchuk's voice dripped scorn. "Only a simple-minded folk could devise so silly a scheme."

Milo's telepathy ferreted out the first stirrings of angry indignation bubbling just below the surface of Hwahltuh Linsee's consciousness, and he decided to put an end to this dangerous discourse before it provoked what otherwise it inevitably must between the hot-blooded pair.

Starting up work again on the stirrup-to-be, he remarked in a deliberately casual tone, "And yet, Tchuk, although the practice is slowly spreading, still only some score or so of our Kindred clans reckon descent through the maternal line and so pass the chieftaincy to the son of the former chief's eldest sister. And it is perhaps most fitting that you, Tchuk Skaht, should hold and defend the practice, since it was your very forebears who first brought it among the clans of the Kindred."

Hwahltuh Linsee snapped up this bit of information avidly, crowing, "Then it was true, what my sire used to say, it was all true! These Skahts truly are *not* come of the true Kindred, are not of the seed of the Sacred Ancestors at all!"

Tchuk Skaht growled wordlessly and tensed, his right hand pawing behind him in search of the hilt of the saber that now lay across his saddle and bedroll.

The soothing broadbeam of Milo Morai was far and away more powerful than that of the still-singing Gy Linsee; moreover, all of it was directed squarely into the minds of the two would-be antagonists, below conscious level. Still in his calm, casual voice, he spoke aloud, saying, "Be you not so full with pride and that arrogance of your supposed lineage, Hwahltuh, for neither were you Linsees of the Kindred in the beginning. Both the Linsees and the Skahts did not join the tribe until long years after the Sacred Ancestors and their children came down to the prairies. I'll tell you just how it happened . . ."

Young Karee Skaht, whose mindspeak abilities chanced to be better than those of many of her fellow clansfolk, dragged the glue pot well back from the fire and stood up, wiping her hands on the legs of her baggy breeches. To Rahjuh's questioning look, she answered, "Crooktail mindspoke that Uncle Milo is about to recount a tale of long ago, of the early years of the Kindred. I would hear this tale myself."

Chapter II

Colonel Ian Lindsay appeared a good ten years older than his actual fifty-three years. Not stooped with age, mind you—six foot four in his stocking feet, with a deep chest, wide, thick shoulders, arm and leg bones well sheathed in rolling muscles and still capable of splitting a man from shoulder to waist with that well-honed broadsword that had been his great-grandfather's pride—but his craggy face become a collection of permanent lines and wrinkles, his once-black hair now a thick shock of snow-white and even his flaring mustaches and bushy eyebrows now thickly stippled with gray hairs.

He was a man beset with problems, problems of such nature as to seem often insoluble to his orderly mind, but somehow he and his staff and the civilian intendant and his staff always came up with some ploy or some substitute for something no longer in supply that would work after a fashion.

Still, as he sat worrying and figuring in his office within the fort designed by his grandfather and built by the battalion of that day with tools and materials that had ceased to be available fifty years ago, he frequently wished that he might have lived in Granddad Ian's day when things had been so easy—motorized vehicles, vast stocks of petrol to run them and the electrical generators, other huge, underground tanks of diesel fuel and heating oil, thousands of rounds of ammunition for the rifles, pistols, automatic weapons and mortars, fine, powerful explosives of many differing varieties. Then, too, in that earlier Ian's time, there were almost double the number of people hereabouts, with the battalion at well over full strength. In that halcyon era, the "(Reinforced)" suffix to the unit designation still had real meaning.

Belowstairs somewhere, the notes of a bugle call pealed, sounding distant and tinny through the thick walls.

"Must be the guard detail making ready to march out to the far pastures and relieve the men guarding the sheep and shepherds," Colonel Lindsay thought. "God grant that they don't have to fight men, this tour, or that if they do, there're no more casualties borne back here to die." He sighed and shook his head. "If only those damned nomad scum were still afraid of us, here."

Leaning back in his chair for a moment, closing his lids over his bright-blue eyes and absently stroking his mustaches with the joint of his thumb, Ian Lindsay thought back to a day now more than thirty-five years in the past, when he had been a subaltern and junior aide to his grandfather, Colonel Ian James Alexander Lindsay. He recalled that day well, did that Colonel Ian's namesake.

The winter preceding had been an extremely hard and long-lasting one—the hardest one in the available records, in fact, a winter which had seen hardly any wild animals abroad other than the wolves— great marauding, hunger-maddened packs of the slavering beasts—on the prairie. There had been precious little sun for weeks at a time, with one long, bitter blizzard after another sweeping down from west and north and east, even, and a full meter thickness of hard ice covering the river bank to bank for the most of the winter.

The fort had then been in place for about fifteen years—it had been begun during the week of the present Ian's birth and had been three or four years in the completion—but all of the other buildings and habitations had been erected even before the first Ian's birth. They were solid and weathertight and well capable of retaining heat generated by hearth fires, stoves and other, esoteric devices then in use.

Even so, the folk and animals living in these sound structures of concrete and brick and native stone, adequately fed on their stocks of stored grain, canned or dried vegetables and fruits, smoked and pickled meats, silage and hay had suffered the effects of the long, hard winter to some degree. But the sufferings of the nomadic rovers—mostly existing in fragile, drafty tents, eating their scrawny, diseased cattle and sheep for lack of game and battling the huge, savage wolf packs for even these— must have been well-nigh unimaginable.

Nor had the following spring done much to alleviate the preceding months of misery and hunger and death. For one thing, it had been a late spring, a very late spring; for another, it had been an exceedingly rainy one and these torrential rains, coupled with the copious snow and ice melt, had transformed ponds into lakes and lakes into virtual inland seas, sent streams and rivers surging over their banks and rendered many square miles of prairie into swampland that discouraged the quick return of game.

Halfway through that terrible spring, the prairie rovers, from hundreds of square miles around, converged upon the fort and the other buildings and sprawling crop and pasture lands.

Young Ian remembered how the tatterdemalions looked from the wall of the fort, through the optics of a rangefinder. They went through the drizzling chill in rags and motheaten furs and ill-cured hides. The few whose horses had not gone to feed either them or the wolves were mounted, but the majority went afoot. There were thousands of them, it seemed, but mostly ill armed. Here and there was an old shotgun or ancient military rifle, bows of varying designs, a few prods and crossbows, but most of them bore nothing more than spears, crude swords, axes and clubs.

Later on that day, Ian had felt—still felt—both pride and despair at the dignified mien of Colonel Ian James Alexander Lindsay—pride, that he was himself come of such stock, despair, that he could ever affect such demeanor, could ever be so cool, so obviously self-assured in confronting the scruffy but deadly-looking leaders of the huge horde of invaders.

Flanked where he sat by his son, the younger Ian's father, First Captain David Duncan Robert Lindsay, and the battalion second-in-command, Major Albert MacKensie, with the three other captains—Douglass, Keith and Ross—ranged along the paneled wall behind, Colonel Ian J. A. Lindsay had seemed to his grandson the very personification of all that an officer should represent: calm dignity, authority and long-established order.

In his mind's eye, the present colonel could see that long-dead old officer as if the years intervening had never passed. The full-dress coat that had been Colonel Ian J.A. Lindsay's own father's was spotless, and its polished brass insigniae reflected back the bright electric lights. Ruddy of countenance, his dark-auburn hair and mustaches liberally streaked with gray, he had sat behind the very desk and in the very oaken chair now occupied by his grandson. A short, but stocky and big-boned, powerful-looking man, he had eyed his "visitors" in silence over steepled fingers.

Finally, he had rumbled in his no-nonsense tone of voice, "I agree that the winter past was a devilish hard one, gentlemen. But it was hard, too, on us, here. Our reserve stocks of nearly everything are reduced to a dangerously low level, far too low to allow us to even think of extending any meaningful amounts of aid to you all, even were you and your folk our responsibility . . . which you are not.

"And, gentlemen, none of the problems mitigates the fact that you are trespassing illegally upon a military installation *and* a classified experimental agricultural station of the Canadian government. Consequently, you are all . . ."

A cackle of derisive laughter from the paramount leader and main spokesman of the gaggle of ruffians —a tall, cadaverous, almost toothless man with dull, lank shoulder-length brown hair and a skimpy beard through which fat lice could be seen crawling—interrupted the officer.

"Canuck guv'mint, my ass, mister! It ain't been no kinda guv'mints nowheres sincet my paw was a fuckin' pup! An' everbody know it, too, so don' gimme none your shit, mister."

Completely unflustered and in icy control, Colonel Lindsay had continued, "It is true that we have been out of touch with Ottawa for some years now, but this means—can only mean to a soldier such as I— that the last recorded set of orders to this battalion still stands. And gentlemen, do not mistake my purpose of commitment. I will see that those orders are carried out; I will protect the MacEvedy Experimental Agricultural Station from your inroads and depredations if I have to see each and every one of you done to death to do so. Do I make myself clear, gentlemen?"

Ian well recalled the feral gleam in the deep-sunk, muddy-brown eyes of that prairie rover headman. "You talks good, mister, real purty-like, but you don' unnerstan' too good. Look, it ain't no deers nor nuthin' out there to hunt no more and the damn wolfs got all our cows and horses and all what we didn' eat our own selfs, las' winter. We all is starvin', mister, and we knows damn well you all got food. If you won't give it to us in a peaceable way, we'll kill ever man jack of you and take it. We ain't got no choice, mister."

The old colonel had sighed and nodded slowly. "Do not think, please, that I do not realize your quandary and personally sympathize, gentlemen, but . . ."

"Wal, then, mister, you jest give us all your wheat and corn and all. Let us take our pick out'n your cows and sheeps and horses, see, and give us some good guns and bullets for 'em and we'll jest go on 'bout our bizness, see, an' . . ."

It had been at that point that Colonel Lindsay's broad, calloused palm had smote the desktop with a sound like a pistol shot. "Preposterous, sir, utterly preposterous! Do not attempt to overawe *me* with your threats. You are not now dealing with some hapless, helpless community of those poor, wretched farmers on whom you and your despicable ilk are habitually wont to prey. All that you will be given by us, here, sir, is a richly deserved death, long overdue.

"I am Colonel Ian James Alexander Lindsay, officer commanding the 228th Provisional Battalion (Reinforced). Our orders are to provide support and protection for and to the MacEvedy Experimental Agricultural Station and all its personnel. An attack upon the station or upon my fort will be considered by me to constitute an attack upon the Canadian government itself, and I shall repel such an affront with all necessary force, treating you all as the criminals that such actions will have irrevocably branded you."

The first attack came howling and screeching at the walls a bare hour after the leaders had been shoved out the gates of the fort. It had been repulsed, of course, bloodily repulsed, and the remainder of that day and the night that followed it were made hideous by the moans and cries of wounded, dying, untended rovers and by the screams of injured horses.

But there had been another attack, headlong, no whit different from the initial exercise in futility and mass suicide; this second attack came at dawn of the next day. Bare hours later, they came at the walls once more, and once more the bullets from the rifles and the automatics, shrapnel from mortar bombs and rockets cut down the starveling rovers long before any one of them had won to within bowshot of the embattled fort. They attacked one more time; then they had had enough.

Colonel Lindsay had had patrols follow the retreating raiders, and when he received the report that they had set up a camp some miles southeast of the fort, he had led out his command in two motorized columns, taking charge of one and turning over the other to his son. They moved slowly that night, so as not to wear out the horse-mounted unit of Captain Keith. Nonetheless, by false dawn, everyone was in position and Colonel Lindsay gave orders to commence firing on the sleeping encampment.

The defeated rovers, never suspecting that the victors might pursue them and complete the butchery, had chosen their campsite on grounds of comfort rather than easy security. The few sleepy sentries they had posted on the low hills almost surrounding the camp had quickly succumbed to wire garrotes and sharp knives, and cautious, silent patrols had established that there existed no second line of sentinels closer to the camp.

Muttering under his breath about rank amateurs playing at the game of war, Colonel Lindsay supervised the emplacement of the mortars and the two armored vehicles mounting 75mm guns; the few rockets brought along were all of the hand-held variety and could therefore be easily shifted to targets of opportunity when once the slaughter had commenced.

Then it was only waiting, waiting until the bursting double star of a purple flare told that First Captain Lindsay and his group were in place. With the bright glare of a rising sun hot on the backs of Colonel Lindsay's bombardment group, most of the rovers could not see even the four-yard-high spouts of flame from the discharging mortars, so had no idea whence was coming the rain of explosive death, and the vast majority of them died within a few minutes there in that hill-girt vale, torn asunder by the explosive shells and bombs and rockets, shredded by the shrapnel, trampled to death by loosed horses mad with pain and terror or cut down by their own bemused comrades all stumbling about in the dusty, smoky, chaotic slice of very hell that they just then were occupying.

At what he felt was the proper time, the colonel had lifted the brutal barrage and Captain Keith's horsemen had come into view over the crest of the hill, between the gun and mortar emplacements, forming up among the low-growing brush that clothed the easy slope down to the blood-soaked, cratered vale. Sabers were drawn, lances leveled, to the peal of a bugle. Even in their shock, the surviving prairie rovers below could see just what horror next was coming their way, and it was just too much for them. They broke and streamed westward toward the second broad break in the circle of hills, where the stream ran southward.

No one of them made to try to catch one of the few sound hores, they just took to their heels, one and all, many discarding their weapons as needless encumbrances to flight. They ran like the formless mob they were become and fell in high windrows before the murderous crossfire of First Captain Lindsay's group, equipped with almost all the automatics.

The few hundred who got out onto the prairie did so either by purest chance or by clawing their way up the steep inner slopes of the southern hills and circumventing the line of troop carriers and machine-gun positions. But few of even these escaped with their lives, not for long, at least, for the vehicles, the horsemen of Captain Keith and, where necessary, foot patrols pursued and harried the scattered survivors relentlessly for many a mile. They took no prisoners and left the flea-bitten carcasses where they had fallen, that their picked and bleaching bones might serve as mute warning to other prairie rovers of equally larcenous intent.

A few got away, of course, and they and those who heard them had spread word of the savage extermination of the original pack of thousands far and wide on the prairies and plains. For three decades, no band of nomads, no matter how desperate, seriously considered trespass within range of that grim, implacable band of proven man-killers.

But time passes, a new generation slowly displaces the older generation, bones crumble away to dry dust, and memories of long-past disasters dim and fade.

During the most of those thirty-odd years, the present Ian's father, Colonel David Lindsay, had commanded, and, under his aegis, the sinews of war so long unused had ceased to be hoarded against a future need that might (he strongly felt) never again come. He had died in a land at peace, secure in the belief that his way had been the right one.

But now his successor, his only son, who had loved him and who still honored his memory, had to face the fact that his late father had been wrong, that fort and station and the folk therein soon would face foemen as deadly as those of long ago, but this time without the tools and machinery of warfare which had given them so easy and complete a victory the last time.

The irreplaceable petrol and diesel fuel had been expended many long years ago, mostly to power farming machinery, the generators and the vehicles sent out to garner anything still usable from towns and settlements within cruising range. Small-arms ammunition had been used in defending these expeditions from the bands of skulkers, as well as for bagging game.

As the supplies of fossil fuels had dwindled, Colonel David Lindsay had taken the heavy armored tracked vehicles out of use, turning the two light tanks into nothing more than immobile pillboxes— sunk into the ground and partially covered with logs and earth—while the troop carriers became aggregations of spare parts for any wheeled vehicle or farm machine that could adapt those parts to its use.

When the time had finally come when there was no more powder to reload cartridges for small arms, an attempt was made to use the propellant from dismantled artillery shells. This had been an unmitigated disaster, resulting as it had in ruined weapons and dead or permanently crippled soldiers. The colonel had then gone back to the old books and gleaned from them a formula for a form of gunpowder that could be manufactured with easily available ingredients and equipment.

This powder did work most of the time, and it would propel a bullet with sufficient force to bring down men and game. However, it would not for some reason cause the rifles and automatics to operate properly, as had the original loads, so that a man was required to pull back the operating handle between shots, which fact vastly reduced the firepower of the 228th. This, coupled with their by now almost nonexistent mobility made them sitting ducks, perfect, tailor-made victims-in-waiting—too slow to run or maneuver and too weakened to fight—and this sorry state of affairs preyed long and often upon Colonel Ian Lindsay.

Soon after his father's death, a routine inspection

of the bunkers had disclosed that a large number of the infinitely dear percussion caps used to reload the small-arms cartridges had somehow been exposed to long dampness and were mostly unusable. Faced with a vastly straitened supply of ammunition in the foreseeable future, Ian had retired every automatic and allowed only the very cream of sharpshooters to retain their rifles. Now, the bulk of the men of the 228th were armed with and trained in the efficient use of pikes and crossbows, if dismounted, and lances and sabers, if mounted; additionally, those horsemen demonstrating an innate ability were issued and trained to the proper employment of one of those beautiful, far-ranging and very deadly recurved-reflex hornbows fashioned by some folk to the south and traded by the merchant-wagon caravans that occasionally wended their long, arduous and dangerous way up here.

The sabers of the horsemen and the straight-bladed swords of the infantry were not so lovely and well balanced as were the ancient, patrimonial, basket-hilted blades born by officers and warrants, but they were every bit as effective in the hot little actions that resulted on occasion from brushes of patrols, hunting or foraging parties with prairie rovers. To fashion the needed swords, dirks, pike and lance heads and ferrules, helmets and a modest amount of body armor for each man, it had been found necessary to strip off the now-perforce-stationary armored vehicles all of the protective plates, along with steel tracks, wheels and every other bit of metal that did not have a direct bearing upon the use of the 76mm guns. The useless automatics, too, went to the forges; lacking proper ammunition, there was simply no point in retaining the heavy, unwieldy things, Ian felt.

He had read and reread and committed to memory as much as he could of certain of the ancient books

of his great-grandfather's extensive, well-thumbed
library, then he had undertaken the retraining of his
command . . . and barely in time, too.

After being sanguineously repulsed by the fort and
the well-defended inner perimeter of the station
compounds, a mounted band of some thousand or so
prairie rovers began to despoil the lands and
pastures round about the station, whereupon
Colonel Ian Lindsay marched out his infantry
and cavalry to do battle. The pikesquare stood rock-
steady under charge after furious charge, while the
crossbowmen at the corners and the mounted horse
archers massed in the center emptied saddle after
rover saddle.

When, finally, the rovers broke and began to
stream away from the field of battle, the square
opened and the mounted troops poured out to
pursue and harry, half of the pikesmen trotting in
their wake with swords and axes, while the other
half went about dispatching wounded foemen on the
stricken field before returning to the fort. There had
been counted over five hundred bodies of dead
rovers, but Ian Lindsay had lost nearly a hundred
killed on the field or in the pursuit and half a
hundred more who had died since of wounds. He still
mourned them all.

At a brief rap upon his door, Colonel Ian Lindsay
broke off his rememberings. "Come."

The man who entered was about Ian's own age,
with close-cropped yellow-gray hair and a red-and-
gray mustache plastered to a sweaty face drawn by
deep lines of care and worry and discouragement.

As Ian Lindsay was the hereditary colonel of the
228th Provisional Battalion, so was Emmett
MacEvedy the hereditary director of the station and
therefore in official charge of all nonmilitary
personnel. Emmett and Ian had been good friends in
childhood, and the two worked closely together at all
times, as indeed they must in order to keep their

people alive, secure and reasonably well fed in this savage world.

Colonel Lindsay poured an old, chipped mug half full of a straw-pale whiskey and pushed it across the age-darkened desk, waving toward a facing chair. The newcomer sank wearily into the chair, drained off a good half of the whiskey, then simply sat, staring moodily into the mug.

"Well, Emmett?" queried the colonel, after a few moments of unbroken silence. "Say you have some good news for me."

The man sighed deeply and slowly shook his head, then sighed once again and looked up. "I do have news, Ian, but it's hardly good. It's not just the wheat and the barley this year, God help us. The rye is affected, too, and the oats, and even the maize. Not a spear or an ear I examined that doesn't show signs of the damned blight . . . and I was through most of the fields. We might get silage out of those fields, but that'll be about all."

Knots of muscle moving under his ears as his clenched jaws flexed, the colonel stared at MacEvedy from beneath bushy brows, cracking his big, scarred knuckles one by one. At long last, he spoke.

"Well, we'll just have to make do with potatoes again, I suppose."

Once more the director sighed and shook his head. "I'd not count on it, Ian, not even on that. I checked the potatoes, too. The foliage is discolored and stunted, and those tubers that I had pulled up had none of them developed properly . . . and the beets and turnips seem to be similarly afflicted."

Through force of habit, the colonel cast a quick glance around the office, then leaned forward, lowering his voice and speaking swiftly.

"Emmett, these last two years have not been at all good—you know it and I know it—and if we lose all of the grains *and* the potatoes this year, all of us will be in the shit for fair, for there simply are not enough

remaining reserve foodstocks to feed everyone—
your people and mine own—through to the next
harvest. I know this for true fact, Emmett. I personally inventoried the fort stocks *and* those of the
station quite recently."

"I suppose we'll just have to send out more
hunting parties, Ian, and foragers with wagons, too,
you know, for nuts, acorns, wild tubers, potherbs
and the like. Hell, the prairie rovers have lived on
them for generations—we ought to be able to subsist
likewise for a few months, one would think."

The colonel heard out his friend, then said,
"Emmett, we can't depend on game or on foraged
foodstuffs, not unless we are willing to pay the price.
That price is high and becoming higher and I, for
one, think it's already too high. My estimate of the
situation is that each and every hundredweight of
dressed game is costing us one man killed or
wounded in brushes with the damned skulking
rovers' hunting parties, with whom ours are
competing. If we start vying with them for plant food
as well, every wagonload we bring back here is going
to be paid for in blood."

"Well . . ." The director hesitated, his brows
knitted up as he carefully thought of his next words,
then he let them go, all in a rushing spate. "If worst
comes to worst, Ian, there are cattle and sheep can
go to table without trimming the herds too much.
And rather than see folk starve, we could eat the
shire horses and the riding stock, as well, I suppose."

The colonel snorted derisively. "And if we
slaughter the shire horses, just what, pray tell, Mr.
Director, will provide draft for the harrows and
plows, come spring, eh?"

MacEvedy squirmed a bit in the chair. "Well . . .
ahh, Ian . . . ahh, the really ancient peoples used oxen
for draft work, you know, back before horses were
bred up big enough to be worthwhile, and some of

the prairie traders use them to draw wagons, too, you know, you've seen them."

The colonel chuckled. "Yes, I've seen them, but they were an entirely different breed from our cattle. I know I'd not care to be the man who took it upon himself to try to hitch Old Thunderer to any plow or wagon."

"Ian, Ian," the director remonstrated, a bit wearily, "Old Thunderer is a stud bull, far too old and set in his ways to do more than what he's always done. But I have quite a number of young steers that would be much more amenable to training for draft purposes. And the traders say that on level ground, a good draft ox can provide a stronger, steadier pull than even the best shire horse or mule."

The colonel grunted and shrugged. "Emmett, the shire horses are yours and the cattle, and if you want to reverse the order of things—eat the horses and train the cattle to draft—that is purely your pre-rogative, but the shire horses will be the only horse-flesh eaten, my friend. I draw the line at my horses."

He raised a hand, palm outward, when he saw the heat in the other man's eyes. "Wait—don't explode at me yet. There are very good reasons why you can't slaughter my horses. Drink your whiskey and cool down enough to think rationally, Emmett.

"Those troops of mounted archers and lancers constitute the only really mobile forces under my command anymore, and without them there will be no farming or herding at all. The damned prairie rovers will butcher every man and boy, carry off every woman and girl and drive off every head of stock that leaves the immediate protection of our inner perimeter, if they have no fear of my mounted patrols. Take away my horses and you doom every man, woman and child in station or fort to death or slavery."

"But . . . but your pikemen . . ." began the director.

"Emmett, no one of those brave men—weighed down with his pike, sword, dirk, armor and helmet—can move as fast as a horseman. And my pikemen are only really effective in numbers of sufficient size to form a defensive square and thus have a good chance of repelling the charges of horsemen.

"No, Emmett, my horses cannot join yours in the stewpots, that's all there is to the matter."

The director drained the dregs of the mug and set it down hard, his mouth drawn in grim lines. "Then, Ian, there will be half as many of us . . . if that many, this time next year!"

Chapter III

"We had ranged far and far to the north, that summer," Milo Morai began. "In those days, the entire tribe numbered about as many as do four or five clans, today, and so all traveled and camped close together for the safety and the strength provided by many warriors. We had followed the caribou herds north in the spring and were heading back southward in the hazy heat of midsummer, lest an early onset of winter trap us in those inhospitable latitudes."

Dung chips and all the wood scraps available had been heaped upon the coals of the nearest firepit, and in the flickering light thus cast, it could be seen that every man and boy and girl in the camp had formed a circle around that fire and Uncle Milo. Only the herd guards, camp guards and those few prairie-cats still out hunting were missing from the conclave of quiet listeners.

"The council and I had decided that the tribe would winter upon the high plains that year, so we had swung much farther to the west than usual. We then had no cat brothers, and so the warriors took turns scouting our line of march, flanks and rear, least we be surprised by dangerous beasts or twoleg enemies.

"Then, on a day, just as Sacred Sun had reached

midday peak, three of our scouts came riding in. One of them had been arrowed, and their report was most disturbing."

Wincing as he shifted, trying in vain to find a comfortable position for his bandage-bulky hip from which the fiendishly barbed arrow had been extracted, Sami Baikuh said, "Uncle Milo, a small river lies ahead, but between us and it are several warbands of nomad herdsmen, and at the very verge of the river there sits the biggest farm that I ever have seen anywhere, in all my life. Some of the houses have walls raised about them—not stockades of logs like many farms, but real walls of stones—and I thought to espy men on those walls. But the fields are all overgrown; they have not been sown or even plowed, this year, I think.

"A roving patrol of the nomad warriors spotted us, and for all that we tried to bespeak them in friendship, they loosed a volley of shafts at us. I was wounded, and since they were a score or so to our three, we felt it wiser to withdraw."

Milo laid a hand on the arm of the wounded man. "A most wise and sensible decision, Sami. The tribe will exact your suffering price from these men, never you fear."

At this, the other two scouts exchanged broad grins and one of them said, "Part of that price already is exacted, Uncle Milo. Even as his flesh was skewered, our modest Sami loosed a shaft that took the foremost of those unfriendly bastards through the left eye. I put an arrow into another's belly— and I warrant he'll be long in digesting that bit of sharp brass. Even Ilyuh, here, who is not the tribe's best bowman, gave one of them a souvenir of sorts to take home with him."

In in-saddle council, it was decided to attempt one time more a peaceful parley with the strange nomads and, if that should fail, to arm to the teeth, ride down upon them and hack a clear, broad path through them, for it was not the wont of the tribe to try to bypass hostile men who were just as mobile as were they themselves; sad, very painful experience had shown that such attempts always bred attacks to flanks or to rear of the vulnerable columns of wagons and herds.

Milo and the chief who had been chosen to head the tribal council for the traditional five-year term of office, Gaib Hwyt, rode out, flanked by half a dozen other chiefs, one of them bearing a lance shaft to which had been affixed the ancient sign of peaceful intentions—a yard-square piece of almost white woolen cloth. Some twoscore yards behind this peace delegation came a mixed troop of warriors and female archers, all fully armed and armored, their lance points twinkling in the sunlight.

As Milo, Chief Gaib and their immediate escort crested a gentle slope and walked their horses down its opposite face in the direction of the mile-distant river, a contingent of warriors sighted them, and while some of them reined hard about and set off toward the east at a punishing gallop, the bulk of the party rode to meet the newcomers, but slowly, in order that they might string bows and unsling targets and otherwise prepare for imminent blood-letting.

When some fifty yards separated the two groups, Milo raised his right hand, empty palm outward, then he and Chief Gaib and the flagbearer moved at a slow walk out into what they hoped was neutral ground, silent but for the stamp of hooves, the creaking of saddles and the jingle-jangle of equipment.

After a few moments of seeming confusion among themselves, punctuated by shoutings and obscenities, three of the stranger horsemen separated themselves from the main body and rode out to meet Milo and the two chiefs.

At easy speaking distance, both mounted trios

halted, then one of the strangers kneed his big, raw-boned dun slightly ahead of his two companions and eyed the three tribesmen with open, unveiled hostility. In dress or in overall physical appearance, he differed but little from Gaib and the other chief, his build being slender and flat-muscled, his visible skin surfaces—like theirs—darkened by sun and wind and furrowed by old scars. His hair was invisible under his helmet, but his full beard was a ruddy blond. The baggy trousers were of soft, if rather filthy, doeskin, his boots of felt and leather and his shirt, with its flaring sleeves, of faded cloth. He sat his mount easily and held his weapons with the ease of long familiarity, and his demeanor was that of the born leader of men.

He answered Milo's smile with a fierce scowl. "I'm Gus Scott. Are you the head dawg of this here murdering bunch of bushwhackers, mister?"

The very air about them seemed to crackle with deadly tension. Milo sheathed his smile, but was careful to make no move toward his weapons, despite the insulting words and manner. "My scouts were fired on first, Scott. They only returned fire in order to cover their withdrawal."

Scott shook his head. "That ain't the way I heared it, mister."

"My tribesmen do not lie!" Milo replied brusquely. "Anyhow, there are only the three of them, and one of them now lies in my camp severely wounded in the *back* of his hip. Does that sound to you like the kind of wound that an ambusher would sustain, Scott? And also think of this: Would any rational man ambush a score of warriors in open country without considerably more force than three men?"

"Well . . ." Scott waffled. "I didn't see it, mister, and I ain't saying I did, hear? It was ackshully some of old Jules LeBonne's boys. Could be they drawed bow and loosed a mite too quick. But that still don't go to say who you is and what you doing hereabouts, mister."

Milo shrugged. "We're a tribe of wandering herders, just as you would seem to be, to judge by your personal appearance, Scott. We followed the caribou north in the spring and now we're returning southwest to winter somewhere on the high plains. We have no desire to fight, only wishing to move our herds and our families south in peace. We will not, however, be victimized by you or anyone else."

Scott snorted. "Mister, I don't give a damn whereabouts you go to, but you better not plan on using that ford down yonder to get there, is all I got to say."

Grimly, Milo demanded, "And just how do you intend to stop us, Scott?"

"Hell, it ain't me or mine, mister. You want a peaceful crossing, you better just head twenny mile east or twelve mile nor'west, 'cause that fort yonder, she covers the only decent ford atween them, and them bugtits down there on them walls'll start picking you off four, five hunnert yards away."

Milo frowned. "They still have guns, then?"

"Damn right they has! And they knows how to shoot them and they purely hates ever living critter on earth . . . 'cepting maybe theyselfs."

Milo did not doubt the stranger's assertions as regarded the other strangers down by the river ford. There was more reason to believe than to doubt, in this case, for he had experienced many times in the last century groups and individuals who were plainly homicidal for no apparent reason.

The brief, savage nuclear exchange which its survivors had called a war had directly caused very few deaths or physical injuries among the hundreds of millions of human beings then on the North American continent; most of the calamitous losses of life had occurred weeks or months after the last missiles had struck target and had been the result of

starvation, various diseases and fighting among the
survivors themselves. In many cases, those who had
survived to the present day were the direct descendants of men and women who had withdrawn to
secure or secluded places and defended those places
with deadly force against all would-be intruders. The
children, grandchildren and great-grandchildren had
imbibed such sentiments as "Death to all strangers"
with their mothers' milk and now could not be hoped
or expected to behave other than as the rabid killers
Gus Scott had described.

The encampment of the warbands was situated in
a fold of ground cupping a small tributary to the
river, which just there widened to the dimensions of
a modest lake and lay a half hour's easy ride from the
farthest fields and pasturelands of the riverside
settlement and fort. Gus Scott's was the only one
that included women, children, wagons and herds; it
also was the largest contingent of warriors. All of the
other chiefs had brought along just male fighters,
spare mounts and a few head of rations-on-the-hoof.
Lacking tents, these bachelor warriors slept in the
open in good weather and in soddies—circular pits
some eight to twelve feet in diameter and three to
four feet deep, with rough blocks of sun-dried sods
stacked in layers around the rim to bring the interior
height to an average of five feet, then roofed over
with poles, green hides and finally more sod blocks—
on wet nights.

It was in an open space between the Scott encampment and the bachelor camp that Milo, Chief Gaib
Hwyt and the other six chiefs sat or squatted in
initial council with the chiefs and headmen of the
various warbands.

Chef Jules LeBonne's French—which he spoke in
asides to his own cronies, never for a moment dream-
ing that Milo could not only understand almost every
spoken word but could fill in those he did not

comprehend by means of telepathic mind-reading abilities—was every bit as crude and ungrammatical as was his English. He was a squat, solid and power-ful-looking man and seemed to have no neck worthy of the name; his head was somewhat oversized for his body, and the face that peered from beneath the helmet's visorless rim was lumpy, scarred and filthy, nor had his basic ugliness been at all improved by an empty right eyesocket, a nearly flattened nose and the loss of most of his front teeth. He and his followers all stank abominably, and Milo doubted that any one of them had had anything approaching a bath or a wash since the last time they had been caught out in a rainstorm or had had to swim a river.

He lisped and threw globules of spittle when he talked in any language. "You mus' unnerstan', M'sieu Moray, thees we here mean to do, *un affaire d' honneur* ees, also too, ees to rid thees prairie of a always *dangereux. Comprez vous?*"

Gus Scott, who seemed to be of at the very least equal rank and importance to LeBonne, amended, "Mr. Moray, Jules and his folks tawks Frainch so damn much ever day that he don't allus tawk Ainglish too pert. Whut he's trying to say is that that bunch of murderers over to the ford, they done owed us all a powerful blood debt more'n thutty year, now. And we all of us means to colleck in full, this time 'round, we does!"

"I take it that more than a few instances of long-range snipings are involved in this vendetta, then, Mr. Scott?" Milo inquired.

"You fucking right it's more, mister!" Scott replied with vehemence. "Bit over thutty years agone, was a real bad winter—I mean to tell you a *real* bad winter, mister! Won't no game here 'bouts a-tall, I hear tell, and the wolfs was all sumthin' fierce and all a-runnin' in bigger packs than any-body'd ever seed afore. Spring come in real late, too, that year, and the floods was plumb awful, whut with the extra-deep snows and thick ice and all.

"By the time folks got to where they could move around some, all of the older folks was all dead and the most of the littler kids and babies, too. Them critters what the wolfs hadn't got had done been butchered and et for lack of game, so that it wasn't no feller had more nor one hoss left and a lot what didn't even have that one. Some pore souls had been so hard put to it they'd had to eat their own dead kinfolks, just to keep alive theyselfs."

Suddenly, for no apparent reason, *Chef* Jules LeBonne cackled a peal of maniacal-sounding laughter, which was echoed by his cronies. A brief scan of the chief's surface thoughts shook Milo and left him more than a little disturbed, but Scott had ignored the laughter and still was recounting the horrors of thirty-odd years before.

" . . . come late spring and some dry weather, everybody was in some kinda real bad shape, you better believe, mister. Everybody, that is, except them murdering bastards over to the ford. Sassy and pert they all was; even their critters was all sleek. So, anyhow, the grandfolks, afore of us, they all went over to there and they asked just as nice and perlite as you please for them selfish, murdering bastards to help us all out some. You know, give us some eatments and enough of their stock for to start our own herds up again.

"Well, them bastards, they th'owed our chiefs out'n their fort, they did, mister. But them old boys might've been starving, but they still had their pride left and they rode at that fort, three, four, five times over, till it won't enough mens and hosses left to do it no more."

Scott paused and tugged at a greasy rawhide thong looped about his sinewy neck, then pulled up from beneath his shirt a bit of metal. Flattish it was, almost two inches across, two of its three edges rough and jagged-appearing, for all that all edges and surfaces were pitted with oxidation and shiny with the patina of years.

Milo instantly recognized the thing, knew what it once had been—shrapnel, a piece of shell casing—and he could not repress a shudder, for he had hoped that that particular horror of warfare, at least, was long years gone from a suffering world.

Scott resumed his heated narrative. "This here thing, it pierced my grandpa's pore laig, right at the same time that some suthin tore the whole front end off of his hoss. My pa and his brother, they dragged grandpa away then, and they said that was the onliest reason any of them lived to tell 'bout it all, too. 'Cause after them dirty, selfish murderers had done shot or burned or tore into pieces all them pore mens, they come out'n that there fort with rifles and great big guns and I don't know whatall. Some was on horses, but most was on or in big old steel wagons what my grandpa used to call 'tanks' a-shooting faster than you could blink your eyes and throwing out sheets of fire a hunnert feet long.

"Them bloodthirsty bastards, they kept after them pore folks for twenny mile and more. They kilt every man they could and then just left their bodies a-laying out for the coyotes and wolfs and foxes and buzzards, they did.

"And ever sincet then, their riders has done kilt or tried like hell for to kill every man they come on any-wheres near here. For more nor thutty year, they done been killing for no damn reason, mister. We tried to put a stop to it, too, not that it got us all anything, 'cepting for dead relatives and friends and hosses.

"Twelve years ago, when my pa still was chief, we joined up with nearly a thousand other mens from all 'round here on the prairies and we come down on that place down there."

Milo shook his head slowly. "I'll say this, your father had guts—about a mile of them—but he, of all people, considering what he'd been through before, should have realized that you can't successfully oppose armored vehicles with horse cavalry, or use cavalry to attack well-fortified positions equipped with rifles and artillery. How many did you lose on that occasion, Chief Gus?"

"Well," answered Scott, "he'd done heard from the traders and some others that won't none of the steel wagons would work no more, and I guess as how that was right, too, 'cause they come out of the fort—some on hosses, but most on their feet and with great long old spears. They stood up in a square-like bunch and put their hosses in the middle and we rode down on 'em, but them old spears was so damn long that they stuck out way past the lines of men, and when the hosses got pricked with 'em a few times, won't no man could get his hoss to go close again. And all the time, it was bastards standing there with crossbows and rifles and prods and some them fellers on hosses in the middle with real bows just a-shooting down man after man. Finally, one of the bugtits shot my pa and then everybody just tucked tail and ran and the damn bastards come after us with their own damn fresh hosses and killed off a lot more pore mens from ahind. That's the kind of backstabbing, selfish murderers they is, you see, mister."

"So," said Milo, "you've spent ten or twelve years breeding and now you're ready to ride down there and have the most of a new generation of young men butchered and maimed, eh? Well, Chief Gus, this is not my tribe's fight and I'd far liefer ride a few miles out of our direct route to the high plains than to get involved in such a matter, thank you."

Scott shrugged. "I didn't ask for your help, did I, mister? I would of been willing to let you folks ride along of us all and share in the loot and stock and womens and all, but the way I done heard it, it probly ain't going to take all what old Jules and me has got, much less of your folks, too.

"See, Squinty Merman, the trader, come th'ough in early summer and allowed as how them bastards over there at MacEvedy Station is in some kind of a bad way. Seems as how they had bad crops for two years running, then damn near no crops a-tall, last year. They done et up all what they had stored, their seed grain, too—had to eat a lot of their critters and done had a bad spate of a sickness that's done took off a lot and left the rest damn poorly.

"Well, Mr. Moray, I figgered right then and there it couldn't be no better time for to go 'bout paying back the murdering bastards for everything they'd done done to us and our grandfolks and all, so I sent riders out to fetch back old Jules and the rest of the boys. I told them to bring all the fighters they could and that we'd all meet here. Then my own folks and me, we moved on down here and set up our camp and waited for them as was coming.

"Since we all got here, it's been damn few of them bastards has come out of that fort and all, and"—he chuckled coldly—"it's damn fewer of the fuckers what done made it back ahind them walls. 'Course, we did lose us some damn good boys and some hosses, too, afore we came to find out just how god-awful far them frigging rifles can shoot and kill a man at. But since we done learned how far we has to stay away from them, we ain't lost but two men, afore today, leastways, and won't neither one of them kilt by them bastards and their fucking rifles."

Arabella Lindsay laid aside the body brush and the currycomb, dipped the dandy brush into the bucket of water and then after she had tossed the full mane of the dapple-gray stallion over to the off side of his neck, she began to brush his crest.

More than seventeen hands of bone, sinew and rolling muscles, the great beast stood stock-still, occasionally whuffling his physical pleasure, while all the time in completely silent, telepathic communication with this small twoleg creature whom he adored.

"But this horse *needs* to run, to run hard." His beaming was becoming a bit petulant. "Trotting around the inside of the quadrangle is almost worse than no exercise at all. This horse is becoming stiff. We don't need to go far, just a few miles and then back."

"Capull, Capull," the girl silently remonstrated. "I've been through all of this nearly every day for weeks now. There are enemies, evil, thieving, murderous men, camped all about the fort and the station, who already have killed many of our folks and stolen or killed their horses and cattle. There are no longer enough men of fighting age left hale enough to go out and drive these skulkers away, as was done in years past, and so we just must abide within our walls until they choose to go away."

She sighed and laid her cheek against the stallion's glossy neck. "Poor, poor Father—he is so frustrated by it all. He would like nothing better than to take out his pikemen and crossbowmen and riflemen and cavalry and trounce these filthy, bestial rovers as thoroughly as he did years ago, but all the deaths from illness and hunger this last year have so reduced the garrison that he no longer has enough force to even defend these walls, much less to mount a field operation against the skulkers. I think, as do Father and Director MacEvedy, that only fear of the two big guns and the mortars has kept them from attacking our very walls, Capull, but if they knew just how few loads there are remaining for not only them but for our rifles . . . Oh, Capull, I am so very frightened. I'm only fifteen, and I don't want to die, but poor Father is so very, very worried about so many, many things that I cannot but keep a brave face and demeanor in his presence. You are the only friend with whom I can talk freely. I love you so, my dear Capull."

The huge stallion beamed renewed assurances of undying love and adoration for the girl and added solemn assurance that he would stamp the life out of anything on two legs or four or none that ever offered her harm. He meant it and she knew it.

The two old friends, Colonel Ian Lindsay and Director Emmett MacEvedy, were indeed deeply worried, and with excellent reason. So hard had they been hit, so badly had they suffered, that even the worst of MacEvedy's predictions had been more than surpassed in actuality. Only some two hundred men, women and children still were alive in all of the fort-station complex, and not a few of those were ill or convalescent, a convalesence lengthened by the poor and scanty rations available to them all these dark days.

The last of the seed grain was long since consumed, along with every last scrap of canned or otherwise preserved foods. Not a single chicken was left, nor any pigs; the rabbit cages gaped empty, as too did the commodious stalls of the shire horses, most of them. The director was now fearful of allowing the slaughter of any more cattle or sheep, lest there be no breeding stock left when once this string of calamities had at last come to an end; however, unless a way could be found to replace the almost expended silage, it might be a hard choice of slaughtering the last of the kine *and* the horses or of just watching them starve to death. He never, of course, considered surrendering his stock to the besiegers any more than he would have thought of turning over to them his wife or his children.

These days, they all were subsisting on fish from the river, herbs and mushrooms cultivated within the walls and those wild plants gathered from the nearer fields where the riflemen on the walls could keep reasonably safe from the prairie rovers the hardy souls who had agreed to go outside.

This past spring, they had had none of the usual
crop or animal surpluses for the trader caravan.
Rather had they had to trade metal for all of the
jerky the traders would trade, and not enough value
had been left of that transaction to obtain any of the
needed brimstone, so the supply of gunpowder now
was become desperately low. Nor were they overly
well supplied with lead for bullets, though Ian
Lindsay seemed to think that certain other metals
still available—notably, pewter—might be utilized in
a real emergency.

The director laughed to himself at the memory of
his old friend's words, as if there could be an
emergency any more real and pressing than their
present straits.

A flurry of shouts and the sounds of fast-moving
feet made him arise from his desk and stride to his
office door just as a fist smote its panels in a staccato
knock. He opened it to a red-faced soldier.

After a smart salute, the sweaty man said, "Sir,
Colonel Lindsay's compliments. He would have the
director at his office as soon as possible. A prairie
rover is riding in alone under a white flag."

Guided by Scott warriors familiar with the
territory to be covered, the Kindred scouts had not
been long in returning from the two other fords, but
their news had run from bad to worse.

"The ford downstream, to the east, some twenty-
two or so miles from this place," Subchief Airuhn
Lehvee had informed the tribal council, "is narrow
and full of potholes and fissures, and the current is
very swift. We could use it—I have crossed worse, I
admit—but it will be very slow and we will lose
stock, maybe wagons and Kindred, too. It will likely
be better, think I, to use this other, upstream ford
that was mentioned, rather than to waste so much
time and take so much risk as use of the one I just
scouted would entail."

But old Chief Gaib Hwyt shook his head. "Would that we had that option, Kinsman, but I fear it is either that dangerous, treacherous ford you scouted or none. The scouts who rode northwest came back to report that at sometime since this time last year the river changed course up there. There now is no ford, only deep, fast-flowing water in a new bed. So we just must move downstream, to the east, and chance yours, I suppose. There is nothing else for it."

"There just might be, Gaib. Don't be too hasty in this very important matter."

The old man turned his head. "You have advice for the council, Uncle Milo? Ever is your sage counsel welcome and heeded by us, your own Kindred."

It had not been all that easy, of course. Gus Scott had had to be convinced that something might be accomplished to satisfy the vengeful ends of him and his people, and in hopes of effecting that purpose, Milo had had the Kindred throw a feast to which the non-Kindred nomads had been invited.

Life was hard, almost unremittingly hard, for the cattle-, goat- and sheep-herding nomad peoples of the prairies and plains. Summers were hot and dry and harbored the near constant threat of horizon-to-horizon fires, which could wipe out entire tribes and their herds; autumn was usually only a continuation of the summer until suddenly, like as not catastrophically, winter swept down to envelop the lands and all upon them in its icy, relentless grip.

Winter was always the hardest, most deadly season to man and beast, and each succeeding one took some toll of life, mostly of the aged, the very young or the sickly, but sometimes, entire encampments would be wiped out. And even the natural rebirth of spring could bring along with its warmth the peril of flooding.

Hunting, which occupation provided a large proportion of a nomad's meat, could be a deadly dangerous affair, and each year took its own toll in

deaths and maimings and a full gamut of injuries.
Nor were even mundane pursuits really safe, for
horses, mules and cattle are none of them noted as
among the more intelligent quadrupeds and their
native denseness when combined with unreasoning
fear and their inherent strength had cost more than
one nomad his life.

It was because their day-to-day life was so hard,
regardless of the season or the weather, that these
people seldom rejected a chance for some pleasure
or recreation and imbibed of it in long, deep drafts.
Consequently, the invitation of the Ehlai-Kindred
tribe was received no less joyously for the gravity of
the acceptance speeches of the various chiefs,
subchiefs and warchiefs approached. Preparations
immediately commenced for a gala two to three
days' revel, with the finest items of clothing,
weapons and equipment being unpacked, cleaned,
polished and refurbished. Favorite mounts were
groomed until their hides were all agleam, for
personal and tribal honor and prestige demanded a
good and impressive showing of chiefs and warriors,
in particular.

Most large game and much of the smaller had, of
course, been killed off or frightened away within the
immediate environs of the besiegers' camps, so the
Kindred had to ride far, far out to secure provender
for the feasting, but find it they did. The various
parties brought back numerous deer of varying sizes,
a couple of fat bears, wild swine, stray caribou and a
brace of some deerlike ruminant with unusual,
unbranched horns.

It was the hunting party accompanied by Milo,
however, that chanced across the true oddity, a
highly dangerous seven days' wonder.

It was a hunter named Bili Gawn who first found
the singular tracks and led the rest of the party to the
muddy streambank in which they had been pressed.

Milo and the rest squatted about the huge hoofprints.

"They look no whit different from any herd cow's," remarked one of the hunters, "but for the size and the depth of the print. By Sun and Wind, Uncle Milo, the beast must weigh as much as two or three of our biggest bulls. What do you suppose it can be?"

Milo shrugged. "There are two ways to find out. One is to try to track it, but away from this soft ground, out there on the open prairie, it might be a task easier spoken of than done. The other would be to hunt as usual this day long, then arrange to be here when it comes back to drink. But what think you, Bili? You're the best tracker, by far."

The red-haired young man wrinkled his brows. "Well, Uncle Milo, we could try both of your ideas. Follow the beast as far out as we can, then carry on with the hunting, set up an early camp and make sure to be here around sundown, which was when it last came here, when these prints were impressed in this mud."

Luck was with them—they found the object of their search only a mile or so distant, a solitary bovine of impressive proportions. Milo had seen gaur, kouprey, bison and wisent, African and Asian buffaloes, and he had never before set eyes to any bovine of the height or apparent weight of this bull.

The creature was a ruddy-brown-black, with a shaggy hide a bit reminiscent of the bison or wisent. Also akin to those beasts, it had a sizable hump of muscle atop its shoulders, which gave it an overall height at the withers approaching seven feet, Milo reckoned. He also reckoned that figure to be about the span from tip to wicked tip of its shiny-black horns. Although the body was thick and deep-chested, it was held well up off the ground on long legs. The animal gave an impression of immense strength and lightning speed, and the old scars

furrowing his hide showed that he must embody
immense vitality to match that strength.

Had it been up to Milo alone, he would have left
the tough old warrior where he grazed and sought
out less deadly-looking prey. But in the minds of the
other hunters, there was never any question as to
whether or not to slay the gigantic bull, for not only
were wild bulls an ever present danger to their herds
of cattle, this black bovine represented significant
quantities of meat, hide, horn, sinew, bone and
hooves, not to mention the inevitable glory and
prestige of having taken part in the slaying of so
unusual and massive a quarry.

However, none of them being of a suicidal bent,
they planned the attack with great care, eight men
being none too many to try to put paid to so big an
animal. The big question, of course, was whether the
bull would make to flee or choose to fight where he
stood. Both eventualities must be foreseen and
covered in contingency plans.

At last, starting far, far out on all sides, they rode
very slowly toward the bull, two with bolas ready in
case the beast tried to run, the rest bearing bows,
nocked arrows and spare shafts between the fingers
of the bowhand. None had even thought of trying to
ready or use lance or spear, for the beast clearly had
too much power for any man and horse to hold on a
lance, and no one wanted to get close enough to put a
spear into him until he had been seriously hurt by
some well-placed arrows.

The monstrous black bull raised his massive head
several times, turning it here and there to test the
vagrant currents of air, the long, long horns
gleaming in the pairie sunlight. And each time that
he did so, Milo's heart seemed to skip a beat or two,
but each time, the bovine went back to grazing the
grasses among which he stood. And the eight men
rode closer, closer, and ever closer. Already, one or
two had come to within extreme range of their bows.

But then the shaggy bull raised his great head yet again, and this time he did not resume his grazing, but stood tensely while he tested the air, then bellowed an awful, bass challenge and began to paw at the ground.

Chapter IV

The huge wild bull was clearly on the very verge of a charge, which Milo knew could mean one or more deaths of hunters and/or quite possibly the escape of the beast. He thanked his stars that all seven of his companions on this day were mindspeakers, then silently beamed his message to them.

"I doubt that he can see any better than any other kind of cattle. He seems to be dependent on scent and sound, so let's be wolf-wily. Those of you behind him make noise. When he turns, you be still and let those then behind him make noises; in this wise we may be able to keep him confused enough to all get within killing range. But when he does charge, don't any of you try to show how brave you are—get the hell out of his way, if you can. Big as he is, he could likely toss a horse with those horns, and one of you on that horse."

Milo reflected that they should have brought some bigger hounds, which could if nothing else have given the monster something to occupy his mind and energies until the men were all in killing range. But he had never really liked hunting with dogs, and besides, who would ever have thought that the party would chance across so singular a beast as this brown-black mountain of muscle and bone and sinew?

In the end, no man or horse was lost or even hurt. Thanks to Milo's wise counsel, the great bull was never able to make up his mind just which way to charge until it was become far too late for him. One bola and then a second flew, spinning to enwrap those treetrunk-thick rear legs, then the bowmen came swooping in at a hard gallop from either side of the roaring, struggling bovine, to drive their shafts nearly to the fletchings in the heaving, shaggy sides.

When bloody froth began to spray from the bull's nostrils, two horsemen risked riding in close enough to hamstring both the near and the off rear legs, then Milo dismounted and dashed forward, burying the six-inch razor-edged head of a wolf spear in the bull's throat, neatly severing the great neck artery.

Walking, leading horses burdened with the butchered bull, they were very late in returning to the camp, but there was nonetheless tumultuous rejoicing, for no one of the Horseclans folk had ever seen the likes of the massive kill, which equaled or bettered the total in edible meat of all the other beasts slain by the hunters.

The tanning hide and the oversized horns of this particular kill were a wonder to all who got to see them, Horseclanfolk or the other nomads alike. At the feast, Chief Gus Scott and his subchiefs wondered and exclaimed over the trophies repeatedly.

"It's all shaggy, like a buffler, 'bout the color of one, too. But who ever seed a buffler hide thet big, huh? And who ever seed horns like them on any buffler? How tall you say he stood, Chief Milo?"

"Between six and seven feet at the withers, Chief Gus, not counting that hump of muscle and cartilage. I've never seen any bovine just like him before. I was hoping you and your folk might be familiar with the breed—could tell me something of them and warn me of how prevalent they are, hereabouts."

The Scott chieftain just shook his shaggy head.

"Not me, mister. I ain't never seen no critter like thet, not out here on the prairies, nor neither on the high plains. Mebbe he come down outen the mountains? I dunno, but I'm sure glad you and your mens kilt the big bastid is all. The less of his kind a-roaming 'round about here, the better." His subchiefs grunted assent and nodded, fingering the wicked tips of the two yard-long horns. "B'cause thet would be a whole helluva lot of he-cow to have a-coming after you."

In the days between the kill and the feast, Milo had had few spare moments to devote to pondering, but those few he had given to trying to imagine just how so singular a creature as the massive ungulate they had slain might have originated. Although his appearance was that of a man in his mid-thirties, Milo Morai was, at that time, a very old man—he himself did not even know exactly how old, but at least something above two full centuries—and his memories spanned a period from the 1930s to the present, through all the vicissitudes that had afflicted and at least nearly extirpated the races of mankind, killing untold millions in a few, terrible months by starvation and rampant, uncontrollable diseases, a few of these new, but most old.

If the areas of what had been the United States of America and the Commonwealth of Canada were a fair example of the rest of the world, eighty to ninety percent of humanity had been brutally exterminated by various causes in the wake of the brief, horribly destructive spate of hostilities between the allied powers of West and East power blocs.

According to his own witness and things he had heard, Milo knew that very few of the larger centers of population on the North American continent had actually been nuked. Several of the West Coast cities had been, along with Washington, D.C., Boston, Norfolk, Ottawa, Chicago, New Orleans and Houston, but these had all most likely been struck by

missiles launched from submarines, since the High
Frontier Defensive Systems had knocked down most
of the ICBMs and satellite-launched weapons.

The response had been immediate and must have
been devastating in the target areas on the other side
of the earth. Milo had, in his travels, seen countless
deep, now empty silos sunk into the soil and rock
which once had contained the retaliatory missiles
and their mutliple warheads.

For a few weeks during that terrible period of the
past, Milo had had access to powerful radio equipment and had been able to ascertain that few nations
had been spared the destruction and subsequent
turmoil, disease, starvation and death.

The People's Republic of China had had several
population centers nuked, then almost immediately
had found itself fighting invasions across its western
and southeastern borders, as well as a concerted
seaborne invasion of the Nationalist Chinese from
Taiwan, a deadly-serious rebellion in Tibet and
assorted smaller uprisings in every province. None
of the Chinese contacts had, however, broadcast for
long, many only once, and by the end of a month
from first contact, all had fallen silent. The Taiwan
station lasted only some weeks longer, its last broadcast reporting uncontrollable rioting in urban areas
and widespread death from as yet undiagnosed,
plaguelike diseases.

The only station Milo had ever been able to reach
in the area of western Russia had been a strong
signal from Erivan. It had been broadcast in
Russian, Armenian, English, French, Turkish,
Arabic, Farsi, Hebrew and Italian and had proclaimed in all of these the immediate declaration of a
free Republic of Armenia. However, at the end of
three days, the station had gone off the air in mid-
sentence and had never again been heard, nor had
Milo been able to raise a response from it.

London had been nuked, he had discovered, along

.with Paris, Bonn, Berlin, Copenhagen, Rome, Ankara, Tel Aviv, Cairo, Riyadh, Teheran, Bagdad, Damascus, Beirut, Belgrade and countless other European and Middle Eastern population centers, ports and places of greater or lesser military importance. The Russian army had swept across most of Western Europe almost unopposed until a sudden onslaught of the new diseases had more than decimated it and its foes indiscriminately along with the civilian noncombatants around them.

A transmission from Belfast apprised Milo that its decades-long turmoil had, if anything, become unbelievably chaotic. While refugees from devastated England and Scotland poured into every port, the Protestant majority were openly battling Catholic and Marxist rebels in cities and countrysides and trying to make ready for an imminent invasion of its southern borders by the army of the Irish Republic. The transmitter went off the air after the third broadcast, and Milo never could raise it again. He did raise a Dublin station, some weeks later, crowing about a "great, God-sent victory" that had "reunited Holy Ireland and driven the Sassenachs into the sea." But the same announcer had deplored the terrible plague that the army had brought back from the north that was even as he spoke baffling all Irish doctors. Dublin continued to broadcast for several weeks more, but it became increasingly sporadic and its last few transmissions were all in some guttural language that Milo assumed to be an obscure or archaic Gaelic, nor would the station answer him in English. At last, it became silent, no response at all.

The Southern Hemisphere seemed less affected by the diseases and destruction than did the Northern, as Milo recalled. Durban, Johannesburg, Pretoria, Uppington and countless other large and smaller private and commercial broadcasts reached him as long as he had access to his own equipment. Quite a number of South American private, government and commercial stations were also on the air when he, perforce, left it. He was never able to pick up anything from Mexico, Central America or the northern and western Caribbean, but he monitored powerful though sporadic transmissions from some variety of underground research facility located somewhere in central Florida. This broadcaster, too, was still on the air when he had to move on, as were several locations in Antarctica.

According to the South African broadcasts, along with a few isolated signals from other areas, both northern and central Africa, from Atlantic to Indian Oceans, were aseethe with invasions, counter-attacks, rebellions and every conceivable type and size of conflict along every conceivable racial, tribal, religious, political or social line. Egypt, seemingly not at all certain whether the nuking of Cairo had come from Israel or Libya, had launched retaliatory attacks on both countries. Libya was in a vise, being attacked as well by Algeria, Tunisia and a shaky coalition of Niger and Chad.

By the time Milo first monitored African broadcasts, the Union of South Africa's armed forces had already conquered Botswana, Rhodesia and part of Mozambique, reconquered Namibia, and were pushing on into southern Angola and Zambia. Their military successes were abetted by the facts that all these countries were racked by widely scattered rebellions and uprisings, other borders were in serious need of protection from the incursions of other neighbors, and while hundreds of thousands, even millions—civilians and soldiers alike—were dropping like flies from the new plaguelike diseases, the white South Africans alone of all on the continent seemed immune.

Half a dozen Indian cities had been nuked. Nonetheless, the Indian armed forces seemed to be in the process of attacking across borders on nearly every side, even while riots, insurrections and rebellions

on a grand scale vied with disease to kill most
Indians.

Those survivors of the Vietnamese army that had
invaded nuclear-stricken and otherwise beset China
had brought back with them the plaguelike diseases,
and these seemed to spread through Southeast Asia
like wildfire, accompanying boatloads of starving,
panic-stricken refugees to the Philippines and the
islands of Indonesia. Australia had not received a
single nuke, had utilized the harshest of draconian
methods to drive off or kill would-be arrivals from
plague-infested areas, but despite it all, still had
found the incurable disease raging over the island
continent from north to south, sparing only the
scorned aborigines, oddly enough. Milo got most of
this information at second hand from a Wellington,
New Zealand, station, those islands having but
recently somehow acquired the dreaded and deadly
disease.

Military installations on the Hawaiian Islands had
been nuked, and so had Tahiti. Otherwise, Oceania
seemed from its various radio transmissions to be
doing better than the most of the world. He was
unable to get any sort of response from Japan,
however.

South America seemed to be suffering almost as
much as Africa, with a fierce war in progress
between Argentina and Chile, another between
Bolivia and Chile. Bolivia also was fighting Peru,
which was in the process of trying to conquer neigh-
boring Ecuador. Colombia too seemed to have
designs upon Ecuador, as well as on Venezuela.
Venezuela herself had moved into Guyana, taken
over Trinidad, and was in process of marshaling an
assault upon Surinam. Brazil had occupied French
Guiana and was filling the airwaves with a barrage
of nuclear-tipped threats against anyone who tried to
violate Brazilian sovereignty or territorial aspirations. Paraguay and Uruguay both were fighting two-

front defensive wars against Brazil and Argentina. It was from a South American source that Milo learned that the Panama Canal had been struck by, at the least, two nuclear missiles, one seeming to come from somewhere out in the Pacific Ocean, one or more others from the Caribbean side.

It had been later that year when he had chanced across the gaggle of sick, scared, starving children who, under his guidance and tutelage, had become the genesis of the Horseclans folk. By that time, after traveling through countless miles of once-populous countryside that now stank to high heaven of decaying and unburied human corpses, fighting off both there and in the towns and smaller cities where he scrounged for ammunition and supplies the huge packs of hunger-mad, masterless once-pet dogs— these more deadly and dangerous than any pack of wild wolves, since none of them feared mankind and most had recently been dining principally on human flesh—he had come to realize that the immensely complex and interdependent civilization was dead on this continent and quite possibly worldwide for a very long time to come. As for the children he had found, were they to survive and breed more of their race, he would have to teach them to live as savages in a savage, brutal and merciless environment.

Knowing that before too long a time modern firearms and parts and ammunition for them would become unobtainable, he taught them all the bow, at which he was himself expert, taking some of the older boys with him on dangerous expeditions to cities to obtain bows and arrows of fiberglass, metal or wood, even while he experimented with wood, horn, sinew and various natural glues in anticipation of the time when ready-made bows would not be available for the mere taking.

Adept already at living off the wilderness, he imparted to the growing children who now depended upon him some of his vast store of knowledge and skills, then sought through the dead cities and villages and towns for books he and they could read to learn even more. Horses and gear for riding came from deserted ranches and farms, as too did the first few head of cattle, goats and sheep. He had had them bring in swine, too, up until the time he had come across some feral hogs eating the decayed remains of men and women who had died of the plagues; after that, he feared to allow them to eat the flesh of such swine or bears as roamed in the vicinity of former haunts of mankind.

The first generation had grown up, paired off, sired, borne and began to raise a second generation in a settled environment. They farmed and raised livestock, supplementing the produce of lands and herds with hunting game and foraging wild plants, nuts, and the like. They might have stayed thus and there, had not a succession of dry years forced Milo to face the necessity of a move to a place where water still was easily available and the graze was not all dead or dying.

Milo and several of the better riders crossed the western mountains to the valley beyond. There they ran down and caught as many of the feral horses as they could and herded the stock back over the mountains to their holdings. Then Milo led another party back to that same valley, but pressed on farther north, as close as he dared to one of the places that had been nuked.

He found that others had been there long before him, radiation or no radiation, and that all the stores and shops had been most thoroughly looted of anything of utility or value. However, on the outskirts of what had apparently been an industrial park, he and his men lucked across a huge, windowless building. Upon the forcing of a loading-dock door, they found themselves within a cavernous building which had been the warehouse, seemingly, of a department store. It required weeks of work, numerous round trips to thoroughly loot all that they could use from the variegated stocks of artifacts, but by the time that the long caravan of people, horses and herds moved out of the desiccated area that had for so long been their home, the packs and the travoises were heavy, piled high with necessaries for man and for beast.

To everyone's great disappointment, the dusty stock had not included a single firearm or any ammunition of any sort, caliber or description; however, after their thorough lootings, every man, woman and child now was provided with a bow of fiberglass or metal, as many arrows and razor-edged hunting heads and spare bowstrings as could be carried, and two or three knives.

Although Milo and the others had seen no living human on their trips to the western side of the mountains, not even any recent traces of humans, the trips had not been uneventful. On the way back east from the very first one, all walking and leading their heavily laden horses and therefore moving far more slowly than they had on the journey west, they had had the picket line attacked one night, a mule killed and dragged off into the darkness.

Milo and those others armed with heavier-caliber firearms tracked the raider and found themselves, eventually, confronting a huge, full-grown Siberian tiger. But huge and vital as the beast was—some eleven feet from nose to tail tip!—he proved no real match for six crack shots armed with big-bore hunting rifles, for all that the monstrous cat exhibited no fear of man and charged almost immediately. And he was just the first animal they had to kill during the course of stripping that warehouse of things they could use.

They shot two adult leopards within the remains of the industrial park, near the warehouse, while on a solitary, exploratory jaunt, Milo was faced by and had to kill with his pistol a jaguar. He found what he

Robert Adams

thought to be the answer to the existence hereabouts of these non-native beasts during another, longer trip, a wide swing around the radioactive core city. In an area that still was partially fenced, grazed and browsed a mixed herd of giraffes, wildebeests, zebras and several varieties of antelope. Having spent some years, off and on, in Africa, Milo was able to recognize waterbucks, blesboks, springboks, Thomson's gazelles, impalas and what, at the distance, looked much like a huge eland. He kept a good distance, observing the herd through binoculars, because he had come across tracks and immense piles of dung that led him to believe that there were elephants and rhino about the place. A bit farther on, he spotted another mixed herd, this one including wildebeests, ostriches, oryxes, zebras and half a dozen types of antelope or gazelle with which he was unfamiliar, but also some specimens of big, handsome, spotted axis deer, a few other cervines he could recognize by the antlers as Père David's deer and a buck and two or three does that could have been red deer, sambar deer or small American elk. It was when he noticed a pride of lions moving through the high grass that he recalled that discretion was the better part of valor and also the fate of the curious tabby cat.

Upon his return to his party of warehouse looters, he ordered the horses stabled within the huge building by night and well guarded by day.

"I've found one of the places that the tiger, the leopards and maybe that jaguar, too, came from. Some of you men may recall being taken as young children, before the war and all, to drive through huge parks and view wild animals from all over the world. Well, there's one of them—pretty big and well stocked, too, from the little I saw of it—only a few days' ride to the northeast of where we are now. A number of the fences are down, and I'd bet that that's where the predatory cats wandered down here from. As I recall, lions and tigers don't get on too well in the same territory, and since I saw a big pride of lions up there, the tiger may have felt outnumbered and come down here to live on feral horses and deer. Those two leopards and the jaguar may very well be the reason why this area is no longer ravaged by packs of wild dogs, for both cats have a fondness for dog flesh. I'm just thankful that none of the big cats seem to have had the inclination to go east and cross the mountains to our valleys."

The migration proved long and hard and slow, with the same drought conditions that had driven them all from their homes seemingly prevailing all along their line of march. Game was very scarce, and many a night they all had nothing more than a few small bites of rattlesnake and/or rabbit to sustain them until something bigger was unwily enough to fall to their hunters or one or more of their herd animals succumbed to lack of graze and water.

Milo tried to avoid stretches of true desert as much as was possible, traveling on or near highways when it proved at all feasible, adapting a fortunate find in the lot of a long-deserted business of several dozen U-Haul trailers to horse- or mule- or ox-draft vehicles. At length, he decided to head them in the direction of Lake Tahoe, figuring that at least there was certain to be a plentitude of water thereabouts, likely graze and game, and, just possibly, enough arable land to settle down and farm. He faced the possibility that there might be people already there, as well, but numbering as they did some fourscore armed men of fighting age, not to mention quite a few women who were as adept with the bow as any man, he felt certain that they could either overawe or successfully drive off any current residents.

As it developed, the forty-odd families living and trying to exist safely in the environs of the lake under the overall leadership of a middle-aged onetime Regular Army officer and sometime survival buff named Paul Krueger were more than happy to see an additional seventy or so well-armed men added to their numbers, beset and bedeviled as they were by the periodic incursions of a large pack of motor-cycle-mounted raiders some hundred or more strong, heavily armed and mercilessly savage.

Milo had had no stomach for settling down and awaiting the next raid. He and Krueger had pooled their available men and resources and staged a night raid of their own on the cyclists, who had become over the years so cocksure that they no longer troubled themselves to mount perimeter guards. No prisoners had been taken, but quite a hoard of secondhand loot and quantities of arms and ammunition, clothing, boots and gear had been liberated by the allies. Liberated, as well, had been scores of male and female slaves of the bikers, most of the women either with children or pregnant; those originally kidnapped from Krueger's settlement were returned to their families if any relatives still lived, and most of the remainder accepted Milo's offer to join his band. The things that these former slaves told him of their deceased captors caused him to wonder if it might not be wiser to move on—north, east or south, anyplace but west.

He had been informed that the bunch just exterminated had made up only the westernmost "chapter" of a highly organized pack of outlaws most of whom were scattered over northern California and southern Oregon on the western side of the mountains. He had been informed that these human predators numbered upward of a thousand, were very well armed and made regular visits to the now-extinct chapter for the primary purpose of collecting a share of loot and slaves.

"What you and your people do is entirely up to you," he had told Paul Krueger bluntly. "But as soon as this winter's snows are melted enough to allow for it, my people are moving on, northeast, probably.

There's simply not enough really arable land hereabouts to support all of us—yours and mine, plus our
herds—without spreading out so thinly that we'd be
easy victims to those thousand or more bikers just
across the Sierra. I haven't wet-nursed my kids and
theirs for twenty years to watch many or most of
them killed off fighting scum like the pack we were
fortunate enough to surprise up there in Tahoe City.
When the parent chapter gets up here next spring,
you can just bet that they're going to be none too
happy to find out that we killed off every one of the
local biker-raiders, thoroughly looted the head-
quarters and then burned it to the ground, so I will
be a damned sight easier of mind with miles and
mountains between me and mine and those murderous outlaws."

Krueger had sighed long and gustily, replying,
"Twenty years, huh? Then you must be some older
than you look or act, Moray, probably closer to my
age. But, hell, you're right and I know it; our
combined hundred and fifty men and boys would
stand no chance against a thousand, not even against
half of that number, not with as few automatics as
we have and no heavy weapons at all except those
two homemade PIAT projectors and a few hand
grenades.

"You're right about the farmlands and graze, too,
and there's something else that maybe you don't
know or hadn't noticed yet: the rains haven't been as
regular and heavy nor the snows as deep in these last
few years. Some of the smaller streams are either
dried up or are just trickles and the level of the lake
has dropped off several feet, and who knows why? I
sure as hell don't. Maybe all the nukes changed the
climate like the nervous Nellies used to claim they
would if they were ever used.

"So, okay, we all move out of here come spring.
But where? We're almost completely surrounded by
some of the worst, godawful deserts on this

continent and we've got damned little transport and little POL for what we do have. What the hell are we going to do if we run out of gas and there isn't any at the next town or crossroads?"

Milo had found the answer to this conundrum while, mounted on captured motorcycles, he and a party of men scouted the route northeast to the Snake River Valley, their agreed-upon destination. Just north of Carson City, they came across a roadside attraction, a "Pioneer Days Museum." Among other things within the sprawling building were two different types of reproductions of Conestoga wagons, a huge-wheeled overland freight wagon, a Red River cart and several other recreations of animal-drawn vehicles, plus a wealth of printed material detailing their construction, use and maintenance. Complete sets of reproduced harness adorned fiberglass horses, mules and draft oxen.

After Krueger and some of his men, including his blacksmith, had journeyed north and looked over the displays, they had hitched the reproductions onto pickups and jeeps and towed them back home, then taken them all apart and set about turning out their own copies of wheeled transport, harness and other relics, while other men and women devoted themselves to training horses, mules and the few available oxen to horse collar, yoke and draft.

It was at length decided, after a conference with the smith and some of the on-the-job-training wainwrights, that the wagons simply took too much of everything—time, materials and effort—to reproduce properly in the numbers that would be needed, and so with the completion of the wagons already in the works, all of the labor was put to making Red River carts instead.

Other crews were kept busy through the last of the summer, the autumn and the winter bringing truckload after truckload of seasoned lumber from lumberyards far and near, seeking out hardware items, clothing, bedding, canvas sheeting, tents and the thousand and one things needed for the coming trek north.

Unlike most of his companions on these foraging expeditions, Milo had been in or at least through some of the towns and cities they now were plundering in the long ago, and he found the now-deserted and lifeless surroundings extremely eerie, with the streets and roads lined with rusting, abandoned cars and trucks, littered with assorted trash, the only moving things now the occasional serpent or scuttling lizard or tumbleweed. Only rarely did they chance across any sign of humans still living in the towns and cities, and these scattered folk were as chary as hunted deer, never showing themselves, disappearing into the decaying, uncared-for buildings without a trace. Milo suspected that these few survivors had bad memories from the recent past of men riding motorcyles, jeeps and pickups.

Every city, town, village, hamlet and crossroads settlement seemed to have its full share of human skulls and bones and, within the buildings—especially in those closed places that the coyotes, feral dog packs and other scavengers had not been able to penetrate—whole, though desiccated, bodies of men, women and children of every age. Although he and Krueger had come to the tentative conclusion that those humans who lived on in health while their families, friends and neighbors had died around them in their millions must be possessed by some rare, natural and possibly hereditary immunity to the plagues, he nonetheless tried to keep his crews from too-near proximity to the dried-out and hideous corpses, figuring they were better safe than sorry in so deadly serious a matter.

However, the only two deaths sustained by the foragers were from causes other than plague. The first to die was a sixteen-year-old boy who forced open a sliding door on the fifteenth floor of a hotel and was found after some searching by the rest of the party dead at the bottom of an elevator shaft; he had not, obviously, known what an elevator was. The other unfortunate was a man, one of Krueger's farmers and of enough age to have conceivably known better, who had disregarded Milo's injunction to leave alone the cases of aged, decomposing dynamite they had found in a shed. He had been vaporized, along with the shed, in the resultant explosion.

With the explosives that had been stored properly and were still in safe, reliable, usable condition, Milo, Krueger and certain of the older men experienced with dynamite or TNT had chosen spots carefully and then had blown down sizable chunks of rock to completely block stretches of both Route 80 and Route 50, the two routes the former slaves recalled as having been used by biker gangs. They might not be stopped, but they certainly would be considerably slowed down, the two leaders figured, which would, they hoped, give the former farmerfolk more of what was becoming a rare and precious commodity—time.

It had become clear that were they to forsake the trucks entirely, they were going to need more horses or mules, so Milo had gathered his group of horse-hunters and ridden out in search of feral herds. Luck had ridden with them. They had found a smallish herd on the second day, and a week's hard, dangerous work had netted them a herd of some two dozen captive equines, including six that showed the conformation and size of heavy draft-horse breeding.

When they had brought back their catch and turned the beasts over to the breaker-trainers, they had rested for a day, then ridden back out, this time to the southeast. They were gone for two weeks and returned—dog dirty, hungry, thirsty and exhausted—without a single horse . . . but with five towering, long-legged dromedaries. They had found the *outré* animals wandering about an arid area and managed to trap them in a small, convenient box canyon. After a few of the men had been bitten by the savage beasts, there was a strong sentiment to kill one for meat and turn the others free to live or die on their own, but Milo had insisted that they be roped and led back to the farming areas, stressing his experiences in certain parts of Africa, where such as these had often demonstrated the ability to draw or bear stupendous loads on little food and less water.

Paul Krueger had not been too certain of the wisdom of trying to use the camels, remarking, "There's never been a really tame one, you know— not even those born in captivity are ever safe to be around all the time. And we don't have any harness that we can easily adapt to them or time left to make separate sets, even if we had the hands and the material left to make them."

Milo shrugged. "Well, why not try them as pack animals, Paul? We can always turn them loose or slaughter them for food if they don't work out for us. As I recall, the Sudanese could pack loads of a quarter of a ton on each camel, and in our present straits, five animals that can, between them, carry a ton and a quarter aren't to be sneezed at or lightly dismissed."

"Who's going to drive the vicious fuckers?" Krueger had then demanded. "Not me! I've got a care to keep my hide in one piece."

"No need to drive them." Milo shook his head. "Just hitch their headstalls to the tails of as many carts."

Krueger grudgingly consented to the inclusion of the camels and was later to thank Providence that he had so done.

Chapter V

Chief Gus Scott brought all of his folk to the lavish feast prepared and proffered by the Horseclansfolk, but he brought them in relays, so that the herds remained guarded and the necessary camp work got done, despite everything, which signs of organizational abilities and natural leadership qualities served to increase Milo's admiration for the man.

That a few boys and girls of marriageable age of both the Horseclans and the Scott tribe seemed to find the company of one another extremely fascinating pleased Milo no end, for he was become determined that when he and his moved on southwest the Scotts would move with them, winter with them and, he hoped, emerge with the spring thaws as another clan of the Kindred.

Jules LeBonne did come to the feast, but brought with him only his personal bodyguards, perhaps a dozen of them, all as filthy as their chief, all as heavily armed and all almost as arrogant. That LeBonne and all his henchmen were contemptuous of their hosts and of Chief Scott was obvious from the outset. Only by keeping an exceedingly tight rein on his own people was Milo able to prevent open combat which must surely have resulted in the quick deaths of all thirteen of the French-speaking guests; he was later to regret that he had not countenanced their killing then and there, for it would have saved later death and suffering.

Deliberately waiting until LeBonne and most of his entourage were become impossibly befuddled with alcohol and hemp, Milo broached his proposal to Gus Scott bluntly, saying, "Chief Gus, my folk and I have no axes to grind, no blood to avenge, insofar as concerns those folks in that fort, so I want your leave to ride into their settlement and try to arrange a passage across the ford they command for my clans and herds. Winter could come down on us anytime now, and I don't want to be caught by it out on these open expanses, or, even worse, in some mountain pass on my way up to the high plains. Am I success-ful, it just might help you and your aims; do I fail, it certainly won't hurt you and them and it will mean that I and my clans will then have a reason to join our arms with yours in defeating those people and thus opening the ford for our use."

But Gus Scott shook his head. "I like you, Chief Milo, and whatall you a-talking here, it's pure, quick suicide; them damn bastids, they'll shoot you offen your hoss five hunnert yards out! You got no way of realizing jest how damn far them bugtits' guns can shoot—ain't no living man as does, 'cepting of me and Jules and a few others of our folks as has seen 'em."

But Milo was adamant, continuing to argue, and, at length, he gained the grudging agreement of Gus Scott. By that time, the nodding *Chef* Jules would grinningly agree to any questions put to him, not that Milo thought the spaced-out inebriate really under-stood any of it, but at least the forms had been served after a fashion.

The very next dawning, while most of the camp still slept, Milo gathered the clan chiefs and gave them his instructions, then rode out of camp alone, mounted on a borrowed easily seen white horse. He bore only his saber and his dirk, those plus a headless lance shaft to which he had firmly affixed a yard-square piece of the whitest cloth he had been able to turn up in his camp. He set his horse's head toward the northwest, toward the certain death that Chief Gus Scott was convinced awaited him.

As he rode through the main gate of the fort, disarmed and under close, heavy guard, Milo's glances to right and left took in the stripped, rusting shells of the self-propelled guns and other armored vehicles. He mentally noted that as the breeches of the long guns were carefully shrouded and the barrels plugged at the muzzles, they just might still be supplied with shells and capable of being safely fired, which boded exceedingly ill for Scott, LeBonne or any other men who elected to mount a charge in force against the fort.

However, he also noted that of the men manning the wall walks, only a mere handful bore firearms of any sort, most of them being armed with crossbows, recurved bows and polearms. At the corners of the walls and on a wide platform above the gate squatted engines that looked very much to him like pictures he recalled seeing long, long ago of ballistae and catapults. Stacks of short, heavy spears stood by the former and piles of round rocks by the latter.

But although they were well armed for this time and this place, every one of the men he had so far seen had looked thin to the point of gauntness, the eyes of many shining fever-bright, their movements not completely sure, their steps slow and plodding. He attributed this seemingly universal condition to either severe, wasting illness or malnourishment of long standing. With all or even a large proportion of a garrison in such poor health, even superior weapons might not be sufficient to save them from the blood-mad warriors that crouched just out of those weapons' ranges.

Once within the gates, two members of his

stumbling guard fell on their faces and just lay there, gasping and shuddering, clearly unable to arise. As he was led toward a large building of brick and squared stone, he saw women and a few hollow-eyed children, but not one chicken, dog or cat. From somewhere within the complex, a horse whinnied, and his white stallion raised his head, laid back his ears and answered. Milo guessed that these luckless people had eaten every animal with the exception of their cavalry mounts . . . probably more than a few of those, as well.

Perhaps he and the clans might be able to trade these starvelings a score or so head of their cattle for an uncontested passage across the ford? Scott, LeBonne and the rest would not like it in the least, of course, but much as Milo admired Chief Gus Scott, his own people's welfare must and did take first precedence in any matter, at least in any matter of such real urgency and importance.

At the foot of a short but broad flight of stone stairs that led up to an ancient but well-kept set of double-valved doors, the man commanding Milo's guard brusquely ordered the prisoner to dismount and ascend ahead of him and a brace of his men. After securing the lance shaft with the metal hook attached to the pommel for just that purpose in order to free a bowman's two hands, he slipped off the white's back and mounted the first step firmly, his face deliberately blank. He knew not what lay ahead within that ancient pile, but he was pretty sure that did they mean to kill him, they would have tried to do so long before this moment. After nearly two centuries of living among humans, he was confident of his abilities to read human character quickly and to reason, to argue a point successfully. Now if the leaders of these strange, archaic, ill-fed people were only reasonable and a bit intelligent . . .

When the guard commander had gone through a formal report, the middle-aged man to whom he had reported had said, "Thank you, Leftenant Hamilton. You and your men may now return to your duties."

With a salute, a stamp of the foot and a barked "Sah!" the younger man had spun about (a little unsteadily, Milo noted) and marched out of the room, closing the door in his wake.

Dredging up from his memory the rank denoted by the insignia, Milo than addressed the middle-aged man himself. "Colonel, are all your people as half starved as your garrison so clearly is?"

The officer addressed sprang up from his chair and leaned on his clenched fists, his face suddenly suffused, his veins abulge and throbbing with anger, but his voice at least under control. That was when Milo first noted that whereas the other two men in the small office wore what looked to be homespun recreations of battledress uniforms, the older man was clad in a Class A blouse—one that looked to be a much-mended original—and, of all things, a *kilt* and a sporran of a black-and-white fur that looked as if it had come off a spotted skunk—a rare beast this far north. He also was able to drub his memory and come up with the surname that most likely went with that kilt.

Speaking coldly, the officer said, "The conditions of my garrison and that of the people of the station should not be of concern to you, prairie rover. It might be better, all things considered, if I did not allow you to leave here alive."

"I hardly think that an officer of your obvious gentility and training would violate the sanctity of a man who rode in bearing a flag of truce, whatever your reasons, Colonel Lindsay. And please believe me, I had no aim of angering you when I asked my first question. Perhaps, if the hunger of your folk is as severe as it looked to me, we two can be of some service, each to the other."

"Which one of those loose-tongued fools gave you my name?" the officer snapped. "Their orders were to carry on no conversation of any sort with you, other than that necessary to bring you here."

Milo shook his head and smiled to himself at his shrewd guess. "No one of those guards spoke to me of you, Colonel Lindsay. It was, rather, the sett of your plaid told me your clan."

A good measure of the flush drained from the officer's face, and his veins ceased to pump quite so furiously, even as his bushy eyebrows rose a few notches. "Is it so, then?" he said, wonderingly, while slowly sinking back into his chair of dark, ancient wood. "And what may your own clan and patronymic be then?"

"Clan Murray, Colonel Lindsay. My name is Milo Moray, but I'm not a Scot by birth, I am . . . rather would at one time have been considered to be an American, a citizen of the United States of America, that is. Only my heritage is Scottish, like that of a good many of my tribe out there on the prairie."

"Say you so? Sit down, Mr. Moray. Emmett, drag one of those chairs over here for our guest and let's at least hear him out about how he thinks we can help one another.

"Oh, don't frown so, Emmett. This one seems at least head and shoulders above those others in intelligence, and he speaks a decent English, as well.

"Mr. Moray, I fear that I have nothing more substantial than cool water to offer you. We ran out of whiskey some time back, but of well water, we've plenty."

He rapidly scribbled something short on a slip of paper with a quill pen and, after folding it, handed it to the other officer—a captain, Milo noted, probably the colonel's aide—and spoke a few words in the man's ear, words inaudible to Milo. The captain saluted and speedily departed, leaving Milo with the colonel and the man Emmett, who was about of an age with the older officer.

* * *

Colonel Ian Lindsay had first become aware of his daughter's telepathic abilities when, as a child of five years, she had branded a well-meant parental lie the falsehood that it assuredly was and, when commanded by him to tell how she knew, had innocently divulged to him that she could "hear it in her head." Other tests he had devised now and then had affirmed that with age, her rare talent had not faded away but had become both stronger and surer. But he had sworn her to silence and had never himself mentioned it to another soul. Upon a very few occasions, he had had the girl delve into the minds of men in cases in which it had been patent that one of two was lying. Just now, it was very important that he ascertain whether or not this prairieman was trying to lure him, lull him and then entrap or attack him and his weakened people. Perhaps Arabella could get to the full truth of the matter for him, and this was why he had sent for her. He was, of course, completely unaware that this strange man with whom he now was dealing was, himself, a trained and powerful telepath, with far more years of experience than Arabella or Colonel Lindsay, in fact, had of bare existence.

While the colonel talked and Milo sipped politely at the mug of cool water, he felt the first indescribable mental tickling that told him that another of telepathic ability was striving to read his thoughts.

Almost without conscious intent, he raised the barrier that shielded his mind from prying, while beaming out a strong, silent demand: "Who are you, telepath? What right have you to pry into my thoughts?"

Then, simultaneously receiving no reply and realizing that the mind that had made to enter his was open, completely lacking a shield, he penetrated it and read the answers in a matter of seconds.

Arabella, outside, in the hallway beyond the office door, leaned half swooning against the wall, her

suddenly and unexpectedly violated mind in utter
turmoil. What she had done to so many others over
the years—both with and without her father's leave
—had now and with no slightest hint of warning been
done to her! Even worse, her attempt to enter the
mind of that prairie rover had been the most dismal
of failures. It had seemed in a way as if she had flung
herself into a brick wall.

But she was her father's daughter, and she stood
there in weak puzzlement for only a few minutes.
Then she made her way down the hall to their shared
quarters, armed herself and returned resolutely to
the office, using the little-known, seldom utilized
side door that looked from the office to be but a part
of the hardwood paneling.

All three men—Colonel Lindsay, Emmett McEvedy
and Milo Moray—looked up in surprise when the
secret door creaked agape and a gorgeous young
woman with flaming-red hair and a worn but well-
kept .380 revolver strode purposefully into the small
room.

"*Arabella*," began Lindsay in his best command
voice, "what is the meaning of—"

But her torrent of words interrupted him. "Oh,
Father, Father, he . . . this man, this stranger, he
knows! He . . . he's like me, just like *me*. I couldn't get
into *his* mind at all, but he . . . he got into *mine!* He
must be killed, *now!*"

So saying, she held the heavy revolver at arm's
length just as she had seen her father and other
officers do, then pulled the trigger, the heavy pull
taking all the strength that her small hand could
muster. The .380 roared and bucked so hard that she
could not retain her grip on it and it fell to the floor.
All three seated men were showered with granules of
burning powder and so nearly blinded by first the
flash of flame from the muzzle and then the dense
cloud of reeking smoke from the black powder with
which the piece's cartridges had been loaded that for

a moment only Milo was aware that a 130-grain lead bullet had plowed into the right side of his chest, exited below the right shoulder blade, and splintered into the backrest of the chair in which he sat.

Gritting his teeth against the pain, he silently prayed that neither of the other two men would notice that he had been hit, dealt what would have been a fatal wound to any other man in this time and place. But such was not to be. Even as many feet pounded up stairs and down corridors throughout the building, their shouts and commands preceding their arrivals, MacEvedy, furiously blinking his still-smarting eyes, gasped, "Sweet Jesus, Ian, she's killed the poor bastard! See the powder burns on his shirt? And there's a bleeding hole in his chest. Now what do we do?"

Quick of both mind and action and no stranger to wounds, Ian Lindsay tore a slicker from its wall hook behind his desk and, striding quickly to the side of the stricken man, wrapped it firmly around his body, sealing both the entrance and the exit wounds, mildly surprised at the paucity of blood from them, the near lack of air bubbles in that blood and the calm of the victim.

"Emmett? Damn your arse, Emmett, look at *me*, not at him! Go reassure those people in the hallway before they break my door down. Then send a runner to fetch Dr. MacConochie and tell him to come up here prepared to treat an air-sucking chest wound. D'you hear me, damn you? Then *do* it!"

"No, wait, Colonel, Mr. MacEvedy," said Milo in as strong a voice as he could just then muster up. "Do not call anyone else in here, not for a while. But I would appreciate it mightily if one of you would make sure that revolver is out of reach of Mistress Arabella yonder. Her bullet didn't really injure me, but it hurt—*hurts!*—like blue blazes."

Not until he had stripped off his hide vest and his bloody, twice-holed shirt and exposed to three pairs of wondering, wide-staring eyes the rapidly closing, bluish-rimmed holes in his chest and back, however, would any of them credit the fact that he was not speaking to them out of an understandable stare of wound-induced shock, that he really was not in imminent danger of death. Arabella Lindsay just continued to stare at him after that, her heart-shaped face expressing nothing of her thoughts. Emmett MacEvedy stared at the floor, looking up now and again, mumbling incomprehensible things to himself and cracking the knuckles of his knotted, workworn farmer's hands.

Colonel Lindsay, too, stared long and hard at his guest, at the revolver now on the desk before him and at the splintered backrest of the side chair. Then he visibly shook himself and cleared his throat before softly saying, "Mr. Moray . . . if that is really your name . . . *what are you?* Are you a man, a human man? There are old, very old stories, fright tales, of manlike things, evil creatures who can't be killed by steel or lead. I had never before put any more credence in them than I did in the old tales of flying horses, dragons and such obvious fabrications . . . not until a few moments ago, that is.

"I repeat, sir, *what are you?* And what are your intentions with regard to me, Emmett and our people?"

Milo pulled his shirt back over his head and began to tuck its long tails back under his belt and trousers as he replied. "Insofar as I know, Colonel, I am a human man, just like you. I am considerably older than any other man I've recently met, and I happen to be, as you have just witnessed, very difficult to kill, although I experience just as much pain as would any other human so wounded."

"How old . . . just how old are you, Mr. Moray?" asked Colonel Lindsay, his firm voice cracking a bit with the strain.

"Something over two hundred years, Colonel,"

Milo replied, adding, "I was nearly a hundred years old at the time of the War, and I looked then just as I do today; for some reason, I don't age, you see. Don't ask me to explain it, sir, any of it, for I can't; nor could the few carefully selected doctors and scientists I took into my confidence in the last few years before the War. All that any of them were able to come up with were things that I already knew— that I don't die of deadly wounds and, rather, seem to regenerate tissue very fast, that my teeth are of an exceeding hardness and are replaced within a few weeks if I do lose one or more, that I appear to be a man in his middle to late thirties and never age beyond that appearance, and that I am gifted with a very strong telepathic ability. I also seem to be immune to all the diseases to which I ever have to my knowledge been exposed, though I do come down with the occasional mild and short-lived head cold. Once I lost two fingers in a war, and they grew back within a couple of weeks; on another occasion, I had an eye gouged and deliberately punctured by enemies who had captured me. It grew back to full vision within a week.

"But Colonel, you have my word of honor that I am nothing more than a human man, a bit extraordinary in some respects, I freely admit, but still just a man. That you may find it possible to believe me, despite your understandable doubts, I now am going to lower my mindshield, that your telepathic daughter may enter my mind and testify to you the verity of all that I've said here."

Within seconds, Arabella had done that for which she had originally been summoned by her father. She solemnly assured him and Emmett MacEvedy that Milo Moray had imparted to them the full truth, as he knew it, adding that she could discern no malice or ill intent toward any of them—even toward her, who had endeavored to kill him short minutes before —in his mind.

Ian Lindsay sat back in his chair and whistled softly. "Mr. Moray, I know not what to say, what even to think. This entire business is far outside my experience or those of my predecessors, I am certain. You make claim to mortality, yet you freely admit to being of an impossible age and I have just seen not only you survive a fatal bullet wound, but the very wounds, themselves, close up of their own accord. Who has ever seen the like in a mere man?

"Yet you seem a man of honor, and you swear upon that selfsame honor that all you have told me of yourself is no less than true. Further, I have the testimony of my daughter and her unusual talents to back up your oaths, and she never has been proved in error in her reading of others' minds.

"Therefore, Mr. Moray, I can only conclude that you are what you say, a human man, for all that my senses and logic assure me that you must be super-human, at the very least. I am a religious man, Mr. Moray, and firmly convinced that God has a purpose, a plan in all that He does. We here at MacEvedy Station are in dire straits, as you have guessed, besieged and unable to work our fields, much of our livestock lifted by the prairie rovers, our people all ill and almost starving. I believe that the Lord God tested Emmett and me to our utmost capacities, planning from the start to send us you in our hour of darkest need. You may not even know it, Mr. Moray, but I have faith that you are our God-sent savior."

With his tribe of clansfolk camped in and about MacEvedy Station, Milo and a few of his warriors, all heavily armed, rode out to the camp of Chief Gus Scott, Milo grim with purpose. They were received with warmth by the chief and his tribesfolk, and all invited to share food. While the rest ate and frater-nized, Milo closeted with the chief in that worthy's otherwise unoccupied tent.

Gus Scott, smiling broadly, unstoppered a stone

jug, splashed generous measures of trader whiskey into two battered metal mugs and handed one to Milo, then clanked the side of his against Milo's in ancient ritual before drinking.

Handling his half-emptied mug, Scott remarked, "Damn if you ain't a pure whiz, Chief Milo, no shit a-tall, neither. I've come for to like you a lot, and so it pained me some to think the end of the fine feast what you and yourn throwed would most likely be the lastest time I'd set eyes to you with the wind and blood still running in you; I'd of laid damn near anything I's got thet them bastids would've blowed you to hell afore you'd got anywheres near to thet goddam fort. Me and some of my boys, we all watched you ride down there from way off. Damn, but you looked smart on thet big ol' white horse— as straight up in the saddle as the pole of thet white flag you was. When them bugtits come out and led you th'ough them gates and then closed 'em ahint you, I figgered sure thet none of us would ever clap eyes onto you again in thishere life. Yet here you sits with me, big and sassy as ever. How the hell did you cozen your way out'n thet damn fort, Chief Milo?"

A smile flitted momentarily across Milo's weather-darkened face. "It was far easier than you'd probably believe, Chief Gus, far and away easier than I'd dreamed it would be. You, you and the others, you have greatly midjudged and hideously maligned the men of MacEvedy Station, you know; they are in no way the rabid, ravening, bloodthirsty beasts you gave me to understand them to be."

Seeing Gus Scott's hand go to the pitted, disk-shaped piece of ancient shrapnel depending from his neck on its chain, Milo raised a hand placatingly, saying, "Regardless of what these people's parents and grandparents may have done to your own grandfather and his generation, I am convinced that were you but to meet the current war chief of that fort you would not only like him but find much in common with him. *I* have come to like Chief Ian Lindsay and many of his subchiefs as well. In fact, I have moved the camp of my tribe into and around the MacEvedy Station compound."

Scott just sat staring goggle-eyed at Milo, his mug dangling forgotten from his fingers, the precious whiskey trickling from its rim down onto his boot. Then he straightened up, and a smile began to crease his face.

"Heh heh heh," he chuckled. "Had me a-going there for a minit, you did, old feller. Took me some time to figger out jest where you were a-headed, but I see now. It'd take a prairie rover borned to tell the diffrunce 'tween your fighters and mine or LeBonne's or any of the others, so we jest let your hunters ride out day by day, 'cepting more rides back in then went out until we has us enuff fighters hid in your tents and all to massacree ever damn bugtit in thet place, right?"

"Wrong, Chief Scott, completely wrong," Milo replied firmly. "There will be no further attacks or raids against the MacEvedy Station, not by you, not by LeBonne, not by any of the other warbands. If attacks and raids do take place, the attackers and raiders will find themselves up against not just the men of the station but my fighters, as well. Let's get that much of the matter clear right now, at the outset."

"So, you done sold out to the murdering bastids, have you?" Scott declared bitterly. "Sold out to 'em jest to git a clear crossing of their fucking ford. Damn it all, I'd never of thought a man like you'd do a thang like thet to his own kinda folks. And I'd thought you was my friend, too. With your fighters on top of my boys and LeBonne's and the others, we could of jest flat rode over thet place and their fucking rifles be damned."

Milo slowly shook his head. "You're wrong, Chief Gus, wrong about a lot of things. You must learn not to jump to quick and erroneous conclusions.

"To begin, recall if you will that I said at the start that your generations-long feud against the people of the MacEvedy Station was not my fight or my tribe's fight, and that if we could find a way to do so, we would keep out of it."

Scott nodded slowly. "Yeah, I recollect thet, Chief Milo, I surely do, but I still would never of thought you and your tribe would of thowed in with them sonofabitches, made a common cause with the folks who crippled up my grandpa."

"Chief Gus, what if, after a very hard winter, a collection of men rode into your camp and demanded that you allow them to take all the jerky and pemmican you had left, plus all of your best horses and cattle? What would you and your tribe do then?"

"Do our damnedest to kill off every mother's son of the damn fuckers, thet's what!" snorted Scott. "But whut's thet got to do with you selling out to them murdering bastids, huh?"

"A lot, Chief Gus, one hell of a lot," stated Milo solemnly. "All of the station folks both read and write; so, too, do I. I was allowed to read their records, and those ridiculous demands were precisely what the leaders of the force of which your grandfather, father and uncles were a part insisted was their due. When those demands were not met, they attacked the fort and were cut down by rifle and artillery and mortars long before any of them got even within bow range of those walls. So, you see, the then chief, the present war chief's own grandfather, did no more than you yourself admit that you would do under similar circumstances; your grandfather simply suffered for the overweening arrogance of the leaders of that group of massed warbands. So blame them; don't continue to blame the descendants of fighters who were only doing the natural thing—protecting themselves, their families and their stock.

"As I understood from our first meeting, the other thing that you and some of the other war chiefs hoped to accomplish was to once and for all make safe and easy the passage across that ford commanded by the station complex, correct?"

Scott just bobbed his head.

"Well, it is possible that that purpose will be achieved, Chief Gus, and without any bloodshed to accomplish it, either. My subchiefs and I are in process of persuading Chief Ian and the other survivors of the original complex complement to leave those lands on which they have been nearly starving for years, now, and come with us to the high plains, give over farming and become nomadic herders and hunters. We are making some progress, although it is slow and fitful at present, but I entertain very high hopes for this project; they'll come as one, maybe two new clans of my tribe. You and yours could be a third new clan, if you and your subchiefs but indicate interest in so being. I like you, personally, and I admire your leadership abilities; your tribe and the station people added would almost double the size of my tribe, make of us a real power on the plains and the prairies.

"With the strength that such numbers would give us, we could set about clearing the grasslands of all the squatting farmers so that these grasslands would be ours and ours alone, completely free and fenceless for our families and our herds, for our children and their herds to roam at will in peace."

All the time that he was speaking aloud, Milo's powerful and long-trained mind had been projecting into the unshielded mind of Gus Scott thoughts favorable to the merging of the three disparate groups of people. His many years of life had convinced him that any man who failed to make use of any personal advantage in argument or fight was a fool and an eventual loser.

It was, therefore, no real surprise to him when Scott nodded and said, "Whutall you's said, Chief Milo, it all makes a heap of good sense to me. I likes you, too, you know, and that's why it pained me so bad, first to thank you was a-going to get yourse'f kilt, then thet you'd sold out to Chief Ian and his folks.

"I thinks my folks would like being a clan of your tribe, too, and you right, ain't no sense to being little and weak when you can be big and strong. And you right 'bout us having to git shet of them damn dirt-scratching farmers, too; ain't never been too many of the fuckers up nawth, here, but they done been a plumb plague further south and looks like ever year it's more of the sonofabitches, a-plowing up the graze and a-fencing off the water.

"It's a passel of no-count herders, too, ought to be kilt or drove off, but I never been strong enuff to do 'er alone, jest my tribe and me. But let's us plan on taking care of all the damn farmers, first off, like you said, then we can git after them fucking sneak-thieving bastids like of the Hartman tribe.

"But really, Chief Milo, we 'uns should oughta ask Chief Jules to come along of us, too; true, he ain't got all thet big a tribe, but they's all of his fighters good boys."

Milo thought to himself that he would liefer adopt a clan of diamondback rattlesnakes than the scruffy, filthy, constantly conniving Jules LeBonne and his pack of prize ruffians. But just now was neither the time nor the place to refuse a friend of Chief Gus Scott's a chance at joining the projected tribal alliance, so he agreed with what he hoped resembled pleasure. The sad and bloody events of the two ensuing weeks were to give Milo Moray much cause to regret this action.

Chapter VI

With the hunters of Milo's tribe and those of the Scott tribe as well, out all day, every day, while parties of girls, women and younger boys scoured the surrounding grasslands and wooded areas for edible wild plants, nuts and the like, the station people began to eat well and regularly once more, and to recover their strength.

Milo himself spent many a long hour conferring with Ian Lindsay and Emmett MacEvedy, endeavoring to convince them of the futility, the suicidal folly of remaining at the station and attempting to derive sustenance from played-out land for so many people. Ian seemed to be wavering toward Milo's side of the argument, but MacEvedy was adamantly opposed to leaving, and each time Lindsay made a favorable mention of departure, the director was quick to point out that it was the inherent duty of Lindsay and his men to remain and defend the station. The parson, Gerald Falconer, who sat in on a few of the discussions, seemed unequivocally a MacEvedy man. Arabella Lindsay, however, and every one of Ian's officers eagerly favored a mass departure from the station and its barely productive farms for a freer-sounding life out on the grasslands.

Milo saw his plans and arguments stonewalled at almost every turn by the strangely hostile MacEvedy and the even more hostile Reverend Gerald Falconer. He was become so frustrated as to almost be ready to seek those two men out on some dark night in some deserted place and throttle them with his own two bare hands.

Very frequently, Milo was forced to carry on two conversations at one time—his oral one, of course, and a silent telepathic "conversation" with Arabella Lindsay, who, while at least quite interested in the affairs under discussion by Milo, her father, MacEvedy and whoever else chanced to be present at any particular time, was even more avid for bits and pieces of assorted knowledge concerning aspects of the lives of the nomads on prairies and plains.

She did not even have to be present for him to suddenly feel the peculiar mental tickling that told him that her mind was now there, in the atrium of his own, with another question or five. Not always questions, though; sometimes she imparted information to him.

"Milo," she beamed to him early on a Monday morning, "the Reverend Mr. Falconer said terrible things about you in his sermon yesterday. Father probably won't tell you, so I suppose that I must. After all, we are friends now, you and I, and that's what friends are for: to guard each other's backs. Is that not so?"

In his two-plus centuries of life, Milo had but infrequently run across any "man of God" of any stripe, creed or persuasion that he had been able to like trust or even respect; all seemed to have imbibed greed, backbiting and hypocrisy with the milk of whatever creatures bore and nurtured them. Ever since their initial meeting, he had known that Gerald Falconer heartily disliked him for some reason that the man had never bothered to bring out into the open and discuss; Milo judged him to be not the sort of man who willingly discussed any matter openly unless he was dead certain, to start, that he had the unquestioned upper hand.

He replied, "I know his kind, of old, Arabella. What did he have to say about me?"

"He started out by criticizing poor Father most cruelly ," was her answer. "His scriptural text had been the story of Job, and he compared Father to Job, saying that Job had had great faith in God and that Father's faith had obviously been scant, since it had evaporated under mild adversity."

"Mild adversity?" Milo mentally snorted. "Mild adversity is it, now? By Sun and Wind, the man's clearly either a madman or he totally lacks the wits to come in out of the rain! A good half of the station people have died in the last four years of either malnourishment or the plethora of diseases associated with it, most of your crops in this same time have been stunted, blighted or completely nonexistent, your herds have been either eaten or lifted by the rovers, and your leaders have had to strip this place of all luxuries or treasures and of many necessary items of equipment, armor and weapons to barter to the traders for a pittance of food. If these sufferings and privations are to this Gerald Falconer merely 'mild adversity,' I'd truly hate to see what he would characterize as strong adversity, Arabella."

"What he said of you was worse, Milo, far, far worse. His hatred of you, whatever spawned it, seems to be really and truly depthless."

"Well," he prodded, "just what choice cesspit dredgings did the mealymouthed bastard decide applied to me?"

"He declared that the devil can quote Scripture when it is to hell's benefit, then he carried on for some time about how mere mortal men can, under great stress and especially when possessed of little or deficient faith, succumb to Satanic wiles. He went on to say that you, Milo Moray, are without doubt a disciple of Satan, that you bear the mark of the beast, that—although you go about on two legs and project the appearance of being a man—you *are* a beast yourself, an evil, hell-spawned, bestial creature of the sort who dwelt amongst men of old, before men were taught by the humble servants of Christ how to detect them, drive them out and kill them— witches, vampires, ghouls and werewolves, all immune to the sharp steel or lead bullets that would take the lives of mortal men."

"Oho," Milo silently crowed. "Emmett MacEvedy apparently forgot his oaths to your father and me as soon as he and his supersititious mind and his loose, flapping tongue had exited that office. That must be why this Falconer seemed to hate me from the moment of our first meeting, why he wears that big silver pectoral cross constantly and never misses an opportunity to wave the thing around, mostly near to me. I'd wondered about him and what I took to be his idiosyncrasies, Arabella, but I've never been able to read his mind, or MacEvedy's either. I think that both of them are just adept enough at telepathy to have developed natural shields.

"And anent that matter, Arabella, just how many of the folk of the station here are possessed of your telepathic abilities? Do you know?"

"Well, there's Capull . . . but he's not a person, of course."

"If this Capull is not a person, Arabella," inquired Milo, "then what is he?"

"Why, he's a stallion, a Thoroughbred stallion, my father's charger and my best friend."

"And *he is telepathic?* You can actually converse with him, a *horse?*" Milo was stunned.

"Of course I can," she replied matter-of-factly. "And with a number of the other horses, too, though not as well as with dear Capull. I was chatting with that big white stallion on whom you first rode into the fort when I was found and summoned up to my father's office to try to read your thoughts and so determine if the words you spoke were truth."

"Well, I'll be damned!" thought Milo. "Why did I never think of trying to communicate telepathically with any of my mounts? If I did, and if the horse was a cooperative sort, I'd need no bridle at all and could keep both hands free for my weapons or whatever. Nor would there be any need to hobble or picket such a horse, either—you could simply beam your command for him to come to you whenever you were ready for him. Son of a bitch, the things I've learned at this place!"

To Arabella, he beamed, "Do you think . . . Could you teach me how to bespeak this Capull and, perhaps, some of my own horses?"

"Certainly I can," was her quick, self-assured reply. "Your mind is much stronger than is mine in this matter of mind speaking to mind, anyway. Furthermore, I have found myself able to bespeak over half of the horses I have met in your camp already, so there is no reason why you should not be able to so do, whenever you wish."

Then, in a bare twinkling, her mind imparted to his the tiny change of direction necessary to reach the minds of equines. It was so simple, yet it was something of which he would never have thought on his own, he realized and admitted.

"But Milo, this matter of telepathy aside, you must be most wary of Reverend Mr. Falconer, and of Director MacEvedy and his son, Grant. They all hate you and will use any means at their disposal to poison the minds of our people against you and to see you and all your people either killed or driven away, back out onto the prairie, whence you all came."

"I can understand a bit of why Falconer dislikes me, of course, Arabella. You weren't around the day that he demanded to know to just what brand of Christianity my tribe subscribed and I told him bluntly that we are not any of us any form of Christian, Jew, Buddhist, Muslim, Hindu, Jain or anything else that he would recognize, that we neither support nor tolerate parasitic priests or preachers, that the only things we consider to be in any way sacred are the beneficial, life-giving forces of Nature—the sun and the wind, principally—those and the Laws of our tribe. At that point he sprang up, stared at me as if trying to will me to death, then stomped out of your father's office, trying to bear off the door with him, to judge by the force with which he slammed it. Very shortly afterward, MacEvedy left on some flimsy-sounding excuse or other.

"But MacEvedy, he's obviously an intelligent adult man, and I find it hard to credit that he truly believes me to be a warlock or werewolf. So what in the world does he really have against me, Arabella. You know him better, have known him far longer, than I."

"I think, Milo, that he fears you, fears you because he is convinced that you just might persuade Father and the rest of the battalion to leave with you for a new life of herding. If the battalion leaves, he and his people will also have to leave or face death or slavery at the hands of the prairie rovers, for few of them have ever bothered to learn how to fight, always having depended upon Father and the battalion to defend them, the station and the farms.

"Here at the station, Emmett MacEvedy is a big frog in a very small puddle—the only three people with any real authority here are he, Father and the Reverend Mr. Falconer, all of whom inherited the same posts and commands held by their fathers, their grandfathers and their great-grandfathers. I think that Emmett MacEvedy fears that if he is forced to leave, he will devolve into a small frog in a much larger puddle, and as I do know the man, I much doubt that he could bear such a descent to lessened power over people, the status to which he was born and reared."

"I offered him exactly the same status as I offered your dad, Arabella," said Milo. "That of a clan chief, which is the most powerful office that is held by any of our folk in the tribe. He'd still have dominion over his own people—that is, unless he proved himself a poor leader or deficient in some other vital ability and, through mere self-preservation, his clan decided to depose him and elect a new and better chief."

"And that last is probably just what terrifies him, Milo. His late father was a real organizer, a born leader of men, like my own father, but—and I have heard Father say this over and over again—not only is Emmett lacking leadership ability, he also is often possessed by faulty judgment. His son is no whit better than his sire in any way, and, moreover, both are utterly selfish. Only Emmett's heredity has kept him in his exaulted position, and only that same factor will see his otherwise completely incompetent son assume the position upon his demise. He knows full well that he would not long remain a chief in your tribe, the people would replace him and Grant very quickly, once removed from the station and inherited office. Many of the farmers already hate Emmett and Grant, and with good and sufficient reasons.

"When first the harvests began to fail, he and his son so abused their positions as to begin to appropriate foodstuffs from out the common stocks and hoard them away in secret places for their own personal use. For almost three years, these two watched their own people grow thinner and more sickly day by day, week by week, month by month, watched young babes and children and old people die after the last of the seed grain had been made into bread flour and half the poor cavalry chargers had been slaughtered to keep at least some of the people alive until the traders came, yet they never even admitted to holding their hoards, far less offering to share it out amongst those suffering and dying for want of food.

"The truth came out only when an officer of the battalion apprehended this precious pair surreptitiously milling some of their hoarded grain by night and marched them straight to my father. Now, Father and Emmett grew up together, Milo, and were old friends, in addition to the fact that their positions had always required them to work together closely almost on a daily basis, so he had thought that he knew Emmett as well as he knew any man at the station. When he so suddenly discovered his old friend's cupidity, he waxed furious, so furious that I thought for several minutes that he was going to shoot Emmett and Grant on that very spot.

"He did not, of course, though perhaps he should have. He would have been fully justified in those executions, and no man or woman in the fort or the station would have faulted him for it. But he regained control of himself and demanded that the two of them immediately tell where their various hoardings were cached, that his soldiers might fetch them out and distribute them to the people. Instead, Emmett offered to evenly split the stolen stores with Father, noting that as they were the leaders of fort and station, it was necessary and in all ways proper that they two should remain always better fed and therefore more mentally agile than their inferiors.

"Milo, Father's eyes shot sparks of fire, then. He drew his revolver, cocked the hammer and put the muzzle hard against the left ear of Emmett MacEvedy—it looked as if he were trying to actually push the barrel into his head through the earhole. I still can hear the words he spoke then, in a chilling tone that I never before had heard him use to any person, for any reason or under any circumstances."

She opened her memories then that Milo might hear just what she'd heard, just as she had heard it.

"You sorry piece of scum," Colonel Ian Lindsay

had grated in tones as cold as the grin of a winter wolf. "You're a disgrace to the memory of your father, you know. You're a disgrace to the office you hold. You're a disgrace to mankind in general, you selfish, heartless greedy *thing*.

"Only because of our lifelong relationship, that which I foolishly deluded myself into calling 'friendship,' do I refrain from blowing your worthless brains all over the wall behind you, yours and your darling son's, as well.

"For the rest of this night, the two of you are going to bide locked up in one of the strongrooms belowstairs, here in the fort. At dawn, you both are going to lead me and a platoon of my men to all of your hidey-holes. When we have collected all the foodstuffs, we are going to assemble the people in the fort quadrangle and distribute every last grain of it to those for whom it was stored and originally intended.

"Be you warned, Emmett, if you try to balk my purpose, here detailed, in any way, I will surely kill you. You, too, Grant—godson or no, I shall fill your well-fed belly with metal it will not be able to digest."

He then called back into the room the officer who had caught the midnight millers and brought them to him. "Leftenant, have a brace of men called up here and escort the director and his son down to the ground level. Instruct Sergeant Brodie to fit them both with his heaviest sets of fetters, and then confine them to separate strongrooms for the night. They are to be provided with water and nothing else —they are both well fed enough, as they stand, better fed by far than the rest of us, so they should be able to bide for a while off their fat, I should imagine. Should either of them try to escape or should they create a disturbance, both you and Sergeant Brodie have my express permission to beat them."

Closing her memories, Arabella silently beamed,

"The foodstuffs were all found out and equally distributed by my father and Emmett, in his role of director of the station, but word of what had actually occurred on that night leaked out anyway, and now Emmett is a most unpopular man to the most of his very own people, while the officers and other ranks openly sneer at him to his very face.

"After that, Father was cool and proper to Emmett in public, but it was long and long before he deigned even to receive him again in his private office, and never, since that night, has he been in our home at the fort. They only reached something faintly resembling their old relationship when first the fort and the station came under siege of the prairie rovers."

Milo had deliberately connived to keep Chief Gus Scott out of the discussions conducted within the fort, fearing the sure consequences of putting a hotheaded and openly pugnacious man of Chief Scott's water in close proximity to such troublemakers as Emmett MacEvedy and Gerald Falconer. Solemnly, he had entrusted Scott with the full responsibility for all the hunting parties.

"You know this country hereabouts far better than do my own hunters, Chief Gus, so you're much more valuable to us all out here than you might be inside the fort yonder. Never you fear—when the time comes, you'll get to meet Chief Ian and all the others."

As the people of the station and the fort became stronger and more active, they flocked out into the camps pitched under their walls, mingling freely with the folk who dwelt in those camps. Moreover, the continued rantings of Falconer seemed to be accomplishing nothing among the most of his flock, as Milo was never ill-treated or openly avoided by any of the folk of station and fort, save members of the immediate families of his two bitter enemies— the director and the preacher.

* * *

The painfully neat parlor of Gerald Falconer's small parsonage was the usual meeting place for him, the director and Grant MacEvedy, it being the one location in which they could be relatively certain, if they kept their voices low-pitched, of not being overheard by any who might bear their words back to Ian Lindsay. Earlier on, it had appeared that they three might have had a good chance to sway the outcome, to make sure that Lindsay and his battalion would all remain here in the place of their births and not go traipsing off into the unknown wilderness in company with a Satanic man-beast and his godless host of minions. But now it appeared that all of their words had been wasted, for not only the two Lindsays—father and daughter—and their soldiers but all the people of the MacEvedy Experimental Agricultural Station acted willing—nay, avid—to desert the ancient buildings and fields and the safe, secure life that they and their fathers before them had always known. So the mood in the parsonage parlor was unrelievedly glum on this day, as gloomy as the cloudy, drizzly day itself.

In the not too distant past, Gerald Falconer had deferred to Emmett MacEvedy at their rare private meetings in an almost abject manner—installing the director in the only armchair, personally serving him with mint tea and the finest his parsonage otherwise had to offer, seldom speaking unless asked for a reply. But things had changed drastically in the space of the last year. Since the distasteful affair of the stolen and hoarded stores had so disastrously come to light and general knowledge and caused general respect for MacEvedy, personally, to drop to nil, the parson had taken to treating the director as he treated most of the rest of his flock.

On this day, Falconer occupied the old cracked-leather armchair, while Emmett and his son perched before him on armless, backless wooden stools. A pot of mint tea steamed softly on the table, but there was only one cup in the room, that one cradled in the hands of Falconer, while cakes and sweetmeats were longsince become a thing of the dead past.

Grant MacEvedy was suffering from a cold, sniffling and snuffling constantly, perpetually dabbing at his sore, fiery-red nose with a stained and sodden handkerchief. The sallow, soft-handed young man had been born a few centuries too late. Although he was an excellent administrator, he detested all physical aspects of actual farming—the dirt, the heat or the cold, the physically taxing hard work, the dealing with smelly and potentially dangerous animals of the likes of horses and cattle.

He had been sickly from birth, and a brace of doting parents had kept him ever close to home and out of the rough, rowdy games played by his peers. Now an adult, he still cleaved as closely as conditions would permit to his office and his home, spending an absolute minimum of time out of doors. The hair of dogs, the fur of cats, the feathers of birds all had never failed to set him to coughing and sneezing, so he never had had any kind or description of pet and now he feared and hated all animals, although he strove mightily to mask these emotions whenever he was forced to be around the farmers and their beasts.

He had completely missed inheritance of his father's big-boned, powerful physique. He was of less than average height, with a sallow skin that sunburned very easily, muddy-brown eyes that were positioned too close together and teeth that crowded haphazardly in his two-small jaws. His hands and feet were small and slender, butter-soft and usually ink-stained. In better times, he had been pudgy and paunchy, but now he was become as emaciated as the rest of the people. His rat-brown hair was thin, lank and lifeless, and even now, in his mid-twenties, his beard growth was at best sparse and patchy, and his only body hair sprouted in his crotch and armpits.

Unlike all of his peers, who had wed in their late teens or early twenties, Grant—rendered painfully shy by his overly sheltered childhood and youth—had never married, continuing to live on with his father and his elder, widowed and biddable sister, Clare Dundas, whom his father had forbidden to remarry after their mother died of pneumonia.

Annoyed by the young man's snifflings, Falconer set down his teacup and snapped, "Either blow your nose or get out of here, Grant—preferably the latter. You're about as much good to me and your father as you have ever been to us or to anyone else, as much an asset as teats on a boar hog.

"The decision has been made, anyway. You know your duties and responsibilities, or you should. All that is now left to do is for me and your father to work out the details. So get you home and nurse your cold, but just remember all you have been told and be sure to be where I told you to be when I told you to be there."

There was, in Falconer's mind, no need to tell the awkward and ill-countenanced young man to keep his mouth shut anent the plans for the demise of the chief instigator of what he and MacEvedy saw as all their present and possibly future trouble—Milo Moray. The preacher well knew that Grant would not babble to friends, for he never had had one and those who worked with him in the station offices were, at the very best, cool and correct in all their dealings with their disgraced and despised superior-by-inheritance.

"If you and your people all want to stay despite everything, dammit," Colonel Ian Lindsay had declared, "then you and they can bloody well squat here until hell freezes over, Emmett, but my people are all going away with Moray and his tribe . . . and to be completely candid, not a few station personnel have come to me and certain of my officers begging to be allowed to come away with us, rather than stay here and keep trying to wrest a bare living out of this contrary acreage."

"Who?" snapped MacEvedy. "Who were the traitors, the turncoats?"

Lindsay shrugged. "Only most of your really intelligent, innovative and far-sighted types, those who have outgrown the fetters of now-senseless tradition and know they can live the better without either being forced willy-nilly into the molds of their ancestors or being constantly hectored and bullied by the man who now seems to command both you and the station, Gerald Falconer. And you can save your breath in this matter; I'll give you no names, not one, and that's the end of it, Emmett!"

"Then you relinquish your honor as well as, as easily as, you forsake your home, your birthplace, do you, Ian Lindsay?" MacEvedy said bitterly. "It was—it is!—your sworn duty to protect me and my station and its people with your battalion, until such a time as some responsible person rescinds the orders originally given your great-grandfather. If you and the battalion do not stay, neither can I and the station people stay safely, and you well know that as fact. Your departure would condemn us all to death, soon or late, at the bloody hands of the rovers."

Lindsay shook his head. "Not necessarily, Emmett. You'll still have the fort, the rifles, the catapults, the spear-throwers, *and* you'll have the artillery pieces."

"None of which the most of the station people know much of anything about the use of," lamented MacEvedy. "It has always been and it still is your *duty* to protect us and the station, we are farmers, not fighters, and it has always been so."

"Then it's now far past time that you all stood up on your hind legs and began to do your own fighting, Emmett. You and the others who want to stay can be taught the fundamentals of the uses of the firearms and the tension-torsion weapons by the time the rest of us are ready to leave with the tribe."

"But . . . but it is not our place," began MacEvedy. "We are all peaceable, peace-loving farmers, we—"

"Yes, peaceable and peace-loving," Lindsay interrupted him scornfully, "just so long as you had, as you always have had, a group of poor sods to do your fighting for you, save you all from risking your precious necks in war, even while you despised and loathed these men of war, these men whom you have always considered to be your moral inferiors.

"No, don't try to deny it, Emmett. I've known just how you and most of the station personnel felt about us of the battalion for all of my life. My father knew it, too, and my grandfather, and his sire, the first colonel of the battalion to serve with it here at MacEvedy Station. But serve on in spite of it they did. It was their duty and they felt bound by their oaths to the government and the army."

"Just so!" said MacEvedy. "They were honorable men, but you . . ."

"But I, Emmett, do not any longer feel myself bound by oaths sworn by my father's father's father to a government, an army, a nation that ceased to exist some century or more ago."

MacEvedy sneered. "You have only the word of that unnatural devil spawn Moray for that last. What makes you believe him, anyway?"

"It just stands to reason, man, or are you too blind and hidebound to see it? What responsible government of any kind would set a station and troops to guard it up here and then just ignore it and them for more than a hundred years? Moray attests that he was living when Ottawa was vaporized by one of those hellish weapons that they used in warfare in olden times. Why, Moray says that—"

"Moray says this, Moray says that," snapped MacEvedy, mocking Lindsay's speaking voice. "I think that that Satan's imp has gone far toward robbing you of your immortal soul, Ian Lindsay. That's what I think!"

"Emmett," asked Lindsay in a serious tone, "what ever led you to the belief that Milo Moray is an evil demon of some ilk? Such maunderings sound less like you than like that power-mad fool Gerald Falconer."

"Sweet Jesus, Ian," expostulated MacEvedy. "You saw and heard all that I did. He freely admits to having no reverence for the Lord God Jehovah, seems vastly pleased that this tribe of his are pagans, worshiping the sun and the moon and the wind. And you saw, as I did, the eerie, evil occurrences when your daughter shot him in the chest with your own service revolver. Do you not recall what she gave as her reason for fetching the gun and making an earnest effort to kill him, Ian?

"She said that her God-given mind-reading talent had caused her to sense that his mind was unnatural, inhuman, not the mind of a mortal man with an immortal soul. She—"

"Arabella said nothing of the sort, Emmett," said Lindsay. "I think you must have a very selective, inventive memory. But go on with it, get it all out. What else is your 'evidence' that Milo Moray is the devil's disciple?"

Looking a bit abashed, MacEvedy said, "Well, he may not be exactly that, he may simply be a werewolf or a vampire, but both kinds of monsters are servants of Satan.

"You must recall all the horror that ensued after she shot him, put a bullet right through his chest, which would have been the certain death of any natural man. As you may remember, I once used a .380 to dispatch a wounded wild boar, when we were hunting together. I know well what those bullets can wreak on the flesh of natural creatures of God's world.

"But he not only did not die, Ian, we all of us watched while that grievous wound first ceased to bleed, then began to close up and heal itself. Gerald only confirmed to me what I knew as I watched the impossible happen: no one but Satan, the Fallen Angel, could have been responsible, so it must have been Satan who sent Milo Moray here to tempt us, to delude us, to steal away our souls and lead us all down to the fiery pits of the deepest, infernal regions of hell."

Lindsay shook his head slowly. "It seems that I learn more about you with every passing day, Emmett, and most of what I've been recently learning is to your detriment, lowering even farther my opinion of you. Emmett, Gerald Falconer is a superstitious fool, a hypocrite, a type of man whom his father or his grandfather would disown. You must, deep down inside you, be every bit as superstitious as is he—otherwise you wouldn't listen to his dredged-up horror stories and hoary legends.

"Hell, man, all of us heard those tales when we were children, and they scared us, as those who told them meant them to do, but when we began to grow up, we began to realize just what those old tales were and they ceased to scare us . . . most of us. Look, you say that Moray might be a vampire, a bloodsucking living corpse, but think back on those particular tales, Emmett. Vampires have to, it's said, move about only by night because sunlight will kill them. How many days has Moray walked and ridden and stood about this fort and station under the glaring sun, do you think? Did he shrivel up and die? Not hardly, Emmett.

"You attest that there can be but one evil reason for Moray's being the most singular type of man that he most assuredly is: namely, that only Satan could have gifted him with the unheard-of physical properties that he owns. But Emmett, Emmett, both you and Falconer have clear forgot that there is One more powerful even than Satan. I am firmly convinced that for all his different and seemingly unreligious ways, Moray has been touched by God. The Scriptures tell us that 'the Lord moves in wondrous ways, His wonders to perform,' and I believe that Moray is one of those wonders of God, just as I believe that his arrival here, in our time of darkest trouble and deepest despair, was another such Wonder."

"I knew in advance that you would fail," said Gerald Falconer. "The devilish beast has too far cozened Colonel Lindsay for your poor powers to counteract. But I have here that which will truly slay the beast, send him back to his hellish master in the pit."

Opening a small box of carven cedarwood, the preacher took from it a polished brass pistol cartridge. Where the dull gray lead bullet should have been there now was the gleam of burnished silver. Moreover, the nose of the bullet had been carefully made flat and a cross had been deeply inscribed thereon.

"I pored over the ancient books, that my memories might be exact, before I cast this bullet and put it in the case over as much powder as it would hold. A bullet of pure silver marked with a cross is sovereign against witch, warlock, vampire or werewolf.

"This cartridge will fit your revolver—your son fetched me the case from your home, so I know. It is your duty as station director and your honor as a true, God-fearing, Christian man to put paid to the beast, to kill this Satanic thing who calls himself Milo Moray."

Chapter VII

"Oh, Milo," Arabella Lindsay silently beamed, "I'm so very excited about Father's decision. I can hardly wait to ride out of this place of bitterness and hunger and death and start living the free and beautiful-sounding life that your people always have known. Capull can run out there, run as long and as far as he wishes, and never again be forced to endure a box stall."

"Our life is undoubtedly free . . . as you comprehend freedom, 'Bella," Milo beamed, "but it is a freedom that you may in time come to truly curse—freedom to die of heat or of thirst or of cold and exposure, freedom to drown in a river crossing where there is no shallow ford, freedom to be consumed in prairie fires such as often occur in late summer and autumn when lightning strikes tinder-dry grasses or a dead cottonwood tree, freedom to be eaten alive by wolves or bears or predatory big cats, freedom to . . ."

"Goodness, Milo, it cannot be so bad, so gloomy a life as you picture. Your people seem happy enough with it, after all."

"They've none of them ever known any other kind of life, 'Bella, but you have known comforts and safeties of which they have never so much as dreamed. The time may well come when you will heap abuse upon me for persuading your father to give over all this and come with me and the clans-folk. You may well come to yearn for the settled life and bitterly regret leaving such, you know. And our customs are drastically different from those to which you have been brought up. For instance, how will you feel when your husband brings a second wife into your yurt? Or a slave concubine captured in some raid or other?"

Arabella's shock showed in her face as she beamed. "But . . . but *why*, Milo, why would any man do such a thing?"

"Because we are not monogamous, as are you and your people and most Christians, for that matter, for all that your own holy book is chock-full of polygamy and chattel slavery."

"Why aren't you happy with just one wife at a time, you and your people, Milo? And how did you ever get your womenfolk to tolerate such an arrange-ment?" She wrinkled her freckled brow in clear puzzlement.

"For one paramount reason, to begin, 'Bella: better than one out of every three children born in my tribe dies either in infancy or, at best, before it is ten years of age. There is strength and safety only in numbers when you lack stone walls to hide behind, and a woman can bear but once in two or three years, if she is to properly nurture the last child she bore, so it was long ago decided that were we to practice monogamy, it would not be too long before we were become so small and weak that we would cease to exist as a tribal entity.

"Our women were mostly born into polygamous society, so there is no question about it in their minds. Besides, there are never enough hands to do all the daily chores necessary to maintain a nomadic household; multiple wives, a slave girl or two and a plentitude of small children make individual workloads far the lighter in day-to-day existence on the prairie.

"Another important reason for the practice of polygamy and concubinage in nomad tribes is the all-too-frequent death of women in childbirth, or shortly thereafter. It is a sad enough occurrence to suddenly lose a loved and valued member of a household, without losing the newborn babe—if it survived her —and any still-dependent children because no other women are resident to quickly take them to suck or otherwise care for them."

Arabella nodded slowly, then demanded. "But Milo, do not the men die, as well? What then becomes of their many women and the children?"

"Yes," he said, "perhaps as many men as women die each and every year, and others are crippled. Mostly, men and older boys die in war or raidings or the hunt. Some suffer death and disablement while guarding our herds from predators. Others are killed or injured by domestic animals or by mischance, as when a galloping horse happens to fall. Illnesses of assorted kinds take away some, and ill-tended wounds a few more. And there are many other fatal perils facing male clansfolk every day and night of their lives. But I believe your question had to do with the fate of a woman whose husband had died.

"Well, if he chanced to leave one or more sons of warrior age, the household simply goes on as before, with the likely addition of the new wife of this new man of the household. If all of the children are too young to follow that course and if the deceased is survived by an unmarried male sibling, it is quite common for that brother or half brother to marry the widows, adopt the immature children and assume ownership of the slaves and horses and other effects, and the household continues almost as before."

"But what of the cattle and sheep and goats the

dead man owned?" Arabella probed. "Who gets those, Milo?"

"Aside from his horses and his hunting hounds, 'Bella, neither he nor any other individual member of the tribe owns livestock personally. The herds, with the sole exceptions of draft oxen, are owned by the tribe as a whole, and their produce—milk, meat, hides, tallow, wool and hair, horn, sinew and such-like—is all divided as equally as can be amongst the clans and households.

"But, 'Bella, we only butcher our stock for meat in times of direst need. More have been slaughtered here to feed and restore your people to health than the tribe would normally kill in a year or more; it was a major sacrifice for the tribe, but I thought it necessary, under the circumstances, and was able to influence the clan chiefs to support me in it. Even then, the herds were carefully culled so that the best stock remained alive to breed more of their superior kind.

"We usually take only milk, wool and hair from our stock, the rest of our sustenance being derived of hunting and trapping game and foraging for wild plants, augmented by fishing and seining if we chance to be near lakes, ponds or larger running water. Hunting and trapping also give us hides for leather, furs for winter garments, sinew and bone for various uses, antler and horn, down and feathers for filling quilted padding and for the fletchings of arrows. Glue is rendered from fish and from the feet of hooved beasts, both wild and domesticated. The paunches of deer and others of the larger grass-eaters are treated and cured and then used to line waterskins. Intestines of the bigger beasts are cleansed and stretched and cured and then used as watertight storage containers. You see, 'Bella, we are a thrifty people, wasting nothing of any conceivable utility. As chancy as our life can be, it's a case of 'waste not, want not.'"

"Milo, if this nomadic herding and hunting life is so very hard and dangerous, why did you first set the tribe to such a life? Why did you not settle them somewhere and farm, instead?"

He grimaced, beaming, "Oh, I tried hard to do just that, in the very beginning, some century or so back, 'Bella. Indeed I did, I tried hard, believe me; I tried not just the once in the one place but several times in widely scattered locations. But the hideous explosive weapons with which the War that immediately preceded the Great Dyings was carried on must have vastly altered the high wind currents that control the climate here on earth, causing many once-productive areas to become near-deserts over a space of only a few years and also drowning many and many a square mile of arable land beneath new lakes or vastly broadened rivers and other waterways. The first three generations of the tribe wandered from place to place, farming a few years here and a few more there, only to finally have to move on due to unfavorable conditions of many differing varieties. As they and I slowly were forced by circumstances to adapt to a nomadic existence, I decided that that was the only feasible way of the future, and we gradually achieved to our current life and customs.

"Here—come into my memories and learn just how it was long ago and far, far away to the south and west."

The spring came in earlier than usual, and Milo, Paul Krueger and their people and herds moved out eastward from the southern fringes of the shrinking Lake Tahoe, but they had not proceeded far at all, not quite to Silver Springs, when the rearguard came roaring in to announce that they were being pursued by a large pack of bikers, loaded for bear and burning up the steadily decreasing distance.

In the empty streets and buildings of the dead town, ambush points were set up and manned. Their

backs were to the wall, and both men and women—
who all had of course heard of the atrocities wreaked
upon the former slaves of the Tahoe City bunch—
were prepared to fight to the last spark of life, asking
no quarter and expecting to receive none.

The filthy, long-haired and -bearded pack came
pouring into the town along its main street, with no
scouts or flankers, all of them cocksure in their
numbers, arms and rabid ferocity. And they were
butchered like so many rats in a barrel. Bullets and
buckshot and arrows came at them from all four
sides—right, left, front and rear, both on their level
and from above their heads. As the impetus of the
followers packed them in between the dead or dying
or wounded and confused vanguards and those still
speeding into the town, hand grenades were hurled
among them, the resultant explosions not only
spreading a dense and deadly wave of shrapnel, but
setting fire to several motorcycles as well.

The bikers tried hard to return fire with their
automatics, pistols, riot guns and heavier weapons,
but were hampered by their exposed positions and
the nearly complete lack of any targets at which to
aim. The few casualties taken by the embattled
farmer-folk were mostly accidental or pure chance
hits.

By the time the survivors of the outlaw band—
less than half of the original force—finally decided
to pack it in and began to stream, run, walk, hobble
or crawl out of town, back toward the west and
safety, the street between the bullet-pocked facades
of the buildings was heaped with still or writhing
bodies and the long-dry gutters were running with
sticky red blood.

Mounting captured motorcyles and horses, armed
now with a plentitude of weapons of all types, Milo,
Krueger and most of the men pursued and harried
the retreating bikers, cutting down stragglers with
ruthless abandon. As they drew up to within range of

the main bunch, they dismounted to fire long bursts at the tires of the speeding bikes, blowing quite a few, then killing the thus stranded human animals at leisure. Some of the former slaves did not kill the unlucky few who fell into their hands quickly, but rather stripped them of clothing, staked them out under the pitiless sun, maimed them in ways that sickened even Milo, then left them to die slowly of exposure, pain and blood loss, if thirst or coyotes did not do the job first. Yet when Paul Krueger and others of the men would have put a halt to the barbarities and granted the captives a quick death, Milo took the part of the freed slaves.

"Paul, gentlemen, God alone knows all that those poor bastards and their fellows—dead and alive— suffered at the brutal hands of bikers, maybe even some of those they've now got at their mercy. You surely don't think that they've recounted all that was done to them, or even the worst things, do you? No, let them alone, for now, what they're performing here is a sort of emotional catharsis for them, as well as a long-overdue revenge for the loved ones and friends who are no longer alive to savor it."

Krueger and the others, after stripping the dead bikers of weapons, ammunition and any other needed items, draining the damaged bikes of gasoline and removing sound tires and wheels, left in disgust, leaving Milo and the freed slaves plus a few of his own people to continue trailing the much-reduced force of raiders.

There was one short, sharp skirmish with a contingent of bikers who had stopped at a crossroads service station and were in process of trying to siphon gasoline out of an underground storage tank, but the exchange of fire was very brief; the bikers just left their dead and seriously wounded and took off up the road to the west with as much speed as they could coax from their engines.

Milo and his party halted there at the site of the

skirmish for long enough to dispatch the wounded bikers, strip them and themselves complete the task of raising enough fuel from the subterranean tank to refill all of their own bikes and the five-gallon cans that several men carried strapped behind them as a reserve supply.

After that, they never again caught up to the fleeing mob of survivors, though here and there along the roadway they found evidences that the pack still rode ahead of them—men dead or dying of wounds, damaged bikes or undamaged ones with empty fuel tanks, weapons, ammunition, supplies and equipment abandoned in order to lighten loads.

On the southern outskirts of Reno, Milo called a halt to the pursuit and turned about, heading back to Silver Springs. His guesstimate was that some eight hundred to a thousand bikers had descended on the ambush points. Of those, a good four hundred to five hundred had died in that little slice of hell that he and Paul and the rest had made of that main street of the town; those killed along the road and in the skirmish at the service station, plus the dead and dying they had found along the way, added up to half the number that had gotten out of the town alive, anyway. And the skirmish had proved one thing if nothing else: the outlaw bikers had had a bellyful of fighting, for once, and desired nothing more than escape. He felt certain that they had seen the last of the predatory cyclists. The pack had not too many fangs left to break on so tough and danger-ous a quarry; his experience with their unsavory breed was that they were bullies who if hurt badly enough by a chosen victim would run away to find another less capable of self-defense.

On the trip back, they topped off their tanks at the same service station, put a couple of cases of motor oil and some assorted lubricants and tools into the two trailer carts that they had found left behind by the enemy, then headed east once more, pausing only occasionally as the sun sank lower and lower behind them to run down and slay the few stray dismounted bikers they spotted wandering about or skulking in the roadside brush. The victory had been complete, the enemy's rout, utter.

After a long, slow march, with frequent stops of varying lengths, since there no longer existed the horrendous pressure of pursuit by the vengeful bikers, the migrants reached what had been the State of Idaho, crossed the Snake River to the famous Snake River Plain and settled down to farming and ranching for a while. They stayed for over ten years, during which time old Paul Krueger died, to be succeeded in authority by his fortyish son, Harry, a rancher.

Through all those years, just as through the many years that had preceded them, Milo's appearance had never changed; no sign of aging had ever occurred and, indeed, he looked far younger than many of those who had been teenagers when he had taken them under his wing thirty years before. But, oddly enough, they and the Krueger group and all the current crop of youngsters had come to accept Milo's immutability of aspect without giving thought to the matter. He was just Uncle Milo, who had always been there to guide and help them and who, conceivably, would always be there when needed.

For the first five or six years of their ten-year sojourn in the Snake River country, now as devoid of other living humans as had been most of Nevada and southern California, there had been few problems. The land had been productive, the graze abundant; the deserted homes and outbuildings they had acquired through merely moving in had been commodious and comfortable in both warm weather and cold. Early on, Milo and Paul Krueger and some others of the older men had rigged new and existing windmills to provide electricity to most of the farms and ranches, with bicycle arrangements as a backup source of power generation.

What with wells, springs, smaller streams, ponds and the nearby river, lack of water was never a problem to them. Both the hunting and the fishing were quite productive of protein, and other than coyotes, wild dogs and the rare bear, there were few predators about to menace livestock larger than chickens. If things had been fated to stay to idyllic, they might well have remained longer in the beautiful, fruitful area, but they did not.

Each succeeding winter snowfall seemed heavier than the last, and the resultant spring floods began to render the fields soggy and difficult to work at just the wrong time in the cycle of farming. The stupendous quantities of snowmelt also turned burbling brooklets into wide, turbulent torrents, ponds into shallow lakes covering many an acre of fields or pasturelands and the Snake itself into a horrifying flood that bore all on or before it and against which there was no defense.

So terrifying and deadly were the floods of the eighth spring in the Snake River country that Milo, after consulting with Harry Krueger and the half-dozen or so other natural leaders who had emerged from among the maturing first generation, decided that they must move on to a place less prone to annual disaster, in Wyoming, possibly, or Colorado.

The group of leaders agreed upon long and very careful preparations for this impending migration, setting a tentative departure date two years ahead.

"Well, at least most of us still have our wagons and carts and U-Haul trailers. My family's trailer has been a chicken coop for the most of the last eight years, but we can get it cleaned up and scrounge new tires for it somewhere, I guess," remarked Chuck Llywelyn, grinning. "But living in that nice, big, warm, dry house for so long may have spoiled us for going back to trailers and tents and wet and cold."

But Milo frowned. "I don't think we'd be wise to plan on using those trailers any longer, Chuck. These heavy snows and floods are probably not a purely local phenomenon, and everyone here is aware of the havoc that the weather and thirty-odd years of no maintenance have wrought on roads and bridges hereabouts. And Chuck, those trailers were designed for use on hard-surfaced roads, not cross-country. Their axles and wheels contain a lot of needless weight for animals to draw, and their ground clearance is so low that it sometimes seemed on the trek up here that we spent half our time whenever we had to leave the roads unloading and reloading and manhandling the damned things. Also, they are none of them light or waterproof enough for crossing deeper fords or floating across waters that have no ford . . . and those are possibilities we are going to have to anticipate and prepare for, this time around.

"No, I think we'd better start collecting hardware and metal scrap that can be reforged and lots of seasoned wood and set up a wagon works around Olsen's forge and commence the building of more carts as well as renovating and refurbishing the ones left from eight years ago. Parties had better set out on regular foraging trips to every settlement within reach, for we're going to need a veritable host of large and small items, from harness fittings and stirrups to tents and canvas sheeting and a thousand and one other things.

"From what I can recall of the country as it was before the War and from recent study of contour maps and whatnot, I think our best eventual destination would be somewhere in southeastern Wyoming or in eastern Colorado. But, gentlemen, both of those areas are a long, long way from here, and in order to reach either of them we are going to have to nurse our herds and our families and our wheeled transport over and through some of the roughest terrain on this continent. We are going to have to move at a much faster pace than we did coming up here from southern Nevada, too, lest we be trapped up there by an early winter.

"In order to see what the general condition of the roads and bridges and cuts and fills may be, I'm going to be choosing men to ride with me over several alternate lines-of-march to a number of alternate settlement sites. Consequently, a largish portion of the preparations carried on here is going to fall squarely on Harry and Chuck and Jim Olsen and the rest of you. And the usual round of farm and ranch work is all going to have to be performed at one and the same time, mind you; this will all take two years to jell, and everyone has to eat between now and then, as well as put up stores for the journey.

"Harry, you have your father's journals from the first migration, and I'll loan you mine, as well. Pore over them and you'll have an idea what to tell the foragers to bring back here. One thing they all should seek out is coal, hard coal, lots of it, for the forge—it produces a steadier and longer-lasting heat for metalworking than either wood or charcoal."

Jim Olsen, the smith, nodded his agreement wordlessly. He never had seen the sense of wasting words and breath. He was vastly talented at his new postwar profession and continued to perform it every day for all that he now was sixty-two years of age. Despite his advanced years, however, he still was as strong and active and vital as many a man of half his age, and he owned the liking, admiration and respect of every man and woman of the community.

"The seasoned woods are going to be the hardest thing to find—I know they were last time, down south. We need hardwoods, not softwood building lumber, you see—ash, oak, fruit or nutwoods, elm, maple, ironwood, birch and the like. Nor should any of them pass up pieces of solid exotic woods of a usable size—ebony, lignum vitae, mahogany, teak and rosewood, cypress, too.

"Harry, are the camels still on your ranch?"

The man addressed nodded. "Yes, they were Pa's pets, kind of, nasty and ornery and vicious as they are, so they're still around, biting cows and horses whenever they feel like it and scaring the hell out of honest coyotes and bears. Why?"

"I'll be wanting them to pack supplies for me and the advance scouting parties, Harry. See if you can turn up the packsaddles we used on them eight years ago, too. The loads that they can easily carry would break a horse's back—that's the reason that Paul doted so on them. With the five of them to pack our water, supplies and equipment, we won't need any other pack animals, only spare mounts."

"There are now six of them," said Harry Krueger. "A calf or foal or whatever you call it was dropped four years ago. But the critter's not been saddle-broke or even gentled. I wouldn't know how to go about breaking one, and I have too much regard for keeping my hide in one piece to go near those loud, smelly, dangerous abortions."

Milo and his intrepid band of explorers rode back and forth along the tentative routes until winter and snow-choked passes confined them in the Snake River country. The country over which they rode and walked had never been in any way thickly settled, even before the War and the subsequent Great Dyings. Now there were almost no signs that men had ever trod most of it, save for the crumbling roads and bridges that, where not washed out, were often of questionable safety for the passage of anything heavier than a mounted man or a pack animal.

Not one of the scattered habitations and business structures along the routes appeared to have experienced human occupation in twenty or thirty years, being all weatherworn, of warped wood, sun-damaged plastics, oxidizing metals and cracked, deeply eroded concrete. In many places, the roofs had fallen in, and many more seemed teetering on the brink of smiliar collapse.

Not that there was no life at all, for indeed there was. Game of all sorts was more than merely abundant. Deer herds abounded—common black-tails, elk and some spotted cervines that Milo was certain were fallow deer, though how they'd gotten into Wyoming was a question now unanswerable, and even a few bison, though these last were in herds of feral cattle and looked to have interbred with the bovines to some extent.

There were feral sheep and goats, too, now all as chary as the bighorns on the heights. Sometimes pronghorn antelope were to be found in the herds of sheep and goats, as well. Smaller game had prolif-erated unbelievably, for all that there were predators in plenty about. There were, of course, the inevitable coyotes and wild dogs, which here as else-where seemed to be in the process of breeding up into real, sizable lupine creatures that ran in small, extended-family packs. There were bears, both the grizzlies and the blacks. There were cougars, bobcats and the larger lynxes, smaller, long-tailed cats that bore a startling resemblance to the European wild-cat, and the full gamut of well-fed mustelids. Forests and open lands and skies were filled with birds of all sorts, sharp-eyed raptors glided high above on every clear day, and owls hooted from the tall trees as dusk was falling on the party's camps.

The men all lived well on easily harvested game, but they were forced to keep fires burning brightly and armed men alert throughout every night to protect the animals from the plethora of hungry predators. Panicky horses frequently were more of a danger to the men than the cougar or bear that had frightened them. But the camels soon proved

themselves beasts of a different water; on the first
outward-bound trip, the six of them joined to merrily
rip and stamp a pack of coyote-dog-wolves into furry,
bloody paste when said pack assayed an attack
against one of the humped dromedaries. On the way
back, through the mountains, a grizzly came sniffing
around the camp and the camels and suffered attack
and fatal injuries as a result. At morning, Milo and
some of the men followed the blood trail of the
gravely crippled ursine and found him, still warm, a
scant half-mile off. So thoroughly had he been
gashed by the long fangs of the camels that the men
did not even try to skin him, taking only his hams for
meat and his teeth and claws for adornment; the
huge bear was missing one eye and had suffered so
many broken bones from camel kicks that Milo
wondered how he had managed to drag himself off as
far as he had.

Three men lost their lives in the expedition, and
some dozen horses were killed or so badly injured as
to require being put down—though some of these
were able to be quickly replaced by animals run
down and roped and broken from wild herds—but
the same six camels that had left in the spring came
back in the autumn. And a spindly camel colt was
dropped the following March, to boot.

When Milo met again with the leaders of the
people on a late-winter day of the ninth year, he had
an armful of marked maps and a voluminous sheaf of
notes compiled from the experiences of the
expeditions he had led out and back again.

"Gentlemen," he began, "there is good news and
bad news. The good news is that the country, everywhere we went, is virtually swarming with game of
every description, including feral horses and sheep
and goats and cattle, although some few of the latter
seem to have interbred with wild bison.

"As these maps show, there are several equally
attractive destinations to be considered, some

nearer, some farther; should we choose one of the
farther ones, perhaps we should plan on wintering
over in one of those farther west, but we'll all make
that decision later.

"We saw no signs at all of recent human life until
we got to what was once the city of Cheyenne,
Wyoming. The few score people scratching out a
bare subsistence in the decaying shell of that city
seemed overjoyed to discover that someone else had
survived, that they were not the only humans left on
the continent, and their leader, a man named
Clarence Bookerman, wants to join us in our
community wherever we decide to establish it.

"At all of the sites we have recommended in these
reports, the land is fertile and adequately watered,
though not obviously prone to the kinds of flooding
we have suffered from here. There are homes and
buildings on most of the lands, though all of these
are by now in need of repair if not complete rebuild-
ing; the fields and pastures are going to have to be
cleared of the tough grasses, weeds, brush and young
trees that have taken root in them since last they
were worked by men, thirty-odd years ago, but with
due care and caution exercised, we can probably
burn off the larger portions of it, fell any treetrunks
that the fires leave behind, then grub out the roots in
jig time, and all the ashes will make the soil even
richer for the crops we sow in it.

"Now the bad news, gentlemen. The far-northern
route, the first one we tried last year, would be
impassable to wagons or carts. Between crumbling
road surfaces, washed-out fills and bridges, cuts
blocked or partly blocked by rockfall, it was difficult
enough for our party of horsemen and pack animals
to negotiate.

"The central route is little better. We probably
could eventually get the vehicles and the herds
through, but it would be very hard work clearing
cuts and refilling fills, and felling trees to build

makeshift bridges, and this all would require a great deal of time, the one commodity of which we lack are we to get through the worst, highest country safely before the snows are upon us.

"The far-southern route, now, is the one that I and all the other scouts would prefer except for a certain factor. Use of it will require that we either use a less-than-satisfactory stretch of roads to get over into Wyoming and then down to this southern route—roads that are going to require all the aforementioned work that the central route would, though for a shorter overall distance—or choose the following alternative.

"The much easier way to get our people and herds to a point at which we can set our feet to the better-preserved road that will take us east to the richest lands is to take old Route 30 down south, curve around the southern tip of Bear Lake and proceed on into Wyoming. But here lies a serious, a dangerous problem, gentlemen, that cost me the lives of two men and some horses."

Chapter VIII

To men accustomed to stalking close enough to deer and other game to bring them down with a single arrow, the stalking of the nighttime sentries walking the perimeter and the settlement that once had been the Utah town of Laketon proved absurdly easy of accomplishment. Razor-edged knife and deady garrote did their sanguineous tasks of severing or crushing human windpipes, quickly, brutally, but very efficiently, in silence so absolute that not even the domestic animals of the settlement were alerted. Milo and those few older men who had done this sort of thing before, long ago, in another world, were very proud of their proteges on that night.

They had left the wagons, the carts, the herds and the women and children several miles to the north and come in on foot, leading their mounts for the last mile or so in the darkness. When the yodel of a loon, repeated three times, then twice, notified the waiting men that the last of the sentries was down, they mounted, rechecked their weapons and moved out, those with torches lighting them from a watchfire as they walked their horses and mules across the now-unguarded perimeter and into the sleeping town.

All were armed with the automatics, short shotguns and handguns taken from the ambushed motorcycle outlaws years before, for unlike the other rifles and shotguns, these weapons were utterly useless for hunting, their sole utilization being the purpose for which they had been made or adapted: man-killing at very close range. In addition, some of the better archers bore bows, the arrow shafts wrapped near the heads with lengths of rag impregnated with oil, resin, lard and other flammables. Milo carried the last two grenades—one fragmentation, one concussion; the grenades had disappeared over the years in the Snake River country simply because they were a sure way to harvest large numbers of fish from a lake with little or no effort.

At the directions of the leaders, the archers uncased their first arrows, fired them from the blazing torches, then loosed them into anything that looked flammable—roofs, buildings with wooden siding, three half-buried strongpoints roofed with logs and weathered timbers, and the like. Other men dismounted to open the gas caps of vehicles, dip strips of cloth into the tanks, light the outside ends and run back to their horses. Detached units had dealt similarly with the flotilla of powerboats at the lakeside docks, then opened the cocks of the fuel storage tanks, following which—and from a goodly distance away—Milo had used one of old Paul Krueger's homemade spring projectors to send the single available concussion grenade to bounce along the cracked concrete in and out of the widening pools of gasoline for the few seconds it had taken for its fuse to set off the fiery main charge.

The first explosion brought armed men boiling out of five of the larger buildings directly into the withering barrage of automatics, shotguns, pistols and even a few arrows. No unarmed man or woman was shot at—the leaders had so instructed the raiders—but those armed received short shrift in the now well-lit streets. And with the prisoners under heavy guard, needing only to look at the bleeding corpses of their comrades to guess the fate of any who attempted escape or resistance against the invaders from out of the night, Milo and the rest of the men went through every building that was not burning, rooting out any hiding humans and collecting everything that even looked like a weapon of any description as well as every round they could find of ammunition. Those they judged might be useful to them were packed on the mules they had brought along; the rest were heaved onto the nearest fire, there to explode or melt or burn or at the least have their temper drawn by the heat.

As dawn began to streak the sky to the east, the rider was sent north at the gallop to announce to the waiting wagons, carts and herds that the way now was cleared of human opposition and that they might proceed south; the packtrain with a few guards followed close behind the rider. Then Milo had a grimy, middle-aged man with singed beard and hair dragged from out the huddle of terrified, woebegone prisoners and brought before him.

Smiling coldly, he said, "Do you remember me, General Ponce? I told you last year that I'd be back."

"You . . . you murderin' bastard, you!" the big man half-sobbed in frustrated rage, his jowls and sagging belly aquiver, spittle showering through his gapped, filthy teeth and hot rage beaming from his black eyes. "You may crow big now, but you gonna sing a diffrunt tune when my boy gits back here with his calvery p'trol, you. Thishere's *our land*, just like I tole you and your other sonofabitches las' year, and don't nobody pass over it or th'ough it lessen we gets our choice of ever'thin' they got, first."

Milo smiled grimly. "Those days are over for you and your pack, Ponce. We've seen to that this morning, for good and all. Oh, and I'd not advise that you try holding your breath until your boy and his mounted patrol come riding back in, either. If you wonder just where they are, wait until it gets full

light and head for the spot up northwest where you'll
see the buzzards circling.

"We've burned down half your settlement here—
your motorized transport, your powerboats and all
of your fuel, the weapons and ammo we could easily
locate in a short time. Without those things, you
swine are going to play merry hell trying to mount
raids against your neighbors or exact cruel tolls of
travelers, as you bragged of doing for years when
last we met. When my main party arrives, we are
going to loot your settlement far more thoroughly,
believe it, Ponce."

And it was so done. With the arrival of the wagons
and the carts, the settlement—what by then remained of it—was stripped of long years' worth of ill-
gotten gains, food, clothing, usable artifacts and
equipment, animals to add to the milling herds, plus
a baker's dozen of captive women and some thirty
children gotten on them by their captors during the
years of their vile captivity.

With the wagons and carts and riders and herds on
the road to the southeast, Milo had the remaining
inhabitants of the town that had once been a resort
called Laketon tied up and roped together. From his
saddle, he addressed his parting remarks to the self-
styled general, Ponce.

"You know, what I should do is send riders around
to the various nearer settlements to let those off
whom you and your pack have been battening for
years know that you all are now here, unarmed and
with neither motor vehicles, boats nor horses." He
cocked his head, as if in consideration of the matter,
and Ponce paled to the color of skim milk, while
several of the bound men began to struggle vainly
against the ropes.

When he could see the smoldering rage in Ponce's
beady black eyes replaced by fear, Milo shook his
head and said, "But my schedule simply will not

permit me to see real justice done to you and this collection of scum that you've gathered around you, so I suppose that we'll just have to leave you all here the way you now are. Eventually, one or more of you will wriggle loose, out of those knots . . . and maybe they'll then free the rest of you, but don't count on it, Ponce. There's no honor among thieves.

"And even when you do finally get loose, even if some of your former victims don't chance on you and stake you out over an anthill with your eyelids and certain other parts cut off, you all are going to have a rough life for some little time. You'll have to actually do hard, manual labor, just to eat every few days, like as not, but most of you seem to have enough fat to keep you going for a while, at least. And all through your sufferings, both the big ones and the lesser ones, just remember that had you not cold-bloodedly shot down one of my men last year, then stolen his horse and a few others from the remuda, all of this might not have occurred here today. I say only 'might not,' Ponce, for I don't like or even easily tolerate your brand of predatory opportunist. People of your stripe made a terrible situation far, far worse, after the War, for the few survivors of the plagues and the starvation. So I just might have done what I did to your den of thieves on general principles, even had you not murdered young Robin Ogilvie at the conclusion of what you had assured us was to be a peaceful, friendly meeting."

Milo made to rein about, then turned back, admonishing, "Oh, and if you and any of your crew had any idea of following us, forget it. Any of you I catch after this day, I'll turn over to the thirteen women I rescued from you, them and some folks who were held as slaves by a group like yours years ago, down to the south, in Nevada and California."

Without further incident, they crossed the Bear River into what had once been the State of Wyoming and, in the southerly outskirts of the deserted ruins of a close-clinging cluster of small towns, they camped, rested the herds and draft beasts and explored the nearby ruins for anything they might want to use, then headed on, first east, then southeast, to the place at which Route 30 merged with a former interstate road, Route 80.

They halted again, briefly, at the empty town of Rock Springs, rested and scavenged, hunted, fished, performed necessary repairs to the wagons, carts, harnesses and other equipment, washed out their water barrels and laundered their clothing, washed themselves, their riding and draft beasts, collected a few head of feral cattle and even a half-dozen wild horses to be broken and added to their horse herd. They also managed to rope a fine, big burro stallion, which feat Milo and the other leaders considered a very good omen, for their mules were all aging and, as the sterile hybrids did not reproduce more of their kind, younger ones were become impossible to acquire.

Despite the most vociferous urgings, it simply proved an impossibility for the train and herds to average anything in excess of about ten miles per day, so it was thirty-two days before they reached what had been called Cheyenne.

They rolled onto the cracked streets of that all but deserted city to a rousing welcome from some hundred or so people and the mayor, Clarence Bookerman—a wiry little man of indeterminate age and some bare five feet-six inches of height, but full of energy and with intelligence sparkling from his bright blue eyes. He greeted the van of the train mounted on a tall, leggy, splendid red-bay Thoroughbred which he handled with the relaxed ease of a true horseman; both he and his people seemed beside themselves with the pleasure of meeting the folk of the train and quickly proved themselves gracious, generous hosts.

After a sumptuous, delicious dinner, that night, Milo arose and introduced their host to the assembled leaders. "Gentlemen, unlike the most of us, Mayor Bookerman is a highly educated man, holding both an M.D. and a doctorate in biology, and he was, before the War, a professor at a university in Colorado, south of here.

"He it was who organized the survivors hereabouts and got them to farming and rounding up animals to be certain that they could feed themselves after the food stocks they had scrounged and scavenged ran out. He got them formed into a militia to beat off the inevitable marauders that seem to survive any disaster of whatever dimensions. He persuaded them all to take to shank's mare or horseback in order to preserve the available stocks of fuels for heating and electrical generators. He has kept this community going for nearly thirty years now.

"But as he knows this country so well, he now thinks that the climate is changing here just as it has in other places, and not for the better, unfortunately."

There was a single, concerted groan from the leaders of the Snake River folk. The journey here had been long and hard on them, their families and their animals, and they had thought, had hoped, had prayed that they were migrating to a land that was, if not flowing with milk and honey, at least capable with proper care and tillage of sustaining them and theirs for years to come.

Milo held up a hand, palm outward. "Hold on, there, Harry, Jim, the rest of you. Let me finish what Dr. Bookerman told me an hour or so before dinner.

"He is not saying that anyone has to mount up and move on tomorrow or even the day after." He grinned. "No, what he is saying is that we should not hunker down to stay for a generation or two. For as much as five more years, we will all of us be able to wrest a good to fair living from the surrounding land, but we should not plan to stay beyond that time, for the winters here have been getting colder and longer, year by year, just as they did on the Snake, back in Idaho."

Olsen demanded, "Well, where in the hell are we all supposed to go from here, Uncle Milo? Not that I mind traveling—I think if it was up to me alone, I'd travel and herd and hunt for a living full-time. But this stop and go, go and then stop again shit is sure hard on me and a whole heap of other folks."

"I know, I know," said Milo sympathetically. "But we're only talking about one final migration, Dr. Bookerman and I, and that not for three to five more years. When we move on, he is of the opinion that we should move southeastward again, down into eastern Colorado, out of the mountains. He and I looked at the maps he has, and he has made several suggestions as to the eventual destination. When we decide on one, or at least narrow the choice down to three or four, I'll scout out them and the roads just as I did before.

"For now, we all should let Dr. Bookerman's people show us to the better stretches of currently unused farm and pasturelands, do what building or repairs we have to, then get ourselves ready for spring and all that that will entail. But just keep it in mind that we are not going to be here for more than five years, come what may, unless the climate improves drastically."

It did not. That first winter came on suddenly with no bit of warning, and was exceedingly hard, with deep snows and long days and nights of howling blizzards which often left buildings, trees and all other exterior surfaces sheathed in ice. That first winter lasted far longer than should have been normal, to judge by old almanacs and records from before the War, and when at length it did relent, the floodings were massive, with the snowmelt abetted by heavy spring rains, which made quagmires of the fields being prepared for planting and bogs of the pastures. It seemed to the recent immigrants fully as bad as anything that the Snake River country had had to offer. Talking at some length as he worked at his forge for those in need of his services, Olsen began to gather converts to his idea of leading a life-long nomadic existence, rather than trekking from one place to another in search of land that was easier to farm in the face of increasingly hostile weather.

"I was fully aware of the blacksmith's ongoing campaigning, speechmaking and arguments with whomever he had around his forge, but I did nothing, said nothing. You see, I was beginning to agree with him. I was coming to the conclusion that, as the climate seemed to have changed and as few mechanized farming devices were still in usable condition, we were beating our collective head against a brick wall by trying to farm." Milo stopped the flow of his memories briefly to beam to Arabella Lindsay. "It had been my scouting expeditions that had shown me just how much easier it would be to live off the country—off the profusion of game animals and feral beasts, wild plants and, in some areas, volunteer crops of grains and vegetables still growing on deserted farms. And my own people had become pretty good at fabricating functional, well-made, tough and capacious wagons and carts, stout running gear and finely fashioned harness. They had learned through practice to make tents very comfortable and weatherproof. Furthermore, some looms had been scrounged while we abided in the Snake River country, and some few of the women had become quite adept at fashioning cloth starting with only raw wool sheared from our own sheep, and others had experimented with and developed the art of felting assorted varieties of hair and fur. We'd been tanning, of course, for many years and working the resultant leather. If we supplied Olsen with the proper amounts of good-grade fuel and metal scrap, there was damned little that he couldn't fashion for us in the way of hardware. We also, of course, numbered among us many fine, if self-taught, wainwrights, carpenters and cabinetmakers, wheelwrights, horse leeches, midwives, trackers, horse tamers, seamstresses and the like. I reckoned that we could, if necessary, be as good as self-sufficient and could learn to live as well off the country as the American Indians had done for thousands of years, probably better, due to the fact that we had a resource available to us that they had lacked utterly —our herds. So I just allowed Olsen to maunder on, doing my work for me, as it were."

Once more, he opened his memories of events long years in the past.

They all nearly starved to death the third year, when an early winter came down too soon for the necessarily late planted crops to be harvested properly. They only squeaked through the dark, bleak period by slaughtering all of the swine and a larger number of cattle and sheep than Milo, Bookerman and the other leaders liked to see go down. The following spring was when the Cheyenne people started collecting the materials to build carts and wagons with the help of the experienced newcomers from Idaho.

Olsen, perforce, moved his operation and his gospel into a place prepared for him in the city, closer to the supplies of fuels, timber and metals and in the hub of the activities of the wainwrights, wheelwrights, carpenters and their new, willing, but mostly unskilled apprentices.

Almost all of the Cheyenne people had become riders, because of Dr. Bookerman's dictates against the use of fuels in the remaining motor vehicles, but none of them had any experience in driving horses for anything other than plowing or short-distance draft of agricultural implements, hay wagons and the like. So Milo and others began a school in the arcane arts of the long-distance trek. As soon as the crops were in, they broadened the courses to include maintenance of wagons, carts and harness; the pitching, striking and care of tents and other camping gear; the proper laying and making and feeding of cookfires; and the basics of archery, afoot and ahorse, for even though they would leave the Cheyenne area well supplied with arms and ammunition, their stock of cartridges would not last forever and there was no assurance that wherever they stopped to scrounge and scavenge, they would be able to find more of the correct calibers and still usable after years of improper storage.

Supplied with antique weapons from a Cheyenne museum, Milo taught some of the better horsemen of both groups of people the basics of saber-work on horseback and resolved to himself to see to it when the then-overworked men had the time that Olsen turned out blades for similar sabers and for light horsemen's axes, as well. He considered lances, which would have been easy enough to fashion, even without the services of the smith, but he had never used one on horseback and felt that he should give himself time to digest a couple of books he had dug from the stacks of the main Cheyenne library before he began to try to teach the use of the tricky weapon. Best to confine his instruction to weapons he did know—bow, saber, light axe.

Dr. Clarence Bookerman quickly proved himself to be the most adept of Milo's pupils. His horsemanship had been consummate, from the start, and after a few days, he handled the heavy saber as if it were a mere extension of his wiry arm. Milo was amazed, at first, that so old a man—to judge by his experiences and attainments both before and since the War, the mayor had to be somewhere between sixty and seventy years of age—could handle so difficult a weapon so well within so short a time, and he told his accomplished pupil just that.

Smiling faintly, Bookerman said, "True, I have not held a hilt in many years, Milo, but it is not an art which once fully mastered one forgets easily. I studied for some years in West Germany, you see. You have heard of dueling societies, perhaps?" The old man outlined with one fingertip two scars—one over his left cheekbone, the other low on his right cheek, a bit above the upper perimeter of his carefully trimmed chin-beard.

"In the *Verbindungen*, we used a straight blade without a point, of course, but I can see the advantages to a horseman of a cursive, pointed blade, especially if his opponent be on foot."

Milo relaxed in the supportive stock saddle, resting the flat of his blade on the top of the horn. " 'Bookerman,' Doctor, has a decided Teutonic ring to it. Are you, perchance, of German origin or descent?"

The mayor smiled again, a bit more broadly. "And I had thought, I had imagined, that I had gained complete mastery of standard American English, Milo; I thought that I spoke it with the fluency of a native."

"You do, Doctor," Milo assured him. "Look, it's none of my business, really, and . . ."

"No, no." Bookerman shook his head rapidly. "Are we two to live out the remainder of our two lives in close proximity, it is proper that you should know such things. And this particular thing is no longer of the slightest importance.

"Yes, I was born in Germany and lived the most of my youth on one of my father's estates in Niedersachsenland. I took my M.D. in Germany and came to the United States in order to pursue a course of study which interested me. I met and married a fine American woman and decided to stay and become a citizen. For a number of reasons, we Anglicized our name to Bookerman, rather than staying Bucher-mann, and at the same time, I changed my baptismal name from Karl-Heinrich to Clarence.

"But please believe me that it all was aboveboard and most completely innocent, Milo." He grinned, adding, "I was born far too late to have had anything to do with the Third Reich, along with anyone now still living, although several relatives of my father were, rightly or wrongly, adjudged war criminals after World War the Second—two of those men were hanged and one was sent to prison, solely for being good officers who remembered their oaths and their honor and followed the lawful orders of their military superiors. However, as I have said, my friend, none of this now is of any slightest importance—not to you, not to me, not to any of our dependent peoples and not, especially, in this new and strange and possibly deadly world within which we all now must live . . . or die."

Then, still smiling, the elderly little man whirled up his saber and delivered a lightning-fast overhand cut with the dull and padded edge which Milo barely managed to stop with a parry in the sixth, the force and shock of the blow tingling his hand and wrist and arm clear up to the shoulder.

Bookerman laughed. "Your reflexes are excellent, Milo. Your style is most unorthodox, however; I can tell that you learned the blade in no *Fechtsaal*. There is a veneer of the Olympic to your style, and that is what you have been teaching here. But when you are not thinking, then comes out an entirely different mode of combat and defense from your subconscious, an instinctive one, if you will, that I think was learned from no modern master."

Many long centuries later, Milo was to recall these words.

As that year's crops were tended and finally harvested, the schools went on. So, too, did the work in and around Olsen's forge. So, too, did Olsen's preachments anent the giving over of the settled, farming life for the existence of nomadic herders. The smith was forceful and voluble, and by the coming of winter, he had managed to convince and convert Harry Krueger and most of the other leaders of the immigrants, not a few of the lesser heads of household and even a few of the Cheyenne people, none of whom had ever before lived for more than a few days at best in portable housing, which last feat was, in itself, something of a real accomplishment.

At the first meeting of the council following the first hard freeze of the early winter, Milo readily yielded the floor to Olsen, who had come to the conclave directly from the still-operating forge and wagonyard, grimy with coal dust and from the ever-constant wreaths of smoke in which he and his helpers labored. His presence filled the small room with the mingled odors of smoke, sweat, wet woolens and singed hair.

Olsen arose, standing and resting the weight of his thick torso on the skinned knuckles of his two clenched fists as he leaned on the table of what was become the council chamber. He cleared his throat and began, "All right, let's us get the bitching out of the way, first. I know that Les Folsom means to complain to the rest of the council that when some of his folks brought me and the wainwrights sheet metal they'd scrounged to have their cart bodies fashioned of it, I junked the aluminum and had the sheet steel cut up to make straps and whatnots."

Folsom, a blond, clean-shaven man of early middle years, grunted and nodded and looked on the verge of speaking, but Olsen just spoke on—after all, he had the floor and he knew it. "Les, boys, there is a damned good reason or three that I ordered what I did. When we first emigrated up to Nevada from southern California, years ago, we found us a whole bunch of U-Haul trailers, which were better than the travoises we were all using back then, but that's about all.

"Because we were then in danger, pressed hard for time, we used those same damn trailers on the march up to the Snake River country from Lake Tahoe. But when we knew we were headed east, coming here, we built new wooden wagons and carts and left every damned one of those old sheet-metal trailers to molder in the Snake River Valley.

"Les, your folks ranted and raved about how heavy and thick wooden wagon bodies were and how messy the waterproofing we used of tar and resin and oakum is, and they're right, for as far as their thinking and the limited experience that that thinking is based on go.

"But, Les, boys, when a sheet-metal body is holed —and they are, too, damned often—it ain't any way to patch it, short of taking it off the running gear, dragging it over to my travel forge and trying to hammer-weld a piece of steel over the hole, and that fails as many times as it works, I've found; besides which, I'm generally up to my ears in trying to do really urgent, important things like keeping the draft beasts and the riding horses decently shod so they don't turn up lame at a bad time for everybody.

"Wooden boards, now, if they get holed, you just stuff the littler ones with oakum and resin or break a chunk off the nearest road and render it in a pot for the tar. Bigger ones you might have to nail a short piece of wood over and then recaulk it. If a board is smashed bad and there is no seasoned lumber to replace it, you can straighten it out, reinforce it lengthwise with long steel or iron straps, then use short straps or angle straps or whatever you need for that job to give the repair support from the whole lumber around it, then just caulk it all up so's it's watertight again."

"It sounds like a hell of a lot of needless work, to

me," said Folsom dubiously. "I still think that a properly welded sheet-metal body would be better in all ways than a wooden one. Look at the automobiles and trucks—they took a hell of a beating, but the manufacturers never stopped using sheet metal to make them, Olsen."

"Have you got any conception of how long it would take us to hammer-weld all the seams of a ten-foot wagon body, Mr. Folsom?" Olsen demanded in controlled heat. "With cars and trucks, back before the War, it was a body shop in damn near any direction you looked all over the country, and mostly, they didn't repair as much as hang new fenders or doors or whatever, even then. If it came down to welding, they had oxyacetylene torches. Man, I don't!

"You tell your people to bring me all the sheet metal they can find—except that thin aluminum, which is good for nothing. I need it at the forge, as much of it as I can get. But if they or you think I'm going to waste time and energy and fuel to try to make them welded sheet-steel wagons, they better find them a way to put in an order to Deetroit—maybe Ford or Chrysler is still in operation up there."

Folsom's long-fingered hands clenched into fists on which the prominent knuckles stood out white as the new snow, and his fine-boned face turned almost livid. It was abundantly clear to all those present that it would not take much more to precipitate open violence between him and the smith.

This was not exactly what Milo had had in mind for the discussion at this meeting, so he moved to halt it before it reached the sure conclusion for which it now was headed.

He bespoke the fuming smith first, since he had known him longer: "Jim, there's no need to be so sarcastic to Les. Recall, if you will, that he and his people have never been on a trek, and that around here they have gotten good service out of their sheet-

metal-bodied farm wagons and buggies and whatnot.
Allow for a little honest, well-meaning ignorance of
just how conditions are from day to day on a
migration. Remember, you've done it three times;
Les and his folks have yet to do it once.

"As for you, Les, the things that Jim Olsen has told
you and your people are nothing less than the clear,
unvarnished truth—wooden wagons or cart bodies
are better, more serviceable on the march and easier
to repair, despite the weight and bulk and the necessity for using frayed rope and resin or tar to pack the
seams and interstices. And none of your arguments
to the contrary are going to change that which is, to
those of us who have made it through several treks,
proven and incontrovertible fact.

"Jim, here, is in or near the last stages of utter
exhaustion, if you need to be told, and his nerves are
as frazzled as the rest of him. He has been working
eighteen- and twenty-hour days for months on end
and really needs to go home and sleep for at least a
week; but his skill, his expertise, his experience,
these all are irreplaceable in that forge and wagonyard down there, and he knows it and is damned
nearly killing himself for the common good—for you,
for all of us and all the other people. Think hard on
what I've said the next time you are moved to ride
Jim, to needlessly antagonize him, Les. We could
probably do it all without him, but it would take one
hell of a sight longer, and be done far less well and at
risks we have not the right to take for the well-being
of families, women, children."

He turned to Krueger, saying, "Harry, I understand that you and Jim and some others have spent a
good deal of time poring over the maps. Have you
come up with any ideas for an eventual destination
for us all?"

Krueger looked at Olsen, and Olsen looked at
Chuck Llywelyn and several others of the Snake

River group, as well as at a couple of the Cheyenne leaders. Then the rancher arose and said:

"Uncle Milo, it wasn't for farming sites we were studying those maps, but for the best grazing lands, whereall they seem to lie and how far from each other, and then we tried to figger out how long it would take a herd the size of ours to use up the grass and force us to move on.

"You see, farming is all well and good and all for them as likes to suffer, but we don't, and we think we could live just as good if not a sight better off game and wild plants and our herds as we do scratching at the dirt and hoping and praying that whatall we plant comes up before the snows come in or before there's an early freeze that kills everything. When that happens—and it's been happening more years than not—we've worked and sweated our asses off and we still have to end up making do until the next harvesttime on game, wild plants and the produce of the herds.

"What it all boils down to, Uncle Milo, is we're thinking of moving out come spring, right enough, but moving only as far as the flatter country in eastern Colorado and only staying where we finally stop until we've used up the graze and the game and all, then moving on to the next good graze and hunting. Does that sound crazy to you, Uncle Milo?"

Chapter IX

Once more, Milo closed the pages of his memories to beam a telepathic encapsulization of the long-ago events for Arabella Lindsay.

"Of course, my dear, it wasn't that easy, that quick a decision. No, the council chewed over it for nearly the whole of that long winter, with shouting, pounding of fists on tables and walls and, occasionally, on each other, exchanges of insults and some very harsh words between the pro-farming and the pro-nomad factions—in other words, all of the usages and forms of polite, gentlemanly discussion. The only thing on which everyone seemed to agree for a while were the facts that we must leave the environs of Cheyenne, that south of southeast seemed as good a direction as any to travel and that the building of the carts and a few wagons were essential, along with the training of teams and drivers. About everything save those few points, they argued endlessly and ofttimes violently.

"Slowly, however, one and two at a time, Jim Olsen and Harry Krueger and Chuck Llywelyn began to wear down and win over their opponents; sometimes it appeared to me that they were managing the feat solely by outshouting them, but nonetheless, it was done. By spring, as the snows began to melt off, a very few diehard holdouts remained adamant about the benefits of farming over those of a nomadic herding and hunting existence, but even these were by then ready and more than willing to accompany the others at least as far as a decent area of arable land to farm and settle upon, and Olsen and the rest were still confident that even these few stubborner cases could be won over once on the march.

Despite a winter of unremitting labor, almost around the clock, in the forge and the wagon works, it slowly dawned on the council that all would not be ready by the time that the countryside had dried out enough to begin a journey of such proportions. Therefore, Milo suggested that he and his scouts set out to ride a reconnaissance of at least the first part of the projected route of the trek. Most of the leaders agreed readily; it was better to know precisely what you were moving into, especially with families, herds and all one's worldly possessions at stake. However, Dr. Clarence Bookerman flatly refused his consent to the venture unless he was included in the party of scouts, and, at length, Milo felt compelled to grant this demand, for all that he was more than a little leery of riding out on what might well be a very rough and possibly dangerous trip with a man of Bookerman's advanced years. Milo consoled his conscience with the thoughts that, firstly, the mayor was in splendid, almost unbelievable physical condition for a man who admitted an age of between sixty and seventy and had not lived anything approaching an easy life during the last thirty-odd of those years, and secondly, that the man was after all a medical doctor who surely would know and recognize his own limitations . . . and whose skills just might come in handy, anyway.

By now, the herd of camels had become just that, there being a full dozen of the tall, long-legged, irascible beasts, and Milo had, mostly by trial and error, trained four of the younger, slightly more malleable and less vicious beasts to riders rather than pack-carrying, constructing traditional camel saddles from pictures and descriptions gleaned from books in the stacks of the main Cheyenne library. The tamest of the quartet were Fatima and Sultan, both of whom he had gotten away from the older camels and bottle-fed when they still were spindly-legged calves, but even these would often end a day of riding with a serious attempt to savage Milo with their cursive canine teeth. He had found out early on why camel riders, no matter what their other gear and equipment, always kept a stout stick ready to hand when around their treacherous mounts.

As his last-ditch argument against Dr. Book-erman's forced inclusion in the reconnaissance party, he remarked that he had intended to use the esoteric beasts not only as pack animals this time, but for riding, as well. They could not outstrip a good horse over a short stretch, but they could keep going for long after hard-pressed horses either had foundered or died; he had dug out records of dromedaries traveling two hundred miles in a day, for many days straight, and on the scouting expeditions into Wyoming, years back, he had found the camels could and would eat anything that a goat would, in addition to many things that a self-respecting old goat would not. There was, if any more plus factors were needed, the fact that camels could easily take care of themselves in confrontations with even the most-feared predators, and this would be no talent to be taken lightly by a small, light traveling, hard-riding party of men.

But Bookerman had just allowed one of his brief smiles to flit across his thin, pale lips. "Wonderful, Milo! It has been far more years than I care to count since last I rode a camel, but I have not forgotten how."

A bit stunned at this sudden revelation by the

multitalented physician, Milo simply acquiesced to what seemed to be the inevitable.

Despite stops to check bridges, cuts, fills, and the general condition of the deteriorating roadway once called Interstate 87, the speedy, long-striding camels bore the reconnaissance party more than sixty miles in the first day of travel, more than halfway to Denver, their goal for the initial portion of the trip. The country through which they passed was breathtakingly beautiful. Game abounded, and fish leaped in the streams and small lakes the waterways sometimes formed with the help of colonies of beaver. But still Milo was saddened by the abundant evidences of the dearth of mankind—the crumbling roads, the tumbling ruins, many with caved-in roofs, now the haunts only of rodents and snakes, the faded, weather-battered highway directional signs and those advertising products and services not available for more than a generation.

Here and there, mixed with the herds of deer, elk and bison, could be spotted feral cattle, sheep and goats, as well as a scattering of the more exotic ungulates—American, African and Asiatic antelope and gazelles ranging in size from tiny to huge. From a distance, with the binoculars, they once watched a herd of llamas, wildebeest and a few zebras and feral horses being painstakingly stalked through the sprouting grasses by a small tiger. Even as the four men watched, fascinated, the feline rushed the suddenly panicky herd, sprang and brought down a shaggy-haired zebra.

As he cased his optics, Bookerman remarked, "A completely wild tiger killing and eating a completely wild zebra—who would ever have thought to see such a drama enacted in North America forty years ago, Milo?"

Milo nodded. "Yes, it would have been unthinkable, back then, before the War. But did you notice the long, shaggy coats of all those beasts—the gnus, the zebras, the horses, even the tiger? They have obviously adapted to this colder, harsher climate far better than anyone, either back then or now, would ever have expected them to do. It makes me wonder just how many more surprises we have ahead, how many other rare animals have been able to make a home in this new wilderness here, in what was once one of the most populous of human civilizations."

They could not approach too close to the place where had stood the city of Denver, for it had been nuked. But they rode well out around the still-radio-active area, cross-country, to the east and thence south, until they came onto Interstate 70. This road, for some reason, seemed to be in far better shape than had been Interstate 87, and they followed it almost to what had been the Kansas border, finally heading north once more on Route 385 to its conjunction with Interstate 76, which they followed the few miles to where it intersected with Interstate 80, the route which led them back to Cheyenne.

Nowhere on their circuitous journey did they sight even a trace of recent human occupancy or passage. The wild game and feral beasts seemed not even to know what a human looked or smelled like. They returned with glowing reports on the countryside they had seen . . . and with three additional camels to boot—two-humped ones.

The three, an elderly female and two younger, but adult, females, had simply drifted into the camp one dawn and, since then, followed the four riding and two pack dromedaries everywhere that the journey took them. At the leisurely pace set by Milo on the return to Cheyenne, the shorter-legged, shaggy Bactrian camels had had no difficulty keeping up with the longer-legged dromedaries.

Figuring that not even a completely wild camel could be any more vicious than their supposedly tame ones, Milo and one of his men had put a halter on the older of the Bactrians with no more difficulty and danger than they experienced every day with their riding and pack dromedaries, then strapped on a packsaddle they had fashioned from scavenged materials and filled it with odds and ends picked up here and there in the course of the reconnaissance expedition. From that day on they had had three pack camels, and Milo wondered aloud if some of the bloodlust might be bred out of the dromedaries by crossing them with the better-dispositioned Bactrians, wondering also if the two were closely enough related to breed naturally or if they might produce the camel equivalent of a mule, a sterile hybrid.

"Oh, yes, Milo," Bookerman had assured him, "the two can be interbred, and often have been in the Middle East and Asia. However, the offspring, though completely fertile and potent, are smaller and less strong than the dromedaries, and most of them have two humps, though one is often much smaller than is the other. However, I never have heard of any improvement in the traditional camel disposition being accomplished by such interbreeding."

"But, Doctor," expostulated Milo, "you saw how docile that camel cow was when Richard and I haltered and saddled her. She only snapped at us a few times during the whole procedure, and those snaps were halfhearted, I thought."

Bookerman just nodded. "Yes, I saw it all, and I suspect that she most likely was thoroughly—well, as thoroughly as any camel ever is—domesticated long ago, before the War, in her youth. You see, Milo, a camel lives for thirty to fifty years, and she is clearly an elderly one, the other two being most probably her daughters.

"Interbreed the camels if you wish, although as the only bull camels we have are dromedaries, I suspect that when next our three volunteers come into their estrus, it would be worth the lives of any of us to try to interfere with interbreeding. But do not expect lamb-gentle offspring, my friend, for you will most assuredly be bitterly disappointed. Those offspring, when once they have achieved their full growth— will be—rather than tall, very strong, long-legged, impressive murderous beasts—relatively short, shaggy, ponderous-bodied murderous beasts."

"How the hell do you know so much about camels, anyway, Doctor?" Milo demanded.

Bookerman smiled another of his fleeting smiles. "Quite easily explained, my dear Milo. My father spent a good bit of time in the Middle East just after World War Two, after having already served some time in North Africa with General Erwin Rommel and, a bit later, in Tuscany, where camels had been in use as beasts of burden for generations. He talked much to me of his experiences, Milo, and he also wrote and privately published a book about those experiences. I studied that book quite often."

In the end, some half-dozen extended families refused to take leave of Cheyenne at all, and a number of others insisted on lading their transport with plows, other tilling implements, seed corn and plant slips; they also carried large items of furniture, in some cases, and drove along, with the help of dogs and children, small herds of domestic swine.

Most of the folk who left, however, drove only cattle, sheep and goats. These traveled far more lightly than did the minority—bringing along tents, bedding, small and easily portable furnishings, carpets, weapons, spare clothing and footwear, cutlery and utensils, here and there a homemade spinning wheel or a small loom, tools of various sorts and usages, ropes and thongs to repair harnesses, tanned hides and oddments of hardwware, jewelry and small personal possessions, perhaps a few books and reference manuals.

Because he had no wife or children to drive it for him, Milo had ordered no cart or wagon for himself; rather, he rode his dromedary, Fatima, and packed his tent and other gear on the bull dromedary, Shagnasty, and the oldest two-humped cow camel, Dishim, leaving his horses to be herded with the remuda. His two baggage beasts hitched behind the carts of friends, Milo himself spent most of every day patrolling the length of the winding columns, from vanguard to rearguard on his long-legged, distance-eating, almost-tireless mount, his path offtimes crossing that of Dr. Bookerman, mounted on the younger bull dromedary, Sultan.

The physician was an enigma to Milo. He gave an age at wild variance to his appearance and physical abilities. Furthermore, conversations with the man were seldom less than surprising to Milo, for the physician usually demonstrated detailed knowledge of subjects, places and events of which it seemed impossible for a single individual of only some seventy-odd years to know.

Bookerman was definitely a skilled surgeon—Milo had seen him at work—but he was also so very much else, besides—natural horseman, crack shot with rifle and pistol or smoothbore, fast and accurate and very powerful with the saber, far better than Milo at use of a lance from horseback, a born leader of men and skilled in the necessary aspects of organization and administration of those he led. The anomalies, however, started with the fact that although he had at one time said that he had emigrated to the United States as soon as he had taken his M.D. in Germany and had then left his adopted homeland but seldom and even then for very short trips, he seemed to know most of Europe in detail, as well as parts of North Africa and the Middle East. The only

languages with which Milo was conversant that
Bookerman was not were those of the Far East—
Japanese, Chinese, Korean, Vietnamese and the like.
Otherwise, the physician could write, read and
fluently speak Latin, archaic Greek, modern Greek,
Hebrew, Yiddish, numerous dialects of German and
Arabic, French, Italian, European Spanish, Portu-
guese, Russian and other Slavic languages, Finnish,
Swedish and Danish and Norwegian, English, Dutch,
Latin American Spanish and God alone knew what
else. The natural "ear" for languages which Bookerman always claimed might have accounted for his
fluency in speech but not, to Milo's way of thinking,
for the concurrent abilities to read and write that
veritable host of widely diverse tongues.

In addition, Milo had spent most of his remembered life in one army or another, the first few as an
enlisted man and the remainder as a commissioned
officer. Bookerman claimed never to have served in
the military, yet continually, certain of his behavior
patterns and comments led Milo to silently question
those claims. Often the physician comported himself
as nothing more nor less than the quintessential
Prussian officer of the old pattern.

Milo honestly liked and highly respected the man,
and he wanted to believe his accounts of his prewar
life, but there were simply too many inconsistencies,
and these seriously bothered him, for everyone knew
that, despite the council, he and Bookerman shared
the actual command and leadership of the people.

While he rode the swaying dromedary and
pondered, Milo had no way of knowing just how very
soon all of the responsibilities of command and
leadership would fall upon his shoulders alone.

The column was quick to scavenge and scrounge
arms, ammo and any other usable artifacts from
homes, farms, ranches, crossroads and small towns
they passed along the way. They had anticipated this
and brought along empty carts to contain the loot,

for to have done less would have been, under the circumstances, extremely stupid. Milo and Bookerman and the council did, however, draw the line at plastic sheetings and containers, for these could not be repaired when holed or worn and replacements would not be certainly available. Containers and utensils of the thicker, heavier grades of aluminum were permitted but not really encouraged, those of iron, steel, copper, pewter or silver and silverplate being preferred by the leaders.

They found that they also were forced to draw a definite line as to the quantities of precious metals, gems and jewelry that any one family was allowed to add to their baggage and personal adornment, else there would not have been enough animals in all the column to pack or draw all the pretty but presently useless baubles. Liquors and wines, too, had to be held down to a certain allowance per person for reasons of space and weight, though Milo and Bookerman agreed to be a bit more lenient on canned and bottled beers, ales and soft drinks, since droving, driving, riding and walking in the warm to hot late-spring days were hot, dusty work and these potables were sovereign thirst-quenchers, good sources of nutrients and needed calories, and either low in alcoholic content or lacking it entirely.

In addition to alcohol, jewelry and arms or ammunition, the choicer items included tents and tarps, especially the larger ones which could house a family, best-quality carpets and bedding, clothing and boots, saddlery and harness, rope, any still-usable foodstuffs, metal canteens and larger flasks, books dealing with identification of edible wild plants, matches and disposable lighters, hunting and fishing equipment of any sort, pipes and still-sealed tins of tobacco and cigars, cigarette papers and snuff and chewing tobacco, horseshoes and any other farriers' equipment found, still-pliable rubber tires that could be cut up to provide traction and protection on the highways for the hooves of horses and the steel rims of wheels, edge weapons such as sabers or swords or longer bayonets, medical and dental supplies and nonelectrical equipment for the use of Dr. Bookerman and the other doctor and the two dentists in their party, all older men and women.

Several times during the cross-country trek, one or another of the diehard farmers announced an intention of settling in a rich-looking, well-watered area, but each time Bookerman was able to discourage these dreamers through the expedient of pointing out that, though well-watered now, following a long winter with very heavy snows and a wet spring, these watercourses were clearly seasonal and no one could predict just how long they might decline in drier weather or conditions. And so everyone continued on, finally coming onto what had been Interstate 70, a little to the northwest of the sometime settlement of Agate, Colorado.

They found, to their general consternation, that the place had not only been thoroughly looted, but burned, as well . . . *recently* burned, for it had been a whole unblemished ghost town when Milo, Bookerman and the other two men had ridden their dromedaries through it bare weeks before.

Following this discovery, a heavily guarded perimeter was marked out around the night's camp and march of the succeeding day was preceded by a well-armed vanguard, flanked by outriders and trailed by alert rearguards.

Milo did not like to be suspicious of the motives of fellow human beings, rare as they had now become in this once-populous land, but the long caravan and the herds raised a dust cloud that could be perceived for many miles hereabouts, yet no one had so far bothered to approach them in peace by day or to come in to the cheery beacons of their fires by night. Nor was he alone; Bookerman and the council shared his trepidation and heartily endorsed all the security measures.

On the second day out of ruined Agate, Milo and a half-dozen other men were riding in a well-spread skirmish-line pattern a quarter-mile ahead of the van, along the fringes of the roadway. About halfway through a narrow draw, a pair of bearded men, rifles slung across their backs, sprang out of the brush. One of them grabbed at Fatima's headstall, while the other—a huge, thick-armed man—extended his ham-sized hands with the clear intention of dragging Milo out of his saddle.

The dromedary cow felt well served, and the smaller of the two bushwhackers immediately learned to his sorrow and agony just what those two-inch cursive fangs mounted in a camel's jaws are intended to accomplish. While he staggered back, bleeding profusely from his torn, ragged wounds, trying vainly to fend off the attack Fatima was eagerly pressing, obviously relishing the rich taste of human blood, Milo first kicked the bigger man in the face, then shortened his grip on the slender lance and drove the edgeless point deep into the barrel chest under a tattered and faded camouflage shirt.

The entire encounter took but bare seconds of elapsed time, and only a few more seconds were required for him to blow a single, long, piercing blast of his brass police whistle, draw the small pyro-technic projector from one of his belt pouches and send a single red star flare arching high to explode in the cloudless blue sky. Having rendered the pre-determined signals for danger, he made to turn Fatima about, but she would have none of it, still being intent on following her prey into the brush, and as her strength and stubbornness were more than he could easily handle, Milo found himself compelled to acquiesce and proceed forward. However, he used his free hand to place the ferrule of the pennoned lance in its socket and loop its thong securely to the saddle, loosen his saber in its sheath, then draw and load and arm the submachine gun and sling it from his neck within easy reach, while gripping the shotgun with its gaping twelve-gauge foot-long barrels—he had discovered the deadly value of shotguns and buckshot loads in Vietnam and in Africa.

As the blood-mad Fatima bore him willy-nilly ahead into unknown dangers, he could hear other whistles passing on his danger signal, quickly followed by the triple blasts from the vanguard acknowledging the receipt of the warning.

All at once, another man nearly as big as the one he had lanced, kneed a short- and thick-legged mount no larger than a Connemara pony out of the concealing, more than head-high brush and fired at Milo with a short-barreled semiautomatic rifle of some sort. Because of the dancing of his small horse, the man could not have achieved any meaningful sort of aim; nonetheless, Fatima squalled once and her rider felt the tugs of swift-flying bullets as they passed through portions of his jacket.

Extending the sawed-off smoothbore at the full length of his arm, Milo squeezed the trigger and saw the puffs of dust as the double-ought buckshot load took the rifleman in the chest and upper abdomen. The stubby rifle went clattering to the ground at the feet of the panicky horse, which suddenly reared and dumped the fatally wounded rider onto his back to be ruthlessly trod upon by Fatima. The unfamiliar stench of camel filling its distended nostrils, the little horse bolted into the brush and out of sight.

As he rode over the jerking body of the rifleman, Milo's keen vision detected a flicker of movement in the thick brush a bit ahead and to his right, and he quickly fired the other shotgun shell at it, to be rewarded by a hoarse scream and a frenzied thrashing about within the heavy undergrowth. Taking

Fatima's reins between his teeth, he broke the double gun, extracted a brace of shells from his bandolier and reloaded it.

And not a split second too soon, either. Four shaggy-haired men, with beards to their chests and clad in a miscellany of old and newer clothing, ran out of the flanking brush, shouting, their weapons spouting flame from the muzzles.

He could feel the impacts of the bullets that struck Fatima's big, virtually unmissable body, and as the stricken beast began to go down, he leaped off her, coming down in a roll into the brush. Immediately he came to a stop, he unslung the submachinegun and dropped the four men with a long burst and two shorter ones. Lying there upon the hard, sun-hot ground, he could feel the swelling thunder of fast-approaching hooves, quite a goodly number of them. He hoped that those riders were his people rather than more of the scruffy bushwhackers, for he had dropped the shotgun somewhere in his roll for safety and he estimated that he now had only half a magazine load or less left in the automatic. There were eight rounds in his pistol, and he would have to expose himself to retrieve either saber, light axe, lance or ammunition pouches from the gasping, groaning Fatima. He then resolved in future to carry his saber and at least one big knife hung from his body rather than his mount's.

Spotting the downed camel, Harry Krueger waved the men behind him into the brush on either side, then advanced up the trail on foot, his reins hooked with elbow, his pump shotgun ready, at high port, as Milo had taught him and the others back in the Snake River country. When he saw the familiar boots sticking out of a clump of brush at the side of the trail, just beyond the felled camel, he felt his heart rise suddenly up to painfully distend his throat. He realized, all in a rush, that he simply could not think of, contemplate, a daily life without Uncle Milo, the man who had been around all of his remembered life, who had taught him and his peers so very much of living and survival. If Uncle Milo now lay dead up there . . .

"Damn fool boy!" Harry heard the well-known voice hiss. "Let that damn horse go and go to ground, before you eat a bullet. These bastards are murderous—no question, just an attack of some kind."

But they found no more foemen that day, just eight bodies and six horses. All of the rifles turned out to be military-issue—M16s of the semiautomatic configuration—though without exception, old, well used and in very poor condition, so they were stripped of magazines, ammunition and any still-usable parts, then rendered useless by Milo and Jim Olsen, who also did the same for the assortment of rusty revolvers and pistols packed by the dead men.

Strangely enough, Dr. Bookerman announced, following a gingerly but thorough examination of Fatima, that he thought her wounds to be superficial, no bones having been broken and none of her vital organs seemingly affected. When Milo remounted the now-kneeling beast and gave her the signal to arise, she did so as grudgingly as always, but she seemed to maintain as good a pace as ever she had, though often groaning, bawling, squalling, hissing, snarling and mumbling to herself. But that night, Fatima dropped a stillborn calf, which Bookerman declared to have been delivered well before its appointed time.

The dawn after the day of the attack on Milo did not see the usual campbreaking and column formation; the camp was left in place and its perimeter heavily guarded while a well-armed contingent rode out eastward to check the highway, the countryside and the nearby town of Limon. These were under the command of Bookerman, it being his day to head the vanguards, as the previous day had been Milo's.

Just before noon, he rode back into camp with a

handful of his men and three strangers. Immediately upon dismounting, he called for Milo and the council.

The spokesman and apparent leader of the trio was of less than average height—about five feet seven, Milo guessed—but big-boned and, for all his thinning white hair, navel-length white beard and posture that was a bit stooped with age, still a powerful man, with broad, thick shoulders and firm handclasp. He identified himself as Keith Wheelock, once a colonel of the Colorado National Guard. Milo thought that while the old man looked distinguished enough, he resembled less an elderly retired officer and more a Cecil B. De Mille version of a biblical prophet.

Colonel Wheelock's voice was strong but controlled, and his speech was literate. "Gentlemen, you and your party must be very wary while passing through this area, for there are roving bands of human scum now in these parts. They have attacked our settlement six times within the last fortnight after overwhelming the smaller settlement that our people had established to the west, in the town of Agate. These renegades are well armed, though lacking any meaningful number of horses. Although it is me and my people that they are really after, having trailed us here from our previous settlements, they are like mad dogs and will most certainly attack you for your horses, weapons and ammo or simply to see your blood flow."

Milo nodded. "I sincerely thank you for your warning, sir, though it comes a bit late. I was attacked as I rode point yesterday; I had to shoot seven of the bastards and another of them was so badly savaged by my riding camel that he bled to death before he got far. We captured six rather sad and ill-kept specimens of horseflesh, some ratty saddles and harness, a few rounds of ammunition and a handful of usable parts off the worst-maintained weapons that I've seen in many a year. Here's the only piece that wasn't all dirt, fouling and rust." He laid a stainless-steel single-action revolver on the carpet.

Wheelock squatted, picked up the weapon and, after opening the loading gate and rotating the empty cylinder, examined the piece briefly. When he raised his head, his eyes could be seen to be abrim with tears. He grasped the barrel and extended the revolver to Milo, butt-first, saying, "Sir, if you will remove the grips from this weapon, you will find the letters *K.B.W.* and the numbers *9-19-71* engraved on the frame. This was once my pistol, then my son's; they must have taken it from his dead body, for I cannot conceive of any man's taking it from him while still he lived and drew breath. He was the leader of the Agate settlement."

The camp and herds were moved into the environs of Limon the next morning, and shortly thereafter, Milo and Bookerman became aware of just how desperate was the true plight of Colonel Wheelock and his followers—almost out of ammunition, very low on food of any sort, their hunters not daring to go outside the perimeter lest they be ambushed and slain by the marauders.

For all that there were thirty-odd families in the settlement, there were only fifteen adult men, including Wheelock himself; augmented, perforce, by a few of the bigger boys, they were all the fighting force now available, in the wake of the numerous and vicious attacks and the subsequent deaths from wounds sustained during them. Trying to farm by day and guarding the settlement by night, and doing it all on little food, these men and boys looked and moved like zombies, all save Wheelock, who seemed to possess depthless reserves of strength and vitality.

Two days after the arrival of the column in Limon, an attempt was staged by the brigands to run off some dozens of horses from the herd. For them it was a failure, exceedingly costly in their blood.

Nineteen of them were killed outright, and three were so severely wounded that they could not escape and so were captured; perhaps six or seven got away, but from the trail that they left, it was clear that at least a few of them bore wounds, too.

Of the captives, one died of a combination of shock and blood loss soon after being taken, and another was shot out of hand when he drew and tried to use a hidden pistol, so there was but one left for Milo and Bookerman to interrogate.

When Bookerman, in his capacity as physician, determined that the prisoner was as ready as he would be at any time soon for a session of questioning, he summoned Milo, Harry Krueger and two other members of the council, about all that could crowd into the cubicle with any degree of comfort.

"Gentleman, this prisoner gives his name to be Junior Jardin and claims the age of twenty-six, which roughly tallies with his physiological development. He follows, he avers, a leader called Gary Claxton, who along with most of his men is from Utah; Junior and a few others, however, were born in and around Durango, Colorado, and joined this group when it passed through their natal territory."

Milo stepped forward to where the propped-up prisoner could easily see him and demanded, "How many men did your pack number as of this morning? And where is your base located? Answer me truthfully, if you know what's good for you, for you're entirely in our power, now."

The bandaged man just sneered, then coughed, hawked and spat a blob of yellowish mucus at his interrogator. "Fuck yew an' all your buddies, yew shithaidid fucker, yew!"

Milo smiled and nodded at Harry Krueger, saying, "There speaks fear, Harry, as I told you. This sorry specimen knows that his chosen leader and the few straggling dunces who trail after him are simply too weak, ill armed and gutless to offer us any real threat. They're likely no more than another of these tiny little knots of skulkers with their pitiful spears and clubs and knives, too stupid and unskilled to make good use of a gun even if one fell into their clumsy hands."

His voice dripped scorn and contumely, and these stung to the very quick and pride of the unsophisticated Junior Jardin.

"An' thass all yew knows, too, yew asshole yew!" he burst out with heat. "Old Gary, he done got hisse'f more'n sixty mens long of us. An' we most of us got real army guns, too, what old Gary brought up from Utah with 'im, an' soon's we gits us more hosses . . . aw, piss awn yew, all yew!"

Then he clammed up. Not one additional word could threats or guile elicit from him; not even several slaps and buffets did any more to accomplish their purposes.

Outside the cubicle, out of range of Junior Jardin's ears, Milo said, "Clarence, have you got any sort of drug that might work on him? We have simply got to know exactly where those bastards are holed up, for forty to fifty men armed with M16s pose a considerable threat to us all, either here or on the march, and Wheelock's people are dead meat the moment we pull out."

Bookerman shrugged. "I've found drugs of the sort you mean, here and there, but they are so old that I'd be afraid to use them, unless we had more than the one captive. However, Milo, I know a few tricks myself. Let me try one of them on him."

Chapter X

At the doctor's direction, they moved Junior Jardin to a heavy, solid wooden chair and secured his arms, legs and body thereto with straps and rope.

Taking a handful of the long, lank, dirty hair, Bookerman tilted the prisoner's head far, far back, then said, "Milo, you are a strong man—take a good grip of his head and keep it in just this position when the time comes . . . should Mr. Jardin here choose to remain uncooperative and force me to do an agonizing thing to him."

After a moment of searching his bag, the physician turned to display a single stainless-steel teaspoon. With a broad, sustained smile, he walked over to stand before the trussed-up Jardin.

Despite the smile, his voice was infinitely sad, regretful, a little chiding, as one might speak just before punishing a willful, stubborn, chronically disobedient child. "Junior, we wish to know the present location of your group's base. Please tell us, now, for if you do not, I am going to have to do something that will hurt you more than any pain you ever before have felt. Nor will that pain go quickly away, Junior. What I do will maim you for life; you never will be able to forget it, either waking or sleeping.

"Well, Junior? We are waiting for you to tell us

where your base is located. Where is your group's camp? Please tell us."

"Shit, yew ain' ascarin' me, fucker!" said the plainly terrified man. "I done been beat on afore this. Yew can go fuck yerse'f." But his voice was not nearly as strong as on previous occasions, and he licked repeatedly at dry lips.

Bookerman sighed. "Oh, Junior, Junior, I am certain that no mere beating would convince you to cooperate with us, and therefore I suppose that I must do what I must do to you.

"Milo, grasp his head and hold it tightly just as I have shown you."

When the prisoner's head was immobile in Milo's strong hands, Bookerman came closer and held the shiny teaspoon before the wide, bulging eyes. "Look well at this instrument, Junior. You see here a simple teaspoon. But with this commonplace utensil, I am going to remove your left eyeball. When once I have begun, I'll not stop until your bloody eyeball is out and lying in the palm of my hand. Do you understand? So if you wish to tell us what we wish to know, if you wish to live the rest of your life with two eyes, rather than with one eye and an empty, ever painful socket, do so now."

He sighed again, admonishing, "No, no, Junior, squeezing tight your eyelids will not save your eye from me and my spoon. Only will the telling of the location of your camp, your base, prevent my permanent maiming of you."

"D . . . don' know!" stuttered the captive, in an agony of obvious terror. "P . . . prob'ly moved on by now, enyhow."

"Oh, Junior, Junior," sighed Bookerman. "You lie so ineptly. But perhaps you will wax more loquacious when you have but one single eye remaining and my bloody spoon is poised to remove it as well. Now, Milo, hold him absolutely rock-steady. You, *Herr* Krüger, assist him, *bitte.*"

Milo could not be certain that the doctor meant to really carry out this threat until, to the ear-shattering screams of the prisoner, the trained fingers of the surgeon slid the bowl of the spoon expertly, precisely between the eye and the socket.

"Oh, sweet Jesus God, no . . ." shouted Jim Olsen, then vomited on the floor with a gush and a tortured retching. The other council member simply fled in horrified silence, slamming the door behind him.

The vials which Bookerman had personally prepared were transported to the isolated farm in a large Styrofoam cooler filled with icy spring water and slung between two smooth-gaited mules in a canvas tarp stiffened with boards.

The volunteer archers had practiced for several days with identical glass vials filled with a liquid of equal weight, so they knew just how to aim arrows to which vials of nitroglycerin had been taped behind the blunt target points.

Milo had been loath even to go near the cases of ancient, deteriorating and thus highly unstable and deadly-dangerous dynamite, but not so Dr. Clarence Bookerman. The doctor himself had boiled the sticks, skimmed off the nitroglycerine, then poured it into glass medicine vials, actions which called for a degree of courage and cool nerve that not even Milo felt he could have summoned up. He reflected yet again that the doctor was simply full of surprises.

The early-morning drizzle of nitroglycerin-laden arrows blew in most of the roof, blew out sections of walls and three doors of the sprawling farmhouse and did even worse damage to the barn, setting it fiercely ablaze. Claxton, who turned out to be a burly, hairy man in his mid-fifties, and his crew, half clad and still groggy with sleep, a few of them clutching their rusty M16s, stumbled and staggered out the enlarged openings where doors had been to face a terrifying and unwavering line of leveled

muzzles—rifles, shotguns and full automatics—
interspersed with the winking points of hunting
arrows in drawn bows.

Milo sincerely wished that they all had come out
shooting. There was no question of the fact that
these predators had to die; they were just too
dangerous—armed or unarmed, ahorse or afoot—in
their numbers and degree of savagery—to let loose
to terrorize any other of the scattered survivors. But
Milo also knew that cold-blooded murder was
beyond him.

It was then proved to not be beyond the man who
stood beside him, Dr. Bookerman. With an
inarticulate shout imbued with a tone of alarmed
warning, the physician opened fire on the mob of
marauders, loosing short, controlled bursts of
automatic fire. And, as he must have known would
happen in the tense, keyed-up situation, every other
weapon joined his within a bare eyeblink.

A few of the band of bushwhackers managed to
flee back into the wrecked, smoldering house, only to
be hunted, rooted out and killed by the now blood-
mad raiders, Wheelock's contingent, at least, set on
long-overdue revenge for past incursions.

Claxton did not look at all imposing as he lay dying
on the bloodsoaked ground before the wrecked
house. The three bullet holes in his torso stood out
markedly against his graying skin, and his thick
beard and furry chest now were thick with blood,
providing a feast for the flies that swarmed the
charnel yard.

There was no fear in the bloodshot eyes that
looked up at Milo where he squatted beside the
fatally wounded leader, only pain alloyed with
wonder.

"How come for you to shoot us all, feller? We
won't no particle of danger to a bunch size of yours,
the way we was out here. The mosta us dint even
have our rifles, you know—them mortar shells or

grenades or whatever it was you used just had plumb
took the fight outen my boys."

"The same reason," Milo replied gravely, "that you
pour boiling water into a barrel of rats—your kind,
you spoilers, are a bane to the existence of folks who
are breaking their asses trying to keep themselves
and their families alive. Or, I could quote you Scripture to the effect that 'those who live by the sword
shall perish by the sword'; you and your pack existed
by violence, and that's how you, most of you, were
killed."

Claxton choked briefly, then weakly pushed
himself up onto his elbows and coughed violently,
sending a frothy, dark-pink spray from his mouth.
Moaning, he eased himself back into a recumbent
posture, breathing raggedly, wheezing loudly, his
eyes shut and a series of strong shudders racking his
body and limbs. Thinking him on the point of death,
Milo had started to arise when the eyes opened again
and Claxton spoke once more.

"How the fuck did you bunch of murderin' bastids
find us, anyhow? It was never no fires was lit here by
day, and even the boys as come back wounded or
dyin' covered their tracks damn good, the way they
was taught to, and I had me three overlapping layers
of guards around this place, day and night."

Milo nodded again. "Yes, I know, Claxton. With an
organizational mind like yours and your leadership
abilities, it's too bad that you didn't choose to work
for people, instead of against them. We had a devil of
a time taking out your sentries without alerting you
here last night.

"As to just how we found you. We . . . ahhh, 'persuaded' one of the raiders who came after our horse
herd to tell us exactly how to find this place."

"Who?" Claxton demanded. "Who finked on us?"

"He calls himself Junior Jardin," Milo replied.

Claxton shook his gory head and snorted weakly.
"No way, feller, no damn fuckin' way! Lissen, I

knows that lil boy, he's done been my lover nearly a whole year now, and I knows he's tough as they come. You could of beat him plumb to death and he wouldn' of finked on me and the boys."

"Yes, Claxton, we tried beating him and he just laughed and sneered and spat at us, for all that he was wounded when we got him. But my . . . my associate was able to prevail upon him to tell us everything."

"How?" asked Claxton, still disbelievingly.

"He pried out the young man's left eyeball with a teaspoon, Claxton," was Milo's answer. "When he showed him his own eye in the bowl of that spoon, dripping blood and other fluids, and promised to do the same to the other eye as well, Junior Jardin decided to tell us everything we asked of him."

Rage and loathing momentarily lit Claxton's glazing eyes. "God damn you, you heartless fuckers! You slanged me and my boys as spoilers and all, but, feller, you bastids is worse than us. I never would of done nothin' *that* bad, *that* common, to *no* man I ever took alive. You all goin' to hell, you knows that, don't you?"

"Quite possibly, Claxton, quite possibly . . . but well after you. As for . . ."

But Claxton could no longer hear him, he saw; the outlaw leader had at last died.

There was precious little worth taking from the farm, save ammunition that might or might not ignite, rifle magazines and parts, and some knives, axes and other tools and utensils. The few head of horses were in such bad, ill-cared-for condition that they were simply turned loose to join the wild herds. The small herd of cattle looked to mostly be diseased, so they were put down, lest their malady spread to the wild cattle and other hoofed game of the region.

Milo thought that he had seen pigpens that had been cleaner than the interior of the blasted house, and he was surprised that disease or infections had not cut down the men who had lived in such filth long before the bullets had done so. Even the sty inhabited by the Tahoe City biker contingent years ago had been scrupulously clean compared to this unholy mess, but that may have been partially because that long-dead pack had had dozens of women and male slaves to maintain their home base, water that still ran from faucets and even electricity.

Claxton and his group, however, had never taken prisoners, male or female, coldly cutting down everyone not killed in an attack, so they had had no slaves to do the household chores that they clearly had never themselves chosen to do, preferring to live in their own stink and slops until they were ready to move on to fresh quarters and recommence the same disgusting cycle.

When the house—what the explosions had left of it —and the dead bodies had been thoroughly searched and anything of any use taken, the men dragged their victims into the structure and then set it afire in several places before mounting and starting the long ride back to Limon.

Subsequent to several heated meetings of the enlarged council, a very important decision had been hammered out. Most of Wheelock's people would move on, out onto the prairies, with the bulk of the newcomers, there being just too many memories of a sad or painful nature now connected with Limon and its environs for them, and their place would be taken by those few Snake River and Cheyenne families still dead set on a settled, farming life rather than the nomad herding-hunting-gathering existence chosen by the bulk of them for their futures.

While Milo hated to leave behind men and women

whom he had known for thirty and more years, men and women whom he first had met as scared, helpless urban boys and girls suddenly marooned in a pitiless wilderness, he also realized that he could no longer guide them. They were all become self-reliant adults, parents of their own children and grandparents, as well, in a number of cases; if they had decided that the settled life was best for them, they were right to choose it, and it would have been unfair to Milo to use his emotional leverage to try to shake that decision. He could only wish them all well and move on eastward with the majority.

This they did. The farmers willingly traded their carts for the lands and buildings that they were taking over, settled on their shares of the herds and immediately commenced feverishly hurried attempts to put in a late crop to help sustain them until next year's harvesttime, their goodbyes to their lifelong friends being necessarily brief.

The long, snakelike column of wagons and carts, of riders and walkers, of herds and herdsmen and herd dogs crawled out, eastward-bond, along the ancient, deteriorating Interstate 70. They made but few miles per day, and detachments halted at each single house or farm or ranch or settlement to search for recent signs of human life and to ferret out anything that might be of use or of value to the people as a whole for their survival.

On the wider, more level, less overgrown stretches of the highway, they were able to travel two and even three teams abreast and therefore increase their speed of march, but then, often as not, they would be forced to wait or to go into camp early in order that the laggards and the fractious herds could catch up. But, sometimes, hours or even days were lost when the entire train found itself confronted by washed-out bridges and broad sections of roadway, necessitating dangerous fording or wide-swinging bypasses or filling and smoothing out sections of former road with earth and rocks and brush and treetrunks.

The buildings and the towns that they passed by and looted of usable artifacts all sat empty, no physical trace of mankind remaining, only his creations. The streets, the buildings, all were now home only to vermin, birds and bats and those beasts for which the lesser creatures were natural prey—mustelids, foxes, bobcats, coyotes, feral cats and a few wild dogs, which last were coming more and more to resemble big coyotes with every succeeding generation, although round, mastiff heads, long, pendulous hound ears, purple-black chow tongues and tight, wiry coats still showed up here and there from time to time.

Of course, many of these predators and others that did not frequent the deserted towns were to be found on the pairies and in the hills and washes, but their combined predations over the years seemed not to have had much if any effect upon the vast wild herds of cattle, horses, pronghorns, a scattering of bison, sheep, goats, unbelievable numbers of fat deer and even a few elk.

Milo quickly noted that the wild cattle, sheep and goats all seemed to sport longer and bigger horns than did most of those in their driven herds. Further, two ewes slain for meat out of two different wild herds showed the beginning development of horns. With the two-legged creature called man no longer about to protect these beasts that he had so prized, they had come again to take up the job of defending themselves against the meat-hungry animals with which they shared their habitat. This task called for as many weapons as possible, as well as increases in size, strength and endurance, the lengthening of legs and the sharpening of the senses of sight, hearing and smell. These now-wild herds demonstrated faster reaction time than did their still-domesticated cousins. Cattle and goats were becoming shaggier, and the sheep seemed to be in the process of exchanging fleece for protective hair in more exposed portions.

From everything he could see, it appeared to Milo that the hosts of nuclear doomsayers had been proved wrong with regard to elevated roentgen counts causing animals to produce monsters. Even in the environs of Denver—the ruins of which might or might not still be radioactive, but which they had studiously avoided nonetheless on general principles —all of the animals they had spied or encountered or killed seemed perfectly normal specimens. Nor were the people producing any significant numbers of abnormal births or stillbirths; quite the contrary, in fact.

Dr. Bookerman summed it up, his opinions concerning it, at least, in a conversation by the fireside one night. "All that occurred in the wake of the War was ghastly, true, but it may have been for mankind as a whole a disguised blessing, friend Milo. With only a few notable and short-lived exceptions, man has been engaged in a shameful pollution of the racial gene pools for a century or more—allowing the worst varieties of mental and physical defectives to live and breed their blighted infirmities back into the species. On the grounds of a misguided sense of so-called 'human rights,' medical science had been put to the perverted practices of keeping alive infants that Nature would have otherwise allowed the mercy of death soon after birth; disgusting, sickening abnormalities were kept alive at staggering monetary costs in a world that was already beginning to be overcrowded, was starting to outstrip its food-production capabilities.

"Certifiable lunatics, criminals, sociopaths were allowed to roam at will, to breed as they wished, perpetuating their unsavory kind; mankind employed selective breeding on his livestock, but seemed to consider his own species not worthy of such effort, and any person or group who suggested such a rational practice was slandered, libeled, vilified endlessly.

"Well, friend Milo, the death of a high degree of civilization has ended that ruinous phase of mankind's history, at least. We can be certain that only the very strongest, least genetically tainted specimens of humanity survived the plagues and hunger of the period immediately following the War, and the hordes of mental and physical defectives were most likely the first ones to die.

"Now there no longer are softheaded bureaucrats to force those few doctors or midwives as remain to expend heroic efforts to keep alive infants better off dead. And in our existing world, at the level of human culture to which that catastrophic war has reduced us, there is scant chance of any save the mentally and physically sound surviving to the age of breeding, so we will be spared the generations after generations of genetically crippled and feebleminded and diseased which so disastrously afflicted the previous civilization.

"With careful safeguards and controls, we now have the God-sent opportunity, my friend, of overseeing the beginning of the birth of a true *Herrenvolk* —a race that will one day be capable of conquering the world and fitted to rule it, as well."

"*Sieg Heil!*" said Milo dryly. "You sound like a 1930s recording of Adolf Hitler, Doctor. Are you sure you weren't yourself a Nazi, before the War?"

Watching the physician more closely than usual, Milo thought to see a start and a forced nonchalance in the reply.

"Friend Milo, National Socialism died in the streets of Berlin in 1945, close to a century ago now. So how could I have been, eh? I was not born until 1956. Though it must have been a very exciting time to be alive . . . for a German, that is."

"Who proceeded to make times even more exciting," added Milo, "for the Czechs, the Poles, the French, the Belgians, the Dutch, the Norwegians and one hell of a lot of other nationalities, Doctor."

Bookerman sighed and slowly shook his head, saying, "Ah, friend Milo, it was but another in a progression of European wars that had been fought since time immemorial, for land, for religion and, later, for politics. America really had no place in it, no reason to get involved at all. It was strictly a war by Europeans against other Europeans and none of the proper concern of the Amis. Had not the then American president *Herr* Rosenfeld, been so very much enamored of that Communist butcher, *Herr* Stalin, and pushed his nation into a position from which war against Germany was inevitable, you know, it is quite possible that the War and the subsequent near-extirpation of most of mankind would never have taken place. The Christian Bible says something about the sins of the fathers, I believe.

"Besides, few of you Americans ever were allowed to truly understand the aims of the National Socialist German Workers Party—"

"Six million dead Jews and gypsies, Doctor, are damned hard to misunderstand," Milo interrupted coldly.

Bookerman's smile resembled a supercilious sneer. "Oh, come now, friend Milo, surely a man as intelligent, as rational as you have proved yourself to be did not swallow that prize bit of Zionist propaganda entire? If so many were killed during the period of World War Two, then from whence came the hordes of Jews who suddenly appeared in Palestine, in America, in Britain and in Australia?

"No, if you want monsters, look not to Germany and our *Führer*, look rather at your former president's great friend and ally. Do you know that Josef Stalin had between thirty and fifty million of his own people murdered in less than fifteen years? And America's more recent ally, Communist China, under

Mao Tse-tung, exterminated close to one hundred millions of Chinese and Tibetans between 1949 and 1967. These figures, of course, pale in comparison with that which was done, worldwide it would appear, thirty-odd years ago. And had Rosenfeld and Churchill and the rest of the meddlers allowed us to do that which was so necessary—scour the world clean of the Communists, the *Untermenschen*—none of this would ever have happened, for there would have been existing no Empire of Soviets to do it, to so destroy all of Western civilization."

"No, Doctor, there would instead have been the hegemony of Shickelgruber's thousand-year Reich, most likely, with all its many and severe faults. It would have been akin to letting a pack of vicious, hungry wolves into the house to protect it from a prowling bear ; the price was just considered too steep to pay."

"I am most sorry to have to say it, friend Milo, but you speak the words of a fool, a silly, soft, sentimental fool, not the realist I had taken you to be throughout all we two had experienced together these past years." The physician looked to truly be sorrowful. "I had, indeed, hoped that after all the decades of frustration, I had at last found a man of kindred philosophy and belief who might be my associate in the beginning and who might then assume my mantle of . . . oh, ahh, of *Führerschaft*, to carry on with the supervision of our folk and to our grand design of a reascension of the West. But you are only another humanistic, egalitarian fool, aren't you? Your baseless slanders against *die Dritten Deutschen Reich* reveal the truth: at your core of being, you are but yet another of a seemingly endless succession of narrow, visionless men, so hidebound in outmoded dogma as to be unable, unwilling to see that nothing of any importance has ever been accomplished in this world without effort, without sacrifice of the few for the future good of the many, without the sacrifice of the individuals for the good of the state and without the sacrifice of the present for the future.

"Although it pains me to say it, I overestimated you, Milo Moray. I, who had thought that so many long years of life and experience had honed my judgment of men to near-infallibility, was wrong in your case."

"If you'd thought that I was going to play Göring to your Hitler, Doctor, you sure as hell were wrong!" said Milo, in a blunt, no-nonsense tone. "A lot of those people you're thinking about breeding like so many dumb cattle are *my* people, kids I've known all of their lives. You try to impose any of that hideous Nazi crap on them, Doctor, and I'll kill you, that is a promise!

"Are you sure you're not a good deal older than you say you are? Nazism died a richly deserved death at least ten years before you claim to have been born, so how you came to be so thoroughly inculcated with its savage, barbaric tenets bothers me more than a little . . . and when things bother me that much, then I make it my business to get to the bottom of them sooner or later, preferably sooner. Perhaps I should take you on as an urgent project, Dr. Bookerman, for my peace of mind and for the future safety of those who depend upon me, for from what you have averred here, this night, I see you as a major threat to the common liberty, if not the very survival, of these few remaining Americans."

After that night, Milo set himself to watch the doings of Dr. Bookerman very closely, but found nothing that seemed at all out of the ordinary. The physician, his co-leader, behaved as if the conversation on that night had never occurred, treating Milo with the same respect or bonhomie as he had since they had been together. Nor was there anything new in his treatment of the second-echelon commanders—Harry Krueger, Jim Olsen and the rest—or his behavior around the lesser folk.

The caravan of wagons, carts, riders, walkers and herds moved on slowly eastward along or closely paralleling the ancient highway. They halted often to rest the herds or to loot the empty towns, now and again setting up Olsen's forge to do necessary repairs, reshoe horses and draft oxen and mules, or where the materials were available, construct new carts to bear away the quantities of scavenged artifacts they were finding. They were in no hurry to arrive at any destination now, or to be somewhere by a certain time of the year.

They continued to follow that crumbling highway, wandering on into the overgrown desolation that once had been called the State of Kansas, its broad prairies now given over to grasses, the beasts that fed on those grasses and the other beasts that fed on the grass-eaters. Now and again, they would chance upon traces of other humans, fairly recent traces—within a decade or so, they guessed—some of them, but most much older, probably twenty years old, possibly thirty or more. These findings were a significant disappointment to Milo, but Bookerman, the other leaders and the bulk of the people seemed not to care whether or not they were the only humans left to roam this vast land.

Milo himself was torn between two goals. One was to try to reach some of what had been the larger centers of population along the Kansas-Missouri border, and the other was a nagging presentiment to head due south before winter caught them in some ill-protected place. In the end, however, they continued their stop-and-go snail's pace eastward, along old Interstate 70, while he salved his conscience with a plan to angle south on Interstate 135 at Salinas. But it was not to be, not that year.

Chapter XI

They did not reach Salinas, not that year. They were surprised by an early storm that became a blizzard, while somewhere between Dorrance and Bunker Hill, Kansas, and they halted and set up camp on the spot. And in their ill-chosen, exposed position, they very nearly froze to death before the weather blew itself out and Milo and Bookerman chivvied them, one and all, into striking camp, loading the transport, harnessing the teams, gathering the herds and moving with all possible speed farther east, to the next town, True, those buildings still standing were in poor condition after thirty-odd years of the worst the elements could offer, but at least they offered frail human flesh and bone more protection from those same elements than did thin canvas tent walls.

When once the people were settled in, Milo began to devote serious thought to something better, more protective than the tents, but equally transportable. It was Dr. Bookerman, however, who came up with the answer.

"Yurts, friend Milo, felt yurts are the answer to this problem. They were designed for just such weather in just such a land as is this—windy and very cold or windy and very hot."

"Now where in the hell are we to get felt, Doctor,

as much of the stuff as we'd need for the undertaking of this project, anyway? Or have you already figured out exactly how many fedoras and billiard-table tops it would take to make each family a home?" demanded Milo.

Bookerman shrugged. "Some of it we will be able to find in the various towns and cities—more in the cities, of course—but the bulk of it we will have to fabricate ourselves. But that will not be so difficult, you'll find, not anywhere nearly as difficult as the fabrication of cloth, yet a good many of the women have learned to do that."

Although Milo still had his doubts, within a few weeks of gathering materials, equipment and volunteers, Bookerman and his crew were actually producing a medium-weight felt from raw wool and animal hair.

"Where in the devil did you learn to make felt?" inquired Milo.

Bookerman allowed himself one of his rare, brief smiles and simply said, "Never you mind, friend Milo. Besides, you'd not believe me if I tried to tell you."

With the felt production in full swing, Milo took the neat, professionally rendered sketches provided him by Bookerman and, aided by some of the cart makers, began to go about turning out the wooden frames and poles of center wheels needed to hold the felt walls and roofs of yurts. When the prototype framing was ready, he turned it over to the doctor.

On a bitter day, with yet another blizzard clearly on the offing for their chunk of prairie, a party rode out of the tiny ruined town on horseback and on two carts to a very exposed place. There they cleared away the snow down to the frozen earth beneath the white blanket, then painfully hacked out a firepit, lined it with stones and laid the fuel for a fire therein.

That done, the physician directed a crew of men in

setting up the supports and frames, locating the doorframe, then beginning the layering of felt and canvas on roof supports and side lattices. The frame and lattices were anchored by being lashed to stakes laboriously driven deep into the frozen ground; the side felts were carefully surrounded with small boulders and chunks of concrete earlier collected.

When once the shelter was set up and the coverings all in place, the ground inside, all around the firepit, was covered first with waterproofed canvas, then with several thicknesses of carpet. Fuel supply was stacked near the doorframe, foodstuffs, cooking utensils and bedding were brought in, along with a kerosene lamp and its fuel, some books, a folding chair and table, a five-gallon can of drinking water, some spare items of clothing and Bookerman's treasured rifle—a bolt-action Steyr-Mannlicher, stocked almost to the muzzle in some rare wood, firing 8x57mm handloaded ammo and, in his skilled hands, more than merely accurate out to chilling distances.

With the wind picking up force by the minute, or so it seemed, the carts and riders headed back into the town at a stiff clip, leaving the doctor within the prototype yurt, by his fire, reading a book. Milo frankly wondered if they ever would see the German again with life in him, for thick as the layers of felt and canvas were, strong as were the sides and supports of carefully fitted, well-seasoned wood, heavy as were the surrounding boulders and deep as had the stakes been driven, still he wondered if the fragile-looking shelter could be proof against the wind—already, knife-edged—and the cold of the fast-approaching storm.

The blizzard raged and howled through the streets of the town for two days, hurling snow and ice on hurricanelike gusts to punctuate the steady blast of arctic air. So bad was it out on the open prairie that the herds were brought into town where they might at least enjoy a measure of protection from the winds, although the only available food for them there was the dried weeds that had grown up here and there through the cracked concrete and macadam, the grain and hay being hoarded for the horses and mules and draft oxen.

Nor, it was soon discovered when the storm finally blew itself out and the people forced a way out into the yards-deep drifts, were the domestic stock the only ungulates which had taken advantage of the shelter of the building walls. There were at least twoscore bison to be seen huddling with the shaggy cattle, deer, native antelope and a scattering of more exotic herbivores, a small herd of wild horses and a smaller one of burros.

Justly fearing the bestial panic that the discharging of firearms might engender, which might cause death or injury to the intermixed domestic animals, Milo saw to it that those wild beasts harvested were taken with bows, or roped in the deep, movement-hampering snow, then dragged away to have their throats cut.

All of the leaders worried themselves almost sick about the fate of Dr. Bookerman, way out there on the open prairie, his low-crouching little shelter unseeable from even the highest of the remaining buildings. And it was simply out of the question, just then, to try to reach him either mounted or afoot, so deep were the drifts, so frigid the air, and so threatening of a new storm was the sky.

But no fresh storm occurred that day, although it remained frigidly cold and, in the following night, dropped even lower in temperature. On the next day, however, the sun rose and the thermometers ascended to a surprising high of twenty-five degrees Fahrenheit. When the wild creatures began to push through drifts and work their way out of the environs of the town, Milo and Harry Krueger decided that they could safely seek out the yurt site and see if Bookerman had survived his ordeal.

First, however, every available man and herd dog was required to try to separate the domestic from the wild beasts. This task proved very taxing and not a little dangerous, as it cost the life of one man, a couple of dogs, and the necessity for—stampede danger or none—shooting dead a huge, powerful, short-tempered bison bull and one feral cow fanatically overprotective of a calf that looked to be about half bison.

Leaving the capture and nursing of the sturdy calf and the skinning and butchering of the bison and the cow to others, Milo and Harry and a hurriedly formed party saddled horses and set out for the site on which the yurt had been situated. They rode, not at all certain that even the intrepid Dr. Bookerman could have survived such hellishly cold and windy weather in so flimsy a habitation, and their worst fears seemed thoroughly justified when, coming within sight of the yurt, they could none of them espy even a wisp of smoke emanating from its peak.

But their fears were proved utterly groundless. When they were invited into the yurt, they all immediately began to sweat in the cloying heat. Bookerman had wisely and long since stripped down to boxer shorts, T-shirt and thick socks, yet the ashes in the firepit were cold and the only heat sources were the lamp and Bookerman himself. That was when Milo and the others began to truly appreciate the concept of the yurt and the degree of assured protection it would offer them and their dependent people from the savage elements of the prairies and the plains.

"So that is how you adopted those curious circular homes," beamed Arabella Lindsay. "But how can anything that your mind tells me is so warm in winter be so very cool and comfortable in hot weather, Milo?"

"Simple, my dear," he beamed back. "Just remove some of the outer layers of felt, then roll up those that remain for a foot or so from the ground; this provides plenty of air circulation, flushes out the heat and such smoke as doesn't go up and out the peak hole, and, with the doorway coverings removed as well, provides plenty of light, even while the roof layers protect from direct sunlight and rain or hail. As I later learned, that old—that very, very old—man Bookerman had done some very terrible things in his long, long lifespan, but his pioneering of the yurt for us did, if anything, at least partially redeem him. I am only thankful that he was on our side, those long years ago, for as ruthless and cruel and brilliant as he was, as he proved himself over and over again to be, he would have made a most deadly and sinister enemy."

She wrinkled her freckled brow in puzzlement, beaming, "But Milo, what made you think the doctor to be sinister, ruthless and cruel? Yes, he did torture the prisoner by the removal of one of his eyes, but had he not done so, how many more lives do you think that the aggressions of his cohorts would have cost you and the rest? As for the other thing that seemed to so upset you, I cannot understand why his wish to breed out any remaining scrubs from your people was so abhorrent to your mind. It's as your memories tell me he said—such a process has been employed for thousands of years in breeding up horses, cattle, dogs, sheep and any manner of other dumb beasts; why should it not have been used to improve the strain of man?"

Milo sighed audibly, then beamed, "Arabella, it was not just that one point that so repelled me, it was the philosophy that clearly showed, that particular night, beneath his surface. I had suspected him, on the basis of things he had said and done and not done, for a long time, and that night's conversation convinced me that I was right. Arabella, Bookerman was a Nazi, the worst kind of Nazi, an international criminal who had somehow managed to escape his just deserts—trial and execution or long imprisonment—and assumed a new identity and lived long and well in the United States of American for who knows how many years before the War."

Once more, the freckled brow wrinkled. "I've seen that word before, Milo—read it, I believe, in some of the older works of military history kept in the fort library. But isn't 'Nazi' just another word for 'German'?"

"Oh, no, Arabella, you've apparently misunderstood that which you read. 'Nazi' no more means 'German'—although most of the Nazis were German nationals—than 'Communist' means 'Russian' or 'Felangist' means 'Spanish' or 'Fascist' means 'Italian' or 'Socialist' means 'Swedish.' Although these groups led, dictated to, the bulk of the populations of these countries, the actual membership in the groups was always a very small percentage of the populations.

"Just how much do you know about what was called the Second World War and the events that led up to it and succeeded it?"

She shrugged. "Not very much, I confess, Milo. I believe that some of my ancestors fought in it, that some were slain and that others were injured, but then there were some of my ancestors in every war that Canada and Great Britain fought for at least a millennium . . . or so Father attests.

"How long ago was this war, Milo?"

"Something over a hundred and fifty years, Arabella."

"And . . . and you truly fought in it, Milo?"

"Yes," he beamed. "Yes, I did."

"Then . . . then just how old are you? Are you human?"

"So far as I know my dear, I'm perfectly human, just . . . different, in some few ways from other men and women. As regards my age, I don't know for certain, not my exact chronological age, anyway. But I have reason to believe that I've roughly two and a half centuries of life and living behind me, although, as I do not perceptibly age, I have no way of telling for sure. I looked no whit different from the way I look today when I soldiered in the United States Army before, during and after the Second World War, and I had just the same appearance during the periods that I just have shared the memories of with you, Arabella."

"What made you the way that you are, Milo?" she begged.

"I have no idea why I differ in the few, but important, respects that I do from the general run of humans. Perhaps I was born different; I don't know. You see, I have no memory at all prior to a point in time a few years before the Second World War. I was found by a policeman one late night in the alleyway in an American city called Chicago. Near my unconscious body he found a wallet—expensive of make, but empty of money or anything else. However, the name Milo Moray was stamped in gold inside it. It appeared to him that I had been struck on the head and robbed, and whoever struck me down hit me hard enough and in just the right place to rob me forever of my memories of my life up until then, a loss of far more real importance than a few paper bills might have had. But I'll tell you more of myself at another time. Let us now get back to the original subject: World War Two and the Nazis and Dr. Bookerman.

"The seeds of World War Two and Nazism were sown in the wake of an earlier war, called World War One. Although the Germans did not really start that first war, they lost it, and then their enemies—notably the French—punished the entire German nation and king and people cruelly hard. The Kaiser—their king—was banished to live in and soon die in a foreign land, then a new form of government was imposed upon the people and nation, a government with which few of the people were ever really happy. Their military forces were disarmed and disbanded; they were occupied by foreign troops and forbidden to have more than a few thousands of men under arms. Their richest mining and industrial areas were taken away from them, as too were all of their overseas colonies. Large chunks of their traditional lands were taken away and given to other countries, some of them very artificial countries, places that never before had been sovereign or enjoyed an independence.

"All of their warships *and* merchant ships were taken from them, all of their aircraft, armored vehicles, rail transport and even many of their trucks and motorcars.

"As if they had not been sufficiently beggared, it was declared by the winners that Germany must recompense all of the costs of the war, and therefore all of the gold that backed the German currency was taken away, making the German mark not worth the paper that it was printed upon."

"Why, that is awful, Milo!" declared Arabella. "How could those poor Germans live? Why would the winners so terribly mistreat the helpless, defeated Germans?"

"Some of the oldest reasons in the human lexicon, Arabella: envy, greed, revenge and hatred. The French were leaders in heaping every possible indignity and humiliation on Germany, Austria and Turkey, which countries had been their principal opponents in the war. Then their occupation troops sat back and watched while the German people starved, sold everything that had not already been expropriated for little or nothing just to keep themselves and their families alive for a few more days or weeks or months. Few Germans had meaningful income, for many factories had had to close because of total lack of capital, and none of the international banking houses would extend credit on reasonable terms to the defeated, robbed and stripped German nation or any of its businessmen and industrialists.

"In such an atmosphere, in a nation aswarm with unemployed men, many of them former soldiers, those extremists who find their most fertile fields to be helpless, hopeless, frustrated and desperate people flourished—Communists, Anarchists, Fascists, religious fanatics of every stripe and persuasion, visionaries, perverts and out-and-out lunatics. Two groups finally emerged from the chaos as the major contenders. One was the Communist Party, which very nearly took over the southern portion of Germany, Bavaria. The other was a group calling itself the National Socialist German Workers Party—the Nazis, for short.

"Both of these major contenders formed bands of armed men—virtual private armies—and waged pitched battles in the streets and the countryside, while the overworked police and the tiny, ill-equipped army rushed madly from place to place in vain attempts to maintain some semblance of order, lest the occupiers take more severe action against the nation and people as a whole.

"Although both parties were made up of extremely violent, sadistic, murderous and clearly psychotic men, large numbers of otherwise sane and ordinary Germans flocked to swell their ranks and to give them support in attempts to legally attain to public office. They did this for two basic reasons, Arabella. The near takeover of Bavaria by the Communists had horribly frightened a great many people, and these Nazis, if they were nothing else, were clearly, openly, avowedly anti-Communists. The other reason was that they offered something that the legitimate, but foreign-imposed, government could not offer. They offered hope—hope of a brighter future in a strong, powerful, respected Germany, a Germany freed of its crushing debts and of its virtual enslavement to alien peoples and nations, a Germany in which all of the traditional German lands would be reunited and all people of German blood would be citizens, a Germany in which there was work and bread for all Germans, a Germany flushed clean of foreign troops and of alien ideologies and once more united behind a single, strong leader—the German word for 'leader' is *Führer*, Arabella—such as their Kaisers had supposedly all been.

"The German parliament was called the Reichstag, and early in the 1930s, a large number of Nazi members were voted into it, whereupon the feeble, dying, politically impotent old onetime field marshal who was the figurehead that the victors had imposed upon the vanquished to govern them had no alternative but to name the leader of that party, one Adolf Hitler, to the Reichschancellorship. Very shortly thereafter, the old field marshal died and then the new Reichschancellor took up all the reins of government and began to shape the nation and its policies to conform to standards laid down by him and his personal advisers and staff.

"In his long and rocky road to power, Hitler had gathered about him a singular crew of men, some of them the very dregs of any imaginable society—sociopaths, sexual perverts, sadists, hatemongers of the worst sort, alcoholics and narcotics addicts, and a few brilliant but mentally and emotionally twisted men. The only thread that had held them all together through so many vicissitudes, through years of difficulties that had included shootings, stabbings, beatings resulting in not a few deaths within their ranks, persecution and imprisonment by the legal government, uncertainty every morning of whether or not the evening might find them in a jail or a coffin, that thread had been their belief in the goals of National Socialism and the personal charisma of their chosen leader, Adolf Hitler.

"Once installed in more or less legal office, however, Hitler found certain of the men who had with their blood and suffering put him where he was a definite liability, and he took care of that liability in a very firm and permanent manner: he had another group of his personal thugs—the Schutzstaffel or SS—murder the most of them, which deed so terrified the rest of them that he never had trouble from them again.

"Now Hitler and certain others of his cronies had early on become imbued with some crackpot theories of inborn racial superiority. That is to say, they had mentally divided all of the world's people into two classes, which they called by the names of *Herrenvolk* and *Untermenschen. Herrenvolk* were all said by them to be tall, muscular, highly intelligent, fair of hair and skin, blue or gray of eyes, with oval skulls, fine facial features and a natural noble bearing—which constituted a type that very few of Hitler's original staff fitted very well, least of all Adolf Hitler himself.

"The so-called *Untermenschen* were made up of everyone else of every race and ethnicity in all of the world. *Herrenvolk* means 'superpeople,' Arabella, while *Untermenschen* has the meanings of 'submen' or 'barely human.' The Nazis felt that it was the inescapable destiny of the few superpeople to rule, be the slave-masters of the vast hosts of subpeople, and in order to make certain that there should be no further mixing of the precious *Herrenvolk* blood with the inferior peoples, they used and abused their power, going to extremes that were ridiculous and lunatic and would have been considered ludicrous, had the end results not been so ghastly, so terrible, so sickening to all decent men.

"It began innocently enough with a form of state-controlled marriage licensing—*Herrenvolk* were not

allowed to marry anyone not of reasonably pure
Herrenvolk descent—and encouragement of *Herrenvolk* wives to breed more of their approved kind,
with honors and money given to those who produced
larger than usual numbers of children. The next step
was to mandate that unmarried *Herrenvolk* women
and girls fornicate with pure *Herrenvolk* men—
mostly officers and other ranks of the aforementioned SS, with the single-minded purpose of producing still more *Herrenvolk* children for the future of
the race, the party and the state. Up to that point, the
Nazi racial-purity obsession could at the very worst
have been considered to be but a form of nationalism
taken to ridiculous, insane extremes, for there was
not then anything approaching a pure race upon the
face of the earth, with the widely scattered exceptions of some few tiny tribes of stone-age primitives.

"But there was another side of the *Herrenvolk*
coin, Arabella, and that other side was far more
sinister and more dangerous to all other races upon
the earth. It consisted of nothing less than the total
extirpation or enslavement of all peoples not, by the
peculiar standards of the Nazis, racially pure
Herrenvolk.

"Soon after the Nazis took power in Germany, and
then in the German-speaking nation of Austria,
camps had been established to contain dissident
elements such as Communists, criminals, deviant
types and the physically or mentally abnormal.
Later, leaders and members of religious groups that
opposed various aspects of state policy were added.
These people all were, in the beginning at least,
legally tried and sentenced to these camps; and,
though primitive and brutal, these camps were really
labor camps wherein the residents worked at
manual labor for the length of their sentences, then
were freed.

"But there was another aspect to the camps. Hitler
and a good many of his henchmen had conceived a

deep and abiding hatred of Jews and gypsies, both of which they considered to be races, although many people of that time thought the Jews, at least, to be a religion, not a race. Of all the various races of the *Untermenschen*, the Nazis considered the Jews to be the very dregs, the lowest of the low, undeserving of anything but enslavement and eventual death. Hitler had written as much in a book he produced while he was imprisoned on one occasion.

"When the Nazis first came to power, the more astute of the German Jews, the born survivors, recalled the words of that book, that savage blueprint for genocide, and got out of Germany with their families and as many of their assets as they could easily bear away. But those were only a few. Most remained, for they considered themselves to be good Germans, whose religion had nothing to do with their German nationalism, and not a small number of them were and had been early supporters of the anti-Communist National Socialist German Workers Party, harboring fully as much desire as any other good German man or woman to once more have their country for their own and at peace internally, freed of the oppressive, foreign yokes of slavery and the totally disruptive radical terrorists spawned by the loss of the war and the subsequently depressed economy.

"But as the Nazis consolidated their power, their stranglehold upon the German nation and people, being a Jew gradually became a crime within the borders of Germany and, a little later, Austria. All of the privations and humiliations heaped upon the German nation and people by the cruel, ill-considered treaty that had followed the war were laid, by the Nazis, at the doors of the Jews, invoking amongst the German people the latent anti-Semitism that had lain just below the surface for generations."

"What is anti-Semitism, Milo?" asked Arabella.

"Another term for hatred of Jews, my dear. I

suppose that its genesis was in the theology, the teaching, of the early Christian Church. Jesus Christ was born a Jew, it is said, but it also is said that he was arrested, condemned and executed at the behest of the Jews, and a frequent epithet referring to Jews was 'Christ killers.' "

"Be that as it may, the bulk of the too-long downtrodden, despised but proud German people undertook the persecution with a vengeance, overjoyed to have a group of scapegoats on whom to vent the angers and frustrations that they had for so long endured in helplessness. At that juncture, emigration of Jews from Germany and Austria was being officially encouraged, and many Jews took advantage of that encouragement to get out, though most of those emigrants were allowed to go only at the cost of almost everything that they owned of any value.

"Now, by this time, many German and Austrian Jews had already been killed—murdered, beaten to death on streets and in jails, convicted on trumped-up charges of capital crimes and then executed with the semblance of legality—but large numbers of them were also beginning to be gathered up and shipped off to the aforementioned labor camps without even the mockery of a trial—old and young, men, women and even children, of every station and occupation, rich and poor. The story given out was that they were being collected to be resettled on the lands that the German armies were then conquering in the countries to the east of Germany—Poland and Russia—but that story was never anything more than a lie designed to prevent resistance and ease the intended transition from living Jews to dead Jews, courtesy of the National Socialist German Workers Party.

"Arabella, in that war and its aftermath, between twelve and thirty millions of human beings died, the numbers only dependent on which nation's figures you credit. Now this is not a large figure, true, not when compared with the losses worldwide caused by the last world war, but it still was a shocking, an almost unbelievable number for those long-ago days and times. And, Arabella, three to six million of them were Jews. So many of the European Jews either emigrated or were killed that, for a long while, Jews were rare in most of Europe and almost unheard of in Germany itself.

"And all of this slaughter and horror and misery because an aggregation of powerful fanatics, trying to practice an insane theory, striving toward a patently impossible goal, were allowed by the people of an unbelieving world to enforce their will upon those over whom they happened to hold sway.

"Can you now understand, comprehend my feeling of loathing, my fear for the liberty and safety of those who depended upon me when I had to listen to Bookerman's oration, that night, my dear?"

"I . . . I think so, Milo. But what ever happened to him? Did you finally have to kill him, after all?"

Once more, Milo opened his memories to the Lindsay girl.

Not much felt could be made that winter, for it was stormy and extremely cold, and consequently the sheep and goats and cattle and horses and mules needed their coats of hair and wool for the maintenance of life-giving body warmth. But with the spring, the shearing and the wide-ranging collection of other hair began in earnest. Parties of hunters and those who carted out to gather wild plants and roots bore along bags for the collection of stray wisps of shedding winter coats from the bodies of wild beasts. All of these many and varied contributions went into the heaps and piles of washed wool and hair—hair of horse and hair of mule, hair of cattle and hair of goats, hair of dogs and even hair trimmed from the heads of men, women and children.

Milo and Harry Krueger and old Wheelock handled all of the mundane affairs of the people, leaving Bookerman free to do nothing but supervise and work with those who were engaged in turning the mountains of fur and wool and hair into sheets of felt.

The physician experimented constantly with mixtures and concoctions of many and sundry natural plant extracts and animal products in search of fullering and hardening agents other than the old and increasingly rare man-made chemicals for which he sent cart expeditions to the empty towns and villages along the route they had traversed as far westward as the outskirts of nuked Denver. He knew that these would not always be available to the fledgling nomads and that even were they now to obtain large stores and cache them away somewhere or try to bear them with the caravan, they would deteriorate sooner or later—probably sooner, for they already were at least forty years old. The records that he meticulously kept of each and every experiment with mineral, animal and vegetable substances were eventually to prove invaluable to Milo and the people of the group that would one day call itself the Horseclans.

But they found themselves unable to stay in the little town for long after the arrival of the warmer weather and new growths, for their herds quickly exhausted the graze around and about, and their repeated incursions against the wild game soon drove those herds beyond their reach. So it was load up and move on again, though this time without old Colonel Wheelock, who had died when the spring was but two weeks old.

By midsummer, they had finally reached the city of Salina, from which the decision had been made to bear due south, if the southbound interstate was still as passable as was the eastbound one. Meanwhile, they camped in the buildings, grazed their herds in the overgrown parks and scavenged, as usual, among the dilapidated, often dangerously decrepit structures.

Two men and a woman were killed and several more people suffered injuries of varying degrees of seriousness when the ground floor of a onetime store collapsed into the cellar below and the remainder of the rickety two-story frame building crashed down atop them all. It required most of two days to dig out the dead and the still-living from the ruins, and, fearing repetitions, the council proclaimed that thenceforth scavenging would be done only by experienced and organized teams of men and women under the overall command of a member of the council. Naturally, there was some grumbling at the announcement of the new rule, but when the councillors presented a united front backing their decision, the people at last seemed to accept it.

Bookerman, alone, had not taken part in the meeting and the decision. This was not considered by any of the other councillors to be odd or unusual, for the doctor had already set up and was supervising a new felting operation. He still was also carrying on experiments, and he still practiced medicine, as well.

The next morning, however, when a felter came to Milo and asked if he knew where Bookerman might be found, he not having been seen at the felting operation, at his experimental lab or at the building set up for use as a hospital for some days, Milo went looking for the physician.

Milo's persistent knocking at the door of the small cottage inhabited by the doctor, however, raised nothing other than echoes, so he proceeded to break in the locked portal, bracing himself for the likely discovery of the aged physician's corpse, cold and probably decomposing by this time.

Chapter XII

But Dr. Bookerman's cottage was empty, completely empty of human presence, either living or dead. Although it was neat as a pin, with everything cleaned and dusted and the bed made up with tight, military precision, items of clothing hung in definite order in the closet and footwear arranged similarly on the closet floor beneath them, it was obvious that no one had resided in the house for two or three days.

A careful search of the place revealed a few facts to Milo. Bookerman's pampered and treasured fine Thoroughbred gelding, Schnellig, was missing from the shed out back in which he had been stabled, and so too were both of Bookerman's saddles and all of his other horse gear. Gone as well was the small yurt that had also been stored in that shed, which facts could mean much or nothing. The doctor could simply have undertaken a search, far afield, for any of the various plants and minerals with which he had been experimenting, though it was not his wont to undertake these trips alone and without informing at least his felters of his plans and of his estimated time of return.

Missing from the cottage itself were a number of items. Not only was the 8x57mm Mannlicher-Steyr rifle, with its fitted case and its scope, gone, but also the manual reloading set and all of the supplies—

bullets, powder, brass cases and primers. Nor was this the only firearm missing from the doctor's collection of them; his Heckler & Koch VP70Z automatic pistol was not to be found, his long barreled Smith & Wesson Model 29 in .44 Magnum, his Rottweil superposed shotgun with its case and all of its accessories, his AR-7 smallbore rifle, and a Spanish-made double shotgun sawed off to twelve-inch barrels and fitted with a pistol grip. His saber was gone, too, along with some clothing and boots, some cooking utensils, a spade, pick and axe, his medical bag and the small chest of surgical equipment.

It appeared to Milo that the doctor had simply packed up and left. The question was, where had he gone and why? When he broke off the lock of the footlocker he found in the laboratory at the felt works, he found some answers, though these answers bred a host of new and unanswerable questions for him.

"Friend Milo,

"You read this only because I at last have decided that the time has come for me to leave. Please do not come after me or send men to track me, for I am well armed and I will shoot any of you that I discover upon my trail."

The very next sentence sent cold chills coursing up Milo's back, covered his skin with gooseflesh and set his nape to bristling.

"Them I will assuredly kill, though I have reason to believe that, like me, a mere bullet would not kill you as it would kill other, more normal, humans.

"I do not know your true age, although I suspect you to be far older than you now aver. My own age, too, is very much more than the one I claim, but if I am wrong about you, you could not believe it were I to herein note it down. Suffice it to say that I have appeared just as I now appear for an exceedingly long time. Nor are you the first friend I have had to suddenly desert due to my noticeable aberration of not aging as do all other human beings.

"Part of what I have told you of myself at various times over our years of friendship has been of truth. I was, indeed, born in Niedersachsenland, to a wealthy, landed family of most noble blood and antecedents; my father was a margrave, a renowned military officer, a very brave man and a widely recognized hero, may whatever God exists bless his gallant spirit.

"Along with all of my brothers and half brothers, I was sent up to University and given the chance at a decent education, then presented a commission in one of the most illustrious of the *Schwadronen* of *Hussaren*, the Kaiser's then-favorite one, in fact. It was during my baptism of fire that I discovered— twice over—that something extremely odd about me there was.

"We received orders to deliver an attack against the flank of the French army opposing us. That charge was delivered with great firmness, driven home, but just as I reached the French at the head of my *Jungen*, a French officer fired his pistol and the ball struck me in the breast. I distinctly felt the hideous pain as that large piece of lead, after passing through my dolmen and blouse and shirt, tore into my flesh, shattered rib bone, lacerated my heart, then exited my back, smashing another rib in the process. Forcing myself to ignore, alike, the agony and the giddiness and the firm knowledge that I was a dead man, I almost decapitated that Frenchman with my sharp saber, then bored into the formation, resolved to take the lives of as many of them as possible before I tumbled, dead, out of my saddle.

"I felt myself to be truly acting out the words of the '*Alte Reiterlied.*' ('*Gestern noch auf stolzen Rossen, Heute durch die Brust geschossen, Morgen in das kühle Grab.*' And then, '*Und so will ich tapfer streiten,*

*Und sollt' ich den Tod erleiden, Stirbt ein braver Reitersmann.')** I set myself to fight until the last drop of my blood had been drained away and the great dark had enfolded my being, as befitted a man of my race and house.

"But, friend Milo, when the recall was winded and I hacked my way back out of the French ranks, my good horse wounded many times over and stumbling under me, my saber blade dulled and nicked and cloudy, my clothing all torn and gashed and soaked through with my own blood and that of many another, the top of my fur busby shorn raggedly away and the heel of my right boot shot off, I still lived, nor was there much deep pain in my chest, as there most surely should have been.

"Then, when almost I was out of the French lines, a wild-eyed, frothing gunner appeared suddenly and jammed the slender finial spike of his linstock into my body, skewering my right kidney and bringing from me a scream of pain. I split the man's head with my saber, the linstock's own weight dragging its point from out of me, then rode on, groaning and grinding my teeth in my agony. My good horse made it back with me still astride him to almost the point from which the charge had been launched, then he suddenly fell dead and a passing troop sergeant dragged me up across the withers of his mount and bore me back to the rallying area.

"The indelible mark of *Fähnrich* Karl-Heinrich von ——— was made on that long ago day, friend Milo. Every officer and other rank of the survivors of

*An old cavalry song:
Yesterday, still on prancing horses,
Today, shot in the chest,
Tomorrow in the cool grave.
And so will I fight bravely,
And should death claim me,
Then dies a brave cavalryman.

that charge treated me with a respect bordering upon awe; my *Oberst* not only presented me with one of his own string of chargers to replace my dead one, but offered a very generous price for a full captaincy in his unit, and immediately my father was apprised of my exploits, he sent the monies to buy me that position, plus funds to pay for uniforms and equipment commensurate with that rank.

"But I here get beyond my story. When, in the privacy of the tent I had shared with another *Fähnrich* who had not come back from the charge, I stripped off my blood-stiff dolmen, blouse and shirt, *I could find no trace of the wounds that I knew I had sustained.* Just below and a bit to the right of my left nipple was a dent that looked like a very old scar, and there was another just below my left scapula. At the place in which the gunner had speared me, there was no mark at all, for all that the blood had dried on my skin and soaked my clothing, which last was holed in just the right places and ways to match my memories of those two deathwounds. Yet I was a living hero, not the dead one that I should rightly have been twice over that day.

"Justly fearing a charge of witchcraft at the very least, I said nothing to anyone in that army about my wounds or their miraculous healings, nor did I mention to anyone aught of the many other severe injuries that I suffered briefly in the course of that and many another war. Eventually, when certain noblemen and comrades began to openly question my imperceptibly slow aging process, I found it expedient to fake my death and move on to another country and army, something that I have been forced to do over and over again across the long years, as I do now, friend Milo.

"But, then, if what I most strongly suspect of you is of a rightness, you, too, are more than familiar with this pattern of self-protection from superstitious or envious human beings. At times, one believes so long a life to be a curse—a curse of seemingly eternal loneliness and wandering amongst strangers—rather than the blessing that normally aging humans would imagine it to be. But there is a very positive side to it, in that it teaches one so very much about humanity in general and the proper psychology to be used in manipulating people both in groups and as individuals. You are different. You are very much like me, and my very first suspicion of you was simply caused by the fact that you did not seem to think, to reason like, a common, normal, short-lived human. I have, I firmly believe, met only two others of our rare kind over my years and travels.

"The first was a French *comte* (although I believe that he did not begin a Frenchman, but more likely as an Italian or a Spaniard), a charlatan, swindler, confidence man, poseur . . . and these constituted his better qualities. But *Monsieur le Comte* briefly took me under his wing, recognizing me for what I was, and taught me telepathy and the arts of mindreading and of hypnotism. He imparted to me the few vulnerabilities of men such as ourselves. For we *can* be killed, friend Milo; anything that prevents the air from reaching our lungs for long enough will render us lifeless as any mere human—immersion under water, strangulation, smothering or a prolonged crushing of the chest and lungs. So avoid these things, friend Milo, and be most wary of fire, as well, for are you consumed faster than the body can regenerate, you will be just as dead as any poor old woman who was burned for a witch.

"Prior to his very precipitate departure from Paris and the French court, *Monsieur le Comte* first sent bravos to kill me, next notified certain sworn and deadly enemies as to my current whereabouts and finally, all else having failed, endeavored to have me taken by the Holy Office for examination on a charge of witchcraft, sorcery and heresy. This last meant that I, perforce, had to depart the court and city and country in some haste myself; but it was as well that I did so then, for within a very short time the rabble of peasants and artisans had arisen and were soaking France in the blood of the better classes, finally even murdering their hereditary king.

"Late in the nineteenth century, I became a physician and surgeon, and I was practicing this profession in Munich in the years after the First World War when I happened to meet the second of our kind, who then was leading a small political party made up mostly of former soldiers. I was able to teach him much concerning himself and how best to use his powerful mind to sway masses of people.

"He had wonderful dreams and plans for his party and his nation and his race. Had destiny allowed for him more time to prepare properly the ground, to lay firmly the foundations of his new and much better order, to draw about him a corps of capable, effective men rather than the flawed fanatics with whom he found himself burdened, then who knows how very grand and great an edifice he might have built for Germany and the world.

"But, alas, circumstances over which he had no control forced his hand, compelled him to launch prematurely portions of his grand design which should have incubated for much longer. And, slipping into a degree of overconfidence bred from his early successes as much as by the lavish praise of the sycophants then surrounding him, he plunged onward, disregarding my advice and even the warnings of his own reasoning abilities.

"As if overextending a finite military were not enough, he allowed certain frothing, fanatic lunatics to destroy certain irreplaceable resources that might, properly utilized, have even so late given him victory. With a wild abandon, henchmen of these fanatics turned potential laborers into corpses, made of would-be allies sworn enemies, even went so far as to cause battles to be lost and German soldiers to die needlessly in order to misuse the rail transport to their own lunatic ends, hauling Jews off to the slaughter, rather than munitions and supplies to the fighting fronts.

"Heinrich Himmler had always hated me and deeply envied my behind-the-scenes influence on my protege, and after the try to blow up the *Führer* failed so disastrously, Himmler accused me of being implicated and ordered my arrest. I fled Berlin and, after assuming the identity of a fellow surgeon who had died only the day before in an air raid on Magdeburg, I used his *Soldbüch* and orders to get me to the Western Front, then arranged to be captured by the American army, which presented no great difficulty in my unit's sector, so fluid was the front then become.

"The medical officer of the Wehrmacht I was become—one *Hauptmann* Klaus Rudolf von Klippe —was well treated by his initial captors, only cursorily questioned by a tired, overworked intelligence officer who spoke very poor German, worse French and most ungrammatical English. After many weeks of waiting and of traveling, *Hauptmann* von Klippe arrived at Camp Trinidad, Colorado, U.S.A., and he there remained until quite late in the year of 1946, practicing his profession (for which he was paid by the U.S. Department of Defense), living quite comfortably and eating better than most any German then still in Germany.

"Repatriated to Germany in 1947, *Hauptmann* von Klippe disappeared, ceased to exist, which was not at all a difficult thing or an unusual occurrence in the Germany of those bleak days of defeat and national dismemberment.

"I then lived in Switzerland for a short while after I had claimed and taken possession of certain funds from a numbered account established years before in anticipation of just such a contingency. Then, by way of contacts in the Vatican, I made my way to South America, supposedly one *Hauptsturmführer* Alois Schmidt, but traveling under the passport of Karl Herbert Bücher provided by the Vatican.

"Friend Milo, I know that many people thought that the *Führer* actually survived the debacle of the defeat of *die Dritten Deutschen Reich*, that he faked his death and escaped to Spain or to South America as did so many others, but I do not, cannot, so believe and I possess the very best of bases for my lack of belief.

"You see, I became connected with the ODESSA network, and I traveled all over South and Central America, as well as to Spain, Portugal, the Near East and parts of Africa, on their behalf, and if he had been in hiding I would surely have found him, for no matter how he might have had his physical attributes changed, he could not have changed his mental makeup, and that I would have instantly recognized.

"Oh, yes, we *are* most difficult to kill. Mere cyanide or a bullet in the brain would not have accomplished the purpose. But, because we know ourselves, a suicide would have been very easy and could have been accomplished most painlessly, as well. Even so long ago, there were drugs available which might have been used by trained personnel in such a way as to have frozen the action of the lungs for sufficient time to cause the organism to run out of oxygen and so die. Then a trusted associate could have fired a bullet into the head and the body could have been borne up to ground level, soaked with petrol and burned.

"This would, of course, have required complete cooperation on the *Führer's* part, but I think that his despondency at the foiling of all his plans and hopes and aspirations nurtured for so very long might have rendered him suicidal, knowing his mind as well as I did. Other causative factors might have been the announced intentions of his friend Josef Goebbels to take not only his own life but those of Frau Goebbels and all of his children, the deaths or desertions of so many men he had liked and trusted over the years and last, but far from least, the unhealthy influence of the Braun woman, who was at best a borderline manic-depressive personality and harbored suicidal tendencies almost constantly. She never was good for him, but he would hear no scintilla of her true nature from anyone, no matter how close or sincere.

"In 1975, I entered Germany on a tourist visa as an Uruguayan citizen, traveled on in slow, leisurely stages to Switzerland and drew upon my last untouched account. With these funds, I returned again to Germany and, through certain persons, was able to purchase a new identity as a citizen of the Federal Republic and a physician.

"Then, in 1980, I took advantage of the shortage of medical practitioners in the United States of America, emigrated and married an American-born woman of Germanic descent. Nurturing pleasant memories of my so-enjoyed and most comfortable captivity in Colorado, I moved there and set up a practice in an affluent suburb of Denver. It so happened that my wife and I were looking over investment property in Wyoming when the missiles were launched and Denver died.

"As I am certain that you recall, friend Milo, 'chaotic' is a very mild term for the two weeks that followed the War, and in the interests of simple safety for my wife if for no other reason, I decided to remain in our hotel suite in Casper rather than try to make it back to who knew what in my home area.

"Then those horrible, deadly plagues began, killing ninety-five or ninety-six out of every hundred who contracted them, and I, like every other person with even a soupcon of medical training or experience, was desperately needed in the overflowing hospitals and makeshift wards in commandeered buildings. My dear wife, Brigitte, had been a registered nurse when I met and wedded her, and she insisted on joining me in my labors despite the risk.

"The emergency brought us all together as equals —doctors, surgeons, nurses, osteopaths, chiropractors, dentists, medical technicians of all sorts, paramedicals, midwives, veterinarians, pharmacists, morticians, orderlies, even sitters and military veterans with antique medical-corps training. But those terribly contagious plagues quickly weeded out almost all of the volunteer staff despite the most stringent precautions, and the man or the woman working beside you in the morning might well be just another dying patient before the fall of that night. Poor Brigitte lasted through three weeks of work in that hellish charnel house, then she came down with a combination of the two worst, most incurably deadly varieties, and, seeing the inevitable, I stole enough of the proper drug to give her a quick, painless death, for she had been to me a very good and loving wife.

"Being what I am, of course, I neither sickened physically nor died. Although I grieved over the loss of my sweet Brigitte and missed her terribly for a while, I did recover in time and then saw for me and my talents a new and a pressing need. No leaders were left alive among the few pitiful survivors still rattling about in the almost empty city of Casper. Food stocks were perilously low, and no one seemed to know just what to do, how to go about the business of remaining alive. So I took over, took command, and won them all over to me with my abilities to so do.

"I organized the survivors, disciplined them, had certain of them do a thorough inventory of our remaining resources and supplies, then set up rationing of food and fuel for the remainder of that mild winter. With the spring thaw, those with any knowledge or experience of farming were set to preparing selected land for the harrowing, plowing and planting, while others were sent out into the surrounding countryside to bring back cattle, horses, sheep, swine, goats, domestic fowl, seeds, farming machinery and equipment and all of the thousand-and-one other necessities.

"Knowing that spoilers would make an appearance, soon or late, I collected firearms and ammunition, trained my people in the proper use of them and waited for the inevitable worst. When it came, each time it came, we drove them back with heavy losses and mounted counterattacks which extirpated their entire strengths, or as good as did so, then appropriated their arms and munitions and explosives to our own use to utilize against the next pack to descend upon us.

"After some years and for a number of reasons, I persuaded my folk to move south to Cheyenne, where we found a few more of the survivors already in residence, but sorely beset by spoilers and overjoyed to be reinforced by trained and well-armed fighters. I was chosen mayor—which should be read to mean 'paramount leader'—and had served as such for a bit over four years when you rode in that day with your scouting expedition.

"Friend Milo, *alte Kamerad*, I had wanted so very much to tell you many of these things over the years we have been co-leaders of the folk. Had you proved less hostile in regard to my rational beliefs about breeding our folk along reasonable lines, I might have told you much of this that night by the campfire. Better yet, I might have awakened your clear, but now latent, telepathic powers and then have opened my memories to you, that you might more quickly have realized the truths, the validities of my beliefs, based as they are upon centuries of experience and of deep thought with which I occupied my mind through countless lonely nights of exile enforced by my differences from humans.

"Now, with me departed, you will just have to

awaken your mind yourself. I have left under this
rather long letter copies of two books which will be
of assistance in this endeavor. Also you will find in
this locker formulae for the fullering and the hardening agents for felt, all derived of natural substances,
all of these native to the prairie hereabouts; this
must be my last gift to the folk once mine and now
yours. I know that you will lead them well, probably
as well as might I have led them, and possibly better.

"I must soon depart, old friend. This typewriter
has surely all but drained the storage batteries and I
can hear the morning shift of felters cursing even
now at the necessity of mounting the bicycles and re-
charging them so early in the day, none of them
knowing that I and my laboratory will no longer have
need of that electricity.

"So, my work—such of it as you would allow—is
done and I now make my exeunt, as it were. I am
taking my Schnellig, of course, two spare mounts
and two of the Bactrian camels to bear my yurt, gear,
food and essentials, grain for the horses, et cetera; I
believe that the folk and you owe me at least this
much, friend Milo.

"I feel most certain that we two will meet again,
one day, be it in a few hundred of years or in a
millennium, but meet we will. As you will then, perforce, be an older, sadder, but much wiser man,
perhaps we can then converse as true equals.

Your true friend,
Clarence Bookerman, M.D.

"Post scriptum: Guard well my sheafs of notes
from my series of experiments, for contained within
them are many other formulae upon which I
stumbled. Included are formulae for the easy
tanning of leather and furred pelts, the best
materials for softening animal sinew (for use in fabricating bows, for instance), several really effective

bonding agents all derived of natural, if not common, ingredients, a number of salves of antiseptic and/or anesthetic properties, some truly fast dyes, a procedure for rendering common cowhide leather almost as tough and impervious as metal, some analgesics, laxatives and a first-rate expectorant. Consider these to be bonus gifts to you and our folk.

                                                    Clarence"

The two books and the notes—ream after ream of them, all as neatly typewritten as the lengthy letter—filled the locker almost to the rim. Even after Milo had read through the notes and removed those which were repetitive, had ended in useless failures or in substances for which he and the people would never have any use, there still were two thick binders of the parchment-bond pages remaining—Bookerman's legacy.

All the while he sorted and sifted the notes, Milo pondered on the letter of the now-departed doctor. Could it all be true? Were there more like himself scattered widely about the world? Never before having found any references to people with like abilities, he had for many long years thought himself to be unique. Now he was not so sure.

Of course, there was always the chance that the letter was all an utter fabrication, cut out of whole cloth, containing no shred of truth, but . . . if it was, then just how had the man so shrewdly assessed Milo's secret agelessness?

And Bookerman's early experiences closely paralleled Milo's own. He still recalled the exact details of the first time that he had been "killed" in combat, though many of the later of such occurrences were become a little fuzzy around the edges unless he consciously set himself to recollect them in detail. One's first "deathwound" simply was not something easily or quickly forgotten.

It had been in France, D-Day+41. While warily

slinking along the shoulder of a narrow roadway with what forty days of hot, vicious, hard-driving combat had left of the platoon with which he and poor little Lieutenant Hunicutter had hit Omaha Beach, they had come within range of a German sniper. And the crack shot quickly proved to them all both his expert-rifleman status and the fact that he was no tyro at combat sniping, which has always been an exacting and often fatal occupation.

The automatic rifleman, Pettus, had slammed into the high grassy bank at their left before any of them had heard the first shot, a bloody hole just under the right rim of his helmet and the now-precious BAR pinned under the dead weight of his bulky body, tobacco juice from his ever-present plug dribbling from the corners of his slackened lips over his blue-stubbled chin.

Then, before any of them could react in any way, the next shot had taken Milo—now, by way of combat attrition, a second lieutenant—under the right arm he had just raised to dash the sweat from above his eyes. The 7.9mm bullet tore completely through his chest at a slight upward inclination, tearing into the right lung, through it, then through the heart before exiting the left-frontal side of the chest and boring through the left bicep as well. Even as he dove to the hard, packed surface of the road-way, Milo had known that he was dead meat.

The lancing agony had been exquisite, unbearable, and Milo had screamed, taken a deep breath to scream once again and ended coughing hot blood, almost strangling on the thick liquid. With only the most cursory of examinations of him, Chamberlin, one of the two remaining original NCOs, had taken over, gotten the men off the exposed stretch of road-way without any more losses, taken one half of the unit, turned the other over to Corporal Gardner and, after they had shed or dropped every nonessential item of equipment, started them out toward the point at which he had seen the muzzle flash of the second shot.

As for Milo, he had just lain still, hoping that by so doing he could hold at bay the pain until he had lost enough blood to pass into a coma and so die in peace. But he did not, could not find and sink into the warm, soft, all-enveloping darkness, and the pain went on, unabated, movement or no movement. In automatic response to his body's needs, he continued to breathe, but shallowly, having no desire to bring on another bout of choking on and coughing up more of his own blood.

Then, as he lay there, composed for the onset of his sure and certain death, the pain began to lessen. Although weak, he felt no drowsiness, no more than he had felt for the long days since the landings, at any rate. He opened his eyes and gingerly turned his head so that he could see—and see very clearly in the bright, summer-sunlit day, which last surprised him —the two contingents of his platoon swinging out wide to converge upon the suspected position of the sniper's nest among the jumbled wall stones and free standing chimney of a burned-out farmhouse.

Feeling the pressing need for a clearer view of the distant objective, he cautiously moved enough to drag from under him his cased binoculars. Through the optics he saw three half-crouching figures, clad in Wehrmacht feldgrau, setting up a light machine gun, an MG42 by the look of it and fitted with the *Doppeltrommel* drum magazine, and the thing was on a rare tripod, which would make its fire far more accurate than from a more usual bipod, too.

With no base of fire to cover them and their advance, Milo knew that those men of his would be slaughtered. They did not even know about that machine gun—after all, they thought themselves to be stalking only a sniper and his assistant and could not see from their positions just what Jerry was setting up for them—wouldn't realize the danger until the fantastically high rate of MG42 fire was ripping the life out of them.

He dismissed his own Thompson submachine gun without thinking; it was a superlative, if very heavy, weapon at normal ranges, but it just could not accurately reach out the required distance, in this case. Forgetting his fatal wounds in his worry for the men in such deadly danger out there, he allowed his body to slide down the bank and then wormed his way up to where Pettus' body lay.

It took no little effort to shift the big man's body enough to get both the BAR and the six-pocket magazine belt off it, but Milo accomplished both. Then, now laden with his own weapons and equipment as well as the automatic rifle and its seven weighty magazines, he crawled up the bank to its brushy top and took up a position that gave him a splendid field of fire. A pair of mossy rocks situated close together provided both bracing for the bipod of the BAR and a certain amount of protection from any return fire, almost like the embrasure of a fortification.

He took time to once more scan his target area with the binoculars and estimated the range at eight hundred yards, plus or minus a dozen or so. With the bipod resting securely on the boulders at either side, he scooted backward and calibrated the sights for the supposed range, then set the buttplate firmly into the hollow of his shoulder, nestled his cheek against the stock and set his hand to the grip and his forefinger to the trigger.

Expertly feathering the trigger so as to loose off only three or four rounds per firing until he knew himself to be dead on target, Milo cruelly shocked the short squad of Wehrmacht who were preparing a deadly little surprise for the two small units of assaulting Americans. As short bursts of .30 caliber bullets struck the fire-blackened stones and ricocheted around the ruined house, the *Gefreite* reared up from where he lay and, using his missing

Zugsführer's fine binoculars, swept the area from which the fire seemed to be coming, nor did it take the veteran long to spot the flashes of the BAR.

The present danger superseding, in his experienced mind, the planned ambush, he pointed out the location of the weapon that now had them under fire to the MG-gunner and ordered return fire. When he had spotted the glint of sun on glass, Milo had anticipated counterbattery fire and had scooted his body behind the longer and larger of the boulders, pressing himself tightly into the hard, pebbly ground, so he had only to brush off stone shards and moss, then get back into firing position. He now had the range.

As Chamberlin later told the tale: "Well, whin I heared that damn tearing-linoleum sound, I knowed it was more than just some damn Jerry sniper up in that place, so I just stayed down and hoped old Gardner would have the good sense to do 'er, too. Then I realized it was a BAR firing from the road, too, and all I could figger was old Pettus, he hadn' been kilt after all and was giving us all covering fire, keeping the damn Jerries down so's we could get up into grenade range of 'em. So I waved my boys on, slung my M1 and got a pineapple out and ready."

Milo was down to his seventh magazine when he saw, then belatedly heard the first grenade explosion within the enemy position, at which point he ceased firing, lest he accidentally make a casualty of one of his own men. Slinging the BAR, he slid down the bank to the roadway and was there to greet the two makeshift squads as they came back to their starting point.

When Chamberlin saw Milo, his eyes boggled and he almost dropped the pair of fine Zeiss binoculars he had stripped from off the incomplete body of the now-dead *Gefreite*.

"Gawdalmightydamn!" Gardner exclaimed, letting the holstered broomstick Mauser that had been the

MG-gunner's sidearm dangle in the dust. "Sarge . . . uhh, Lootenunt, we thought you's daid, fer shure. I know damn well that bullet hit you—I could see the fuckin' dust fly up outen your fuckin' field-shirt. So why the fuck *ain't* you daid, huh?"

Milo had no real answer for Gardner's question, not then, and not now, almost a century after the end of that war. Knowing that he must say something, however, he said that the bullet fired by the sniper had simply torn through his baggy shirt, leaving him unscathed—the first of many such lies he was to tell to explain the unexplainable, over the course of years—and he blamed the bloodstains on his necessary handling of Pettus' body when he took the BAR and magazine belt from off it. The men believed him, none of them able to think of any other explanation, especially when no wounds could be found anywhere on his body.

Milo recalled that he had sustained at least two, maybe three, more dangerous wounds before the end of the war, more during the Korean thing, several more during his years in Vietnam and a couple after the U.S. Army retired him as overage, when he had gotten bored in retirement and became a mercenary. The wounds all had left scars, but these were faint, tiny, almost-invisible things, and he no longer could remember just where or when or how he had come by any particular one of them.

As he packed away the precious notes of the departed doctor, he thought of how much, how very much, the man might have been able to explain to him of their shared affliction, if only he had known of it. He even thought of immediately mounting up and riding out in pursuit of Bookerman, but then he recalled just how many men, women, children and domestic animals now depended solely upon him, upon his leadership, for their continued survival, and knowing the thoroughness of the German, Milo did not think that he would leave an easy trail to follow. Running him to ground might well take weeks, months, if he could catch up to him at all in totally unfamiliar territory.

If only Bookerman had spoken his suspicions months ago, even weeks or mere days ago, then told of his own, identical experiences, rather than imparting it all in a letter intended to be read after his departure.

"Who was it," thought Milo Moray morosely, "who said that 'if only . . .' were the saddest words in any language?"

Chapter XIII

Arabella Lindsay's small freckled hand gently squeezed Milo's bigger, harder hand in sympathy as she beamed, "Oh, my poor Milo, you must have been so very disappointed. Perhaps, for your peace of mind, you should have ridden out after that man, no matter how long it took you to find him. But I, above all others, save maybe Father, can understand why you did not, why you felt that you could not; duty is an exceedingly hard taskmaster, I well know. But it is a shame, nonetheless, for a man or a woman should live around, near to, his or her kindred, not always alone among those different from him or her.

"You never have found, never have come across others like yourself, then?"

Milo sighed, then beamed, "No, although when I learned to use my own telepathy and to help to awaken that dormant trait in other men and women, I assiduously delved their minds in search of certain signs that Bookerman had noted in the margins of some of the pages of the books he had left me. I delved vainly, however; I never found any of the signs in the minds of those around me."

"And mine, Milo?" Arabella questioned silently. "Have you delved my mind, too?"

"Yes, my dear, it's become automatic with me. But

you are human, just like all of the others, pure human."

She smiled. "I am glad, Milo. I deeply sympathize with you, but even so I do not think I could bear the long, searching loneliness of being like you. I could not bear to watch while my little cousins and all of my onetime playmates grew up and grew old and finally died and I remained the never-changing same; I think that I should go mad rather quickly. That you have not done so, and that long ago, shows, I think, the immense strength of your character and mind and will. If anyone can end this deadly enmity between the prairie rovers and the people of the fort and the station, I think it must be you, and I cannot but agree with Father that God and God alone must have sent you to us in our time of greatest need."

The identities of the MacEvedy Station farmers who had chosen to accompany the departing battalion for the nomadic, herding, hunter-gathering life offered by Milo Moray were no longer secret; they could not be, for with the invaluable aid of clan smiths and wainwrights, the farm wagons were being transformed, rebuilt into commodious carts like those of the nomads—with shorter bodies, higher wheels and stronger axles and running gear.

In the cases of the soldier families, carts were having to be built from scratch, using seasoned wood stripped from some interior parts of the fort itself, and from the dismantling of frame outbuildings, the hardware being fashioned of steel from the mortar tubes and baseplates and from the ancient 75mm guns.

When first it had become apparent that more ferrous metal would be needed were the battalion families' carts to be done properly and the colonel had ordered that the necessary steel be stripped from the last remaining intact source, the director and his son had come bursting into Ian's office at the fort, the elder MacEvedy white-faced with rage.

"Now dammit, Ian Lindsay, have you completely lost your mind?" he had shouted. "A squad of your men and some three or four of those godless, heathen nomads are at this very minute dismantling one of the cannons, and they refused to stop it when I ordered them to desist, attesting that it was you who said they could. If you strip us of the two cannons, then how can those of us who still are sane put the fear of God into the plains rovers after you and the rest of those lunatics you lead are gone? The mortars are very short-ranged, and I have not yet figured out just how the catapults and spear-throwers are supposed to work."

There was no longer any trace of either respect or friendship left in the officer's gaze or voice when he answered. "You'll no longer need worry yourself about the tension-torsion weapons, for they've been broken down for the timbers, rope and hardware, and the spear-throwers, too. The mortars have gone to the forges by now, and both of the cannons and their carriages are on the way. If it develops that we need more metal, the rifles will follow."

Grant whimpered, but his father demanded in heat, "And just how are those farmers and their families you and your damned troops are deserting here supposed to defend themselves against the next pack of rovers who come along if you choose to self-ishly destroy all of the real weapons?"

Ian smiled coldly. "You no longer bother to keep abreast of what's happening in the station, do you, Emmett? There aren't going to be any people left in the station or the fort, with the exception of you, your son and Falconer and his family. Why, even your own daughter, the Widow Dundas, has asked if she might accompany us, and I have gladly welcomed her; she'll travel with Arabella and me until one of my officers gets around to marrying her."

"But . . . but . . . but . . ." stammered Grant, looking to be on the verge of tears, "but without Clare in the house, who will . . . will *cook* for us and . . . and wash our clothes and make up our beds and dust and . . . and everything?"

Lindsay snorted in disgust. "Why, Grant, you'll just have to start caring for yourselves . . . unless you can cozen Mrs. Falconer or her daughter into keeping you both in the style to which you have become accustomed."

"But . . . but . . . but . . . Father and I are just too busy running the Station to . . . to . . ." sniffled Grant.

"Why you brainless, ball-less young ninny," snapped Lindsay. "Can't you understand plain English? There's not going to be any station to administer. All of the farmers are going with me and the nomads, *everyone*, excepting only you, your father and the Falconers."

"But . . . but . . . but you . . . you *can't*, Godfather!" Grant sobbed, his tears beginning to come in floods. "Without you to . . . to take care of us, without the farmers to grow food, without even . . . even Sister Clare to . . . to cook and keep the dust out of the house, we'll . . . we'll all *die!* You . . . you just *owe* it to us to stay here and keep us all safe." He ceased to speak then, giving himself totally over to gasping, shuddering sobs of mindless terror.

"My God, Emmett," rasped Lindsay, "for all your other faults, you are at least a man. How in the name of all that's holy did you and Martha Hamilton ever manage to produce a man-shaped thing like this? Get out of my office and out of the fort, and keep out of my affairs, both of you! I'm sick unto death of the sight and the sound of you!"

On the next Sunday following that meeting, the

few older people who had attended divine services arose and slowly filed out when the Reverend Gerald Falconer cleared his throat to commence his sermon. Their departures left only the station director, his son and Falconer's own family, less his eldest daughter, Megan, who had earlier in the week surreptitiously moved into the nomad camp and sent back a note declaring her intention of there remaining and of leaving with the battalion.

What issued from Gerald Falconer's mouth during the next three-quarters of an hour was not a sermon. He ranted, he raved like a frothing lunatic on the disloyalties of parishioners, children and other relatives. He damned every prairie rover ever born or spawned, laying upon them the full blame for every ill that had afflicted the station in the last fifty years. At last, when he had worked part of the frustration and rage out of himself, he paused for a long moment to catch breath.

Then he bespoke his wife. "You get out of here now, and take the children with you. Have my dinner ready in an hour. I needs must have words with Emmett here."

For all that Jane Falconer had been Gerald's wife for over ten years, she still was a young woman—not yet twenty-six—and not even his years of browbeating had worn her down, any more than identical treatment had broken the spirit of his daughter by his deceased first wife. She and Megan had, indeed, thoroughly discussed in secluded whispers the girl's decision to quit the house of her overbearing father and seek a chance of happiness in the nomad camp. She had thought to remain with the husband whom so many had already deserted, not through any sense of love or duty, but because she had felt pity for him. But after today's diatribe, she now entertained serious doubts as to his mental and emotional balance and the wisdom of her and her tiny children's remaining in proximity to him.

She did go home, but she remained only long enough to get together her clothing and that of her children, her Bible and a few especially treasured kitchen utensils. With everything packed in the garden wheelbarrow, her youngest child perched atop the load, she led the other two in the direction of the camp of the nomads.

"It must be done in front of as many of our people as is possible," averred the Reverend Gerald Falconer. "I leave it to you two as to how to assemble them. Lie, if you must. God will forgive you, for it's being done in His Holy Name.

"When we have them and him there, I will advance upon him and offer him the silver cross, demand that he hold it in his hand, kiss it and bow knee to me. He will, of course, recoil in horror and loathing from the sacred cross, and that will be your signal, Emmett. You must then bring out the pistol and place that silver bullet as close to his foul heart as you can, praying hard that God Almighty will guide your eye and hand.

"I will not, of course, be bearing any weapons, but Grant will have a rifle, and—"

"But . . . but Reverend Falconer," protested Grant MacEvedy anxiously. "I . . . I don't know anything about shooting rifles. Besides, the noise is so loud that it gives me headaches for days afterward, sometimes."

"All right, all right," snapped Falconer shortly. "Get yourself a hunter's crossbow, then. That ought to be noiseless and simple enough for even you at the short distance you will be from your father and me. All you have to do is put your bolt in anyone who makes to prevent your father from shooting the Beast. Do you think yourself capable of protecting your own dear father, boy?"

Grant MacEvedy left the chapel meeting and

repaired to the empty, echoing, now-dusty house that he shared with his father. MacEvedy *pere* had, in better times, been a hunter and owned the usual collection of hunting weapons, clothing and equipment.

Grant was not and had never been a hunter. He ate game, just as he ate domestic animals, but he had never even thought of killing his own food, for it was just so terribly *messy* a job. He had always insisted that his meat of any kind be cooked completely through, for the sight—indeed sometimes even the mere thought—of *blood* could render his delicate stomach unable to hold food of any type for some little time. Besides, hunting as practiced by fort or station people had always included dogs—before the folk had had to eat them, the cats and even the rats and mice—and close proximity to any furred animal had always set Grant to sneezing, wheezing and coughing, his eyes so red and swollen and teary that he could not see clearly.

Because of Grant's utter inexperience in the use of and his complete unfamiliarity with the construction and appearance of weapons—to him, all of the prodds and crossbows closely resembled each other —it were perhaps charitable to forgive the born blunderer his grievous error in arming himself for the imminent confrontation into which he had been most unwillingly dragooned.

After all, every person or other living thing that he had ever seen shot at and hit with a fired bullet or a loosed arrow or quarrel bolt or a prodd-pellet had immediately fallen, either dead or mortally wounded. Therefore, the young man had a much-overinflated faith in the never-failing efficacy of all firearms and other missile weapons. He did not for one single minute doubt that immediately his father blasted the holy silver bullet into the breast of the werebeast, Moray, the sinister, unnatural creature would curl up and die, thus proving for once and always to all and sundry of the misled, mutinous people that Director MacEvedy and the Reverend Mr. Falconer had been right all along.

He seriously doubted that he ever would have to actually make use of the heavy, clumsy, terribly dusty weapon he finally chose, but he always had obeyed his father, and his father had instructed him to cooperate in every way with the Reverend Gerald Falconer.

He left the room that housed the director's modest arsenal with a medium-weight crossbow and a belt pouch of quarrels, just as he had been bidden to do. However, that device which he took for a crossbow, because of very similar shape, was actually a double-stringed prodd or stone-thrower, while the pouch of quarrel shafts—which, of course, he had not bothered to check, nor likely would have known for what differences to look, had he checked—were tipped with smooth, blunt horn heads and were intended for use in a lighter, one-stringed weapon when hunting birds or rabbits.

After severely skinning the knuckles of his butter-soft hands while trying to operate the built-in cocking lever of his chosen weapon, Grant brushed away his tears, blew his sniffly nose twice, then carefully washed off the scrapes before donning a pair of pliable doeskin gloves, lest he be again so injured.

Next came the problem of concealing the fact that he now was armed. The pouch of quarrel bolts presented no difficulty; he simply allowed his shirttail to dangle down untucked, as he often did in hot weather. But the awkward and, to him, ill-balanced prodd was something else again. At last, despairing of really effective concealment, he wrapped the ill-shaped weapon in a rain cape and took it under his arm, still uncocked. Then he left the house and set off for the chapel, whence all three of them—Director Emmett MacEvedy, the Reverend Gerald Falconer and he—were to set off together for the fateful confrontation with the Satanic beast and the God-sanctioned, fore-ordained successful conclusion of their deadly purpose.

Soon, very, very soon, Grant assured himself, everything in the fort and the station would be just as it had always been. At the orders of the director, the reverend and himself, the people would join together to kill or to drive off the dirty, smelly, godless, heathen, prairie rovers—keeping their cattle and sheep and goats and horses, of course. Then, with proper order again restored, he and his father and the reverend would firmly reestablish their God-given sway over the deeply repentant insubordinate subordinates. Personally, he, Grant, relished his thoughts of making the faithless folk of station *and* fort squirm for many a year to come as he hashed and rehashed the tale of their faithlessness and gullibility to the wiles of Satan.

As for the arrogant, violent and often—to Grant— frightening Colonel Ian Lindsay, he would be utterly discredited for all time, and whenever Pa died and Grant, himself, became director . . .

So, thinking thoughts of ultimate power and revenge for all real or imagined wrongs done him in his lifetime, Grant MacEvedy trudged on to his appointment with destiny.

The quadrangle of the fort was become an open-air smithy and wagon-building yard, wherein the Clan Ohlsuhn smiths—they being traditionally the best practitioners of the art in Milo's tribe—and the smiths of the Scott tribe labored on as they now had for long weeks at turning archaic steel scrap into useful hardware with the willing assistance of the smiths from fort and station.

In the area near the wide-opened main gate and outside, beyond it, the gathered lumber had been piled, and men scurried like ants around and over those piles, busy with measuring instruments and tools—cutting boards into fellies, turning dowels and then shaving them down for tapered spokes, assembling running gear, bending wood for ox yokes and tying it into its new shape with wet rawhide strips and then hanging it within the heat radius of the ever-glowing forge fires in the quadrangle to set and season.

But carts were not the only uses of the lumber. Thinner, lighter laths were being turned into lattices to make up the sides of yurts, the joints each joined with treenails. Shorter but wider and thicker pieces became doorframes and center wheels, slotted to take the roof supports, the lower ends of which dovetailed into the side-bracing timbers.

Inside a building that had once been a stable, its box stalls now gone for lumber, nomad women of Milo's tribe worked at and instructed the women and girls of the Scott tribe and of the fort and station in the proper making, fullering and hardening of Horseclans felt to cover the yurt frames that the men were constructing. Of course, there would not be nearly enough of the new felt for a long while yet to come, but the generous nomads would share of their own with the newcomers, and the available canvas from tents would be used, layered under and over the felt, along with green hides, worn-down carpets and whatever else turned up to temporarily plug the gaps.

Other women and girls thronged the nomad camps, avidly absorbing the teachings of their new role models in the arcane arts of properly managing a nomad household. An old, wrinkled woman of Clan Krooguh was teaching identification of roots and tubers and leaves and flowers of wild plants relished by the folk of the clans. Another, much younger, woman was instructing a group of younger, stronger young women in use of the stock whip and ox goad; as she spoke, she likened various of her actions to saber strokes and promised to teach the use of that weapon to any interested females, later on, on the march.

Within the fort itself, Colonel Lindsay and some of his officers, helped by Milo, who sympathized and agreed with the commander in many ways, had just finished stowing the last of the books and records of the battalion and its fort in stout copper- and brass-hooped casks, waterproofing them with tar and safely stowing them in a secret space behind a false wall of the strongroom. The colonel had agonized for days in drafting a letter to accompany those records, and he now felt that he had offered the best reasons of which he could think for ordering the desertion of the station, the post to which the last legal government of Canada had assigned the original battalion, then commanded by his ancestor, the first Colonel Lindsay of the 228th Battalion (Reinforced) to guard MacEvedy Experimental Agricultural Station and its government-sponsored research.

The metal sheathing of the strongroom's outer door had long ago gone for body armor, and that double-thick oaken door itself had more recently gone, with its massive frame, to provide the boards for strong fellies for the carts. But the records still were as secure as possible under the circumstances, for with the pivoted section of wall eased back into place and securely latched, the chamber looked to the uninitiated like simply another empty stone-walled room, stripped now like all of the others of furnishings, carpets and all of its wood paneling.

When he rounded the chapel to see only the barest trace of smoke—no more than what could be expected to emanate from a banked fire—arising from the parsonage chimney, Gerald Falconer's righteous wrath, never far beneath the surface anyway, began to arise. A man could not be expected to attempt or accomplish God's work on an empty stomach, and he had issued unmistakably clear orders to Jane that she have a hot meal ready for him in an hour's time, something that would have required the addition of more wood to the stove fire at the very least.

The front door gaped open, and this, too, annoyed him. "Wife!" he roared, in the growling tone that denoted his vilest rage. But there came no answer of any sort, not even the expected whimpering of one of the younger children, who could recognize the tone of his wrath and had felt his kicks and cuffs often enough to fear him when he chanced to be in such a degree of anger and ill-controlled violence toward anything that moved or made a noise.

He searched the parsonage from low attic to root cellar, then opened and entered the semiattached privy, storage shed and stable, but there was no trace of Jane or of the little children. He then searched again, and it was in the course of this second vain search that he noticed the facts of missing clothing items and certain familiar objects from kitchen and cupboard; moveover, the big, capacious wheelbarrow was gone from its designated place against the back wall of the shed. Then the light of knowledge dawned in his narrow mind like the sudden blaze of sunlight emerging from behind dark clouds: *his* wife, *his* own wife, given into *his* service by God Almighty, had taken *his* children—the blessed fruit of *his* loins—and with them left *his* bed and board, deserted him and the Lord for the camp of his nemesis, following in the wake of the backsliding, heretical daughter who had earlier had the effrontery to desert him and the Church and God.

"Well, we will just see about that matter!" he snarled to himself, from between gritted teeth. His stomach agrowl, the Reverend Gerald Falconer stalked off toward the nomad camps, whitefaced in his anger, a two-foot billet of firewood clamped in his hand, resolved to have his wife and domestic slave back even if he had to beat her into insensibility to accomplish his holy purpose. When she came to her senses and fully realized the perdition from which he had saved her immortal soul, she would most abjectly thank him, of that he was more than certain.

At the edge of the nomad camp, an elderly, silvery-jowled and near-toothless hound approached him, its motheaten old tail waggling a greeting. Without breaking his firm stride, Gerald Falconer raised his cudgel and brought it down with such force as to crush the friendly animal's skull and simultaneously snap its neck like a dry twig. He felt much the better for the act as he proceeded on into the camp, threading a way between the haphazard arrangement of openwork wooden-walled and felt-roofed tentlike things in which the heathen lived out their lives of utter damnation.

Deep into the camp, a semicircle of women and girls from fort and station modestly sat or immodestly squatted watching while a trio of nomad women—recognizable by hair first braided, then lapped across their pates, as well as by their terribly unchaste men's clothing—fitted a yoke to a huge but gentle pair of oxen, then expertly attached the stout lines that hitched the device and the animals to a high-wheeled cart.

Falconer's keen brown eyes picked out his errant wife's mahogany-hued hair from a distance, and he stepped around and over the two rearmost ranks of women and girls until he stood just behind the rapt Jane Falconer. Stooping, the parson grasped a handful of that thick hair, hauled her over onto her back and wordlessly commenced to belabor the shrieking woman with the wooden billet still tacky with dog blood, even as he slowly backed from out the aggregation of females, dragging her with him.

At least, that had been his plan, but he had not backed up more than two or three short steps when he himself shrieked in pain and surprise and let go his wife's hair to clap the freed hand to a smarting and now bleeding buttock. Still grasping his cudgel, he spun about to confront a lithe nomad woman who held a cursive saber in a businesslike way, the blade of the weapon an inch back from the fine point now cloudy-pinkish with his blood.

"How dare you, you godless, pagan hussy!" he yelped. "You have no right to interfere with the high and holy work of the Lord. Get you gone ere I smite you." He raised the cudgel in a threatening manner, but she just smiled mockingly at him.

"You try laying that club on my body, dirt-scrabbler, and I'll take off your damned hand at the wrist, for all that your scrawny neck does offer me a most tempting target, and I doubt me not that you could do most comically a rendition of the dance of the headless chicken, to the amusement of all of us."

"Woman of Satan," said Falconer, in a heated anger that completely overrode his fear of this obviously demented nomad strumpet, "you know not to whom you speak. I am the—"

"You are the shitpants coward who needs must have a heavy club to attack a woman half your size from the rear, with no warning," the swordswoman sneered. "That's what you are! And if you don't get out of this camp quickly you're going to be a very dead shitpants coward."

"The . . . she . . . this woman is my wife, and you have no right to interfere in domestic affairs," stated Falconer, conveniently forgetting how often he had done just that to his parishioners, and generally to no real or lasting good effect. "She is my God-given helpmeet, and her proper place is in my home caring for me and our children. It is her duty, ordained by God's Holy Will."

He had hardly finished speaking the last word when there came a *whhuushing* noise from behind him and the long tail of a stock whip suddenly wrapped around his billet and then jerked it from out his grasp. An identical noise immediately preceded what felt to him to be the laying of a red-hot bar of iron upon his shoulder and diagonally across his back. He screamed then and bent to retrieve his cudgel, whereupon the same or another hot length of iron bar was pressed across his already sore and wounded buttocks. Forgetting the billet of wood, forgetting his mutinous wife, forgetting his empty stomach, indeed, forgetting everything save only his unaccustomed pain, the Reverend Gerald Falconer leaped forward in a dead run, heedlessly knocking the lightly built swordswoman asprawl from out his path. His long legs took him with some speed, nor did he stop until he once more had attained the safety of his empty house, with a barred door between him and his tormentors, whose mocking, shrill laughter and obscene, shouted jibes still echoed in his ears, where he leaned against the mantel, panting.

Emmett MacEvedy had been at the door of the chapel for a good half hour, having arrived a bit before the appointed time, when the parson made his appearance, walking slowly and a bit stiffly, wincing every now and again, as if some injury might lie under his black vestments. The large silver pectoral cross hung from his neck on its silver chain, the polished surfaces glinting in the sunlight. Arrived before the chapel, the parson seemed about to climb the four steps up to the stoop, then he apparently changed his mind.

"Are you ill or injured, Reverend Falconer?" inquired the director solicitously. "If you are, perhaps we should postpone our plans until another day, when you possibly will be feeling better." Emmett MacEvedy would just as soon have postponed their act of desperation indefinitely, having experienced some very foreboding presentiments as regarded it.

"No, no, I am well and uninjured, Emmett," Falconer assured him, possibly sensing that did he expect the MacEvedys to act in accordance with his directive in this matter it were best done now, at once. "I . . . I nearly fell and think I have only strained a muscle in my . . . uhh, leg. Yes, that's it, I slightly pulled a muscle in my leg, but it will no doubt improve with careful use.

"Where is your son, Grant? He too should be here by now."

"Oh, he'll be along, Reverend," said MacEvedy. "He's often tardy for things he doesn't care for. You should remember that about him from his school days."

"Yes, yes," Falconer said impatiently, "but it speaks ill of him to be late for this, the Lord's work.

"How of you? Did you do as I told you? Did you spy out the present whereabouts of the Beast?"

MacEvedy nodded. "I could not find him for a while, but then he and Ian and some of the other officers came out of the main building of the fort. Moray and Ian are now in the space before the main gate, overseeing the construction of carts in company with that other prairie rover chief, Scott. Most of the men and bigger boys of both station and fort seem to be thereabouts, too."

"Very well, then," said Falconer, "immediately your son, your laggard son, comes, we will go to the fort and do God's work, perform the task He has set us. Come, come, Emmett MacEvedy, smile. You should feel pride in having been chosen to be an instrument of the Lord."

Although Emmett was able to coax his lips, at least, into a grimace that parodied a smile, the load of encroaching doom was weighing heavier and ever heavier upon him; he *knew*, knew without knowing, that no good would come to him this day, knew that all three of them—him, his son and Falconer— moved in the bright sunlight under an invisible but horrifyingly palpable black cloud of deadly and irrevocable doom.

"Oh ho," muttered Ian Lindsay to Milo. "Yonder comes trouble."

Milo turned to look in the direction indicated by his companion. The Reverend Gerald Falconer was pacing in their direction as fast as his awkward limp would permit, his black vestments swaying about his ankles and the big silver cross bouncing up and down on the front of his torso. Some pace or so behind the parson came Director Emmett MacEvedy, trudging slump-shouldered, his demeanor that of a convicted felon bound for his execution. A few steps behind the director came his son, his shirttails flapping out and his arms supporting an angular bundle that looked very much like a crossbow wrapped hurriedly and most inexpertly in an old rain cape; MacEvedy *fils* did not look any too happy either, and his pale, beardless cheeks both bore the red imprints of recent slapping hands, while tears glittered unshed in his eyes and his lips could be seen to be trembling.

Milo disliked the look of it all. He had already been apprised as to Falconer assaulting his wife and being whipped out of camp by Manda and Sally Kahrtuh, Chief Bahb's two youngest wives. Yes, it had been extreme, to say the least, but he agreed that Falconer had fully deserved every last stripe he had been awarded, for not only had he clubbed to death an old hound for no apparant reason, his vicious attack upon his wife had broken at least three of her ribs, several fingers and her right lower arm, both bones of it.

So now, deserted by all of their subordinates and personal dependents, these three approaching men were become desperate, and desperate men are often wont to do or attempt to do mad, desperate things.

"Chief Gus," said Milo swiftly and softly to the

Scott chief at his other side, "arm as many bowmen as you can quickly and unobtrusively. At least one of those three is armed with what seems to be a crossbow, but he doesn't apparently want anyone to know of that fact."

"Why not let them get a little closer and drop them before they have a chance to do whatever they've come for?" asked Scott. "They hate you and Chief Ian and care little, they've made it clear, for me or Jules or any other rover. You throw a knife every bit as accurately as do I, and Chief Ian has his belt gun, so what need have we three of archers?"

"There may possibly be more than just those obvious three, Chief Gus," said Milo. "They could have infiltrated a few more armed men into this gathering, and we'd never have noticed the fact, probably. So let's play it safe—get those men armed and watch carefully for any treachery from any quarter."

The Reverend Gerald Falconer limped up until he stood only an arm's length from Ian Lindsay and his Satan's-spawn companion. Clearing his throat, he unhooked the silver pectoral cross from its heavy flat-link chain and held it bare inches from Milo's face, intoning in his best pulpit voice, "Begone, imp of Lucifer!"

Milo just threw back his head and laughed, then said, "You superstitious fool. If you really, truly believe me to be some kind of Satanic monster or demon, then you and your two toadies there are the only ones hereabouts so stupid and childish. We're all busy here, as you can clearly see, at men's work. If you try to hinder us, I'll send for two women I think you'll remember; I'll have them whip you back to your kennel, this time around."

Emmett had no idea, of course, just what Moray was talking about. Still heavy with dread and certain doom, he nonetheless was awaiting the words and actions that would be his cue to draw from under his shirt the old .380 caliber revolver with the silver-bullet cartridge carefully set as next to fire in the cylinder. The parson would press the cross even closer to the face of Moray and demand that he kiss it to demonstrate to all here assembled his submission to God Almighty and his abnegation of Satan and all his unholy works. When the Beast recoiled from the sacred silver, Emmett knew that—for good or, more likely, for ill—he must produce the revolver and fire the silver slug into the heart of the thing that called himself Milo Moray.

"If you are not a lover of Satan," said Falconer, "then kiss this cross, take it and press it to your breast, then bend a knee to me and swear that you abjure the Fallen Angel and do truly love and reverence the Lord God Jehovah and that you expect the salvation for which His only begotten Son died upon a cross like this. Do it, and I will believe you."

Grinning, Milo extended a hand and jerked the cross from Falconer's grasp. Bouncing it on his palm for a moment, his grin broadening, he nodded, then thrust it under his waist belt, saying, "Solid, isn't it? Heavy, too—obviously solid silver or at worst, sterling; no hollow casting, this one. I thank you for the gift—it will melt down into some very impressive and valuable decorations for my saddle."

The Reverend Gerald Falconer just stood rooted, gaping and gasping like a sunfish out of water. The damned creature clearly was not harmed in the least by contact with the holy silver. It was on his mind to speak a word that would stop Emmett when the sound of the pistol shot boomed in his ear.

Now sterling—an alloy compounded of about nine parts of pure silver to one part of pure copper—is somewhat harder than is pure silver; and pure silver, alone, is considerably harder than is lead; so this blessed bullet, propelled as it was by a load nearly triple that cutomarily used behind leaden pistol rounds by the fort armorers, sped undeformed through Milo's hide vest and shirt and flesh, went completely through the head of a man standing thirty feet behind him, then blew off toward an unknown lighting place out on the limitless prairie beyond.

His grin became a grimace of pain, Milo drew his big, heavy-bladed dirk in a twinkling and, taking a long step forward, drove its sharp blade deep into Emmett MacEvedy's solar plexus, holding the man's pistol arm tightly and twisting the blade about in his vitals with vengeful relish.

Frantically, Grant MacEvedy unwrapped the crossbow, drew back the cocking lever, then fumbled a quarrel bolt from the pouch under his shirt, managing in the process to spill out all the rest onto the ground at his feet and tear the shirttail jaggedly. Glancing up for a moment, he saw the big knife of the bleeding but patently still living rover leader flash briefly in the sun, then he saw his father start violently, heard him make sickening noises.

Bringing up the crossbow, he tried to fit the bolt into the slot, only to find that it would not, for some reason, stay in place or straight. After frantic split seconds that seemed long as hours to the inept young man, he thought that he at last had gotten it positioned properly and he raised it up to sighting level in shaking hands.

Emmett MacEvedy gurgled and vomited up a great gush of blood. His eyes rolled back in their sockets and his head lolled. When Milo let go the man's right arm, the legs buckled and the bloody corpse sprawled on the ground at his booted feet.

Aiming at his father's killer, Grant MacEvedy squeezed his eyelids tight closed and jerked the trigger of the crossbow. The blunt, unpointed bolt took the Reverend Gerald Falconer in the small of his back a couple of inches to the right of his spine. The quarrel tore and lacerated a way through his right kidney and into the frontal organs beyond. But due principally to the fact that it had been launched from a bow that it did not really fit, it lacked power and did not—as it would otherwise have done at such close range—go all of the way through the parson's body, but rather lodged in its agonizing place, heedless of the shrill screams of the man whose body now harbored it.

Poor, hapless Grant MacEvedy never even got a chance to see the bloody handiwork wrought by his clumsy efforts, for a brace of arrows from nomad hornbows pinned his eyelids shut and bored speedily, smoothly, relentlessly into the brain behind those eyes. He fell into a bottomless pit of darkness and was dead even as he hit the ground.

MacEvedy, *fils et père*, both lay dead, and once Colonel, now Chief, Ian Lindsay regarded the gory bodies of his boyhood friend and his godson sadly, deeply regretting so sad and savage an ending, but recognizing that he had done all within his power to prevent it, done it in vain.

The Reverend Gerald Falconer knelt in a spreading pool of his and Emmett's blood, hunched over the pain, hugging his agonized body and shrieking mindlessly, until Chief Gus Scott stepped forward, grasped a handful of the parson's hair, tilted his head back and slashed his throat almost to the spine. The noises made by the death-wounded man had begun to rasp on his nerves.

Epilogue

For all that fresh wood and dung chips had been added to the central firepit, it now contained only a mere scattering of isolated, dim-glowing coals mixed among the gray ashes. The halfmoon rode high overhead in the star-studded sky of full night, and Chief Milo Morai was tiring, having spoken and simultaneously mindspoken for hours to the assembled boys, girls, cats and clansmen.

The tale that he had spun had been a complex one, dealing as it had dealt with times long past, times before those and snatches of time of even a greater age.

He had told the stories of the War and the Great Dyings of the most of mankind, he had recounted for his rapt listeners—young and old, human and feline and equine—almost the earliest years of the Sacred Ancestors, the progenitors of the Kindred folk known as the Horseclans. And the stories bore the stamp of hard fact, not of mere bard song, possibly embroidered and added to over the long years by who knew whom. For the teller of the tales spun this night had *been* there, and all who had listened to him had known that truth.

But his long, intricate tale had only whetted the appetites of his audience for more, and as he fell silent, a flood of questions broke upon him and washed about him. Some of them were spoken aloud, but a larger number were beamed silently, by cats and horses who could communicate in no other way, as well as by telepathically gifted humans.

"Uncle Milo," Snowbelly, the cat chief, mindspoke, "this cat had never been told that the Kindred had kept dogs. Why did the Sacred Ancestors keep such loud, clumsy, dirty, smelly creatures? When did finally they come to their senses and cease to harbor the yapping things?"

"Uncle Milo," said one of the Linsee boys, "please tell us what the world was like before the Great Dying. Were there then as many people on the land as the bard songs attest, or do they exaggerate?"

Another, a Skaht youngster, asked, "Please, Uncle Milo, is it true that men knew how to fly in those times? That they could even fly up to the moon and . . . and truly walk upon it?"

Then Karee Skahts's strong mindspeak beamed, "Uncle Milo, whatever became of the girl Arabella and the stallion Capull? Did she marry into her own clan or into another?"

"I find it difficult to credit, Uncle Milo," said Rahjuh Skaht dubiously, "that this pack of mere Dirtmen could ever have become Horseclansmen. That Chief Gus Skaht and his tribe became of the Kindred sounds at least reasonable. But Uncle Milo, everyone knows just how slow and dense of mind, how clumsy and slow of action, how ill coordinated of body are Dirtmen, such as were those long-ago Linsees. So how did they manage to survive living as free folk on the plains and prairies long enough to breed any more of their ill-favored kind? Were all of them, then, as oversized and dark and stupid as the Linsees of today . . . as Gy Linsee over there, for instance?"

"Now, damn you, you young impudent pup!" snarled Hunt Chief Tchuk Skaht, coming suddenly to his feet and bulling his way around the firepit toward his insubordinate clansman, his big, powerful hands ready to grab and hold, heedless of whom or how many he stepped upon in getting to his quarry.

But before he could reach that objective, dark-haired Gy Linsee, already, despite his youth, a trained if unproven warrior and far bigger of body than most adult clansmen, laid aside his harp with a resigned sigh. He had taken days of oral and telepathic calumny in silence, tightly controlling himself in hopes that emulating his precedent, his example, his peers and his elders would give over the endless, senseless round of mutual bloodletting between Clan Skaht and Clan Linsee, as Uncle Milo wanted. But this last was the final straw; his personal honor and that of his ancient and honorable clan demanded either public apology and retraction from the sneering Rahjuh Skaht or a generous measure of the wiry young man's blood.

"All right, Rahjuh Skaht," he said aloud in a resigned tone of voice, "you have been relentlessly pressing the matter for long enough. I did not want to fight you—"

"A coward, eh? Like any other Dirtman," said Rahjuh scathingly. "For all your unnatural size, you—"

"No, I do not fear you, though you are a fully trained and experienced warrior who has fought battles and slain men, while I am yet to see my first real fight. But if fight you I must in order to know peace during the rest of this hunt, then fight you I assuredly shall. Choose what mode of fighting and what weapons you will, little man; I'll try not to hurt you too seriously."

"Here and now, with whatever weapons we have or can grab up!" shouted the raging Skaht, at the same time that he plucked a knife from his sleeve sheath and threw it with all his force at Gy Linsee's chest.

But moonlight is often tricky, and the hard-cast knife flew low, striking and skittering off the broad brazen buckle of Gy Linsee's baldric, then falling point-foremost to flesh itself in the tail of the prairie-cat still lying at Gy's feet.

The prairiecat queen, Crooktail, squalled at the sudden sharp unexpected pain and sprang to her feet, her lips pulled up to bare her fangs, her ears laid back close to her skull and every muscle in her body tensed to leap and fight and kill.

And all around the firepit, there was a rapid ripple of motion as boys and girls, warriors and cats, of both clans came to their feet and felt for familiar hilts and hafts. But then Hunt Chief Tchuk Skaht came up to his young and impetuous clansman Rahjuh. Seizing the murderous youngster by the back of the neck, he lifted him from off his feet and shook him like a rat, hissing all the while, "Now damn you for the intemperate fool you are, you little turd! Uncle Milo warned me earlier that you intended to provoke a death match with Gy Linsee, but I had credited you with brains you obviously lack, lack utterly, from the look of things.

"You mean to fight a man nearly twice your size to the death when you can't even throw a knife properly? You shithead—he'd kill you in a bare eye-blink of time, or if by luck you killed him, you would only dishonor yourself and your clan for provoking such a fight, for you are a seasoned warrior and he is not. And either outcome would undo everything for which Uncle Milo and the Council of Chiefs and Hwahltuh Linsee and Gy and I have worked so hard to attain despite your constant badgerings and insults."

He raised his voice and mindspoke, too, "Hear me well, all of you, Skaht and Linsee and cat and horse. This hunt is our last chance to show the Council of Chiefs that we all can live together in harmony and love and mutual respect as Kindred clans should

live. If we fail here, Uncle Milo has told me and
Subchief Hwahltuh that it is probable that the
Council of Chiefs will, at the next Tribal Gathering,
declare both Skaht and Linsee to be no longer
Kindred, disperse our women and children among
other clans, give our slaves and kine to new masters,
strip us of everything, then cast us out upon the
prairie to die in loneliness, far from all that we love.

"I do not mean to end my life so nastily, clans-
people. I know not just when or just how this feud
between our two clans commenced—it started long
before my eyes first saw the blaze of Sacred Sun or
my nose drew in the first breath of Wind—but it is
going to end, here, now, on this hunt, in this place,
this camp by this river. It will end if I have to shake
and break and batter apart every hot-blooded fire-
eater hereabouts. And if any one of you thinks I can't
do just what I've threatened, then come over here
and try me!

"As for you, Rahjuh Skaht, if you're so anxious to
nibble at fire, then here, eat your fill of it!"

All the while he had been speaking and mindspeaking, the huntchief had relentlessly continued to
shake his young clansman, and such protracted mis-
treatment had rendered the boy no more than half
conscious, if that. But when flung into the firepit,
atop and among the still-glowing coals, Rahjuh
abruptly came back to full, screaming, thrashing,
struggling consciousness. While all of the others
only stood rooted, watching the suffering boy,
listening to his mindless screams, Milo and one other
man leaped forward. Between the two of them, Milo
and big, strong Gy Linsee dragged Rahjuh Skaht
from off his bed of pain, thence down to the nearby
riverside, where they brusquely divested him of his
scorched clothing and gently immersed his burned
body in the icy water, holding him firmly there
regardless of his hysterical struggles. Only when
some of the Skahts came down to take over the care

of the injured boy did Milo and Gy wade back onto the rocks at the water's edge and flop down to rest for a few moments.

"I am very sorry for that." Gy gestured toward the knot of men and boys and girls in the pool, as he mindspoke. "Uncle Milo, what happened to that poor boy . . . it was mostly my fault. I should have exercised better control, I suppose."

"Not so, son," Milo reassured him. "You are blessed with a maturity far beyond your actual years, and you controlled yourself far better than do and have right many of your elders in like situations. I mean to keep track of you, for I am certain that you will be a very important and a long-remembered man. I also mean to have words concerning your future with your chief and your sire, for your talents are much too rare to be wasted as a simple warrior and hunter.

"I have scanned your mind while you slept, and I know that you yearn to succeed your father as Linsee clan bard, as you should, for you have inherited and developed vast talents in this area. But, also, I think that you will become too talented as you grow older and mature in your art to be truly happy as a simple hereditary clan bard.

"As I earlier said, when we return to the clan camps, I mean to have converse with your chief and Bard Djimi, your sire. With your agreement, I mean to ask the loan of you for a few years, that you might travel the land with me and the tribal bard, Herbuht Bain of Muhnroh. Would it please you to accompany us on our rounds from clan to clan, Gy Linsee?"

He raised a hand and added, "Wait—don't answer until you have heard it all, son. We travel light, with few comforts, on the sometimes long rides between clan encampments. There are only me, Herbuht and his wives and their children, my two women, three cats and some score or so of horses. We live simply, we sometimes are confronted with savage beasts and, less often, even more savage men, and we fight when we must with no friendly swords to guard our backs. So think you well and long upon your decision, Gy Linsee, and do not give me your answer until we are riding back to the clan camps, the camps of Skaht and Linsee."

"Uncle Milo," said Gy, a bit hesitantly, "if . . . should I make up my mind to . . . you say that you have two women and that Bard Herbuht has two. Well, if I decide to go and if my chief and my father say that I may, then could . . . do you think I could wed a certain girl and take her with me . . . with us?"

Milo smiled. "Gy, if Karee Skaht will have you— and I think she most assuredly will whenever you screw up the courage to ask her, and maybe even if you don't, for she seems a strong-willed little baggage—then Herbuht and I and our ladies would be most happy to welcome a brace of young newlyweds to our jolly little entourage."

"If I do go with you, Uncle Milo," said Gy, "will . . . would you perhaps tell me of your life before the Great Dyings and the terrible War of Fires? Will you tell me of how you and those long-dead other people lived in that distant time? Will you tell more of the earliest years of the Sacred Ancestors and more, too, of the time when my clan first became of the Kindred? Oh, Uncle Milo, there is so very, very much that I feel I must know."

"I know, son-Gy." Milo nodded. "You are indeed, just as I said, a very rare young man, and your driving curiosity, your biting hunger for knowledge, is a true indication of the rarity. Yes, young Gy Linsee, I shall tell you all of it, from as far back in my life as I have accurate memory, never you doubt it.

"Some of those things you and others have asked to hear, I will recount tomorrow night, around the fire, as I did earlier this night. Story-spinning around a fire after a strenuous day and a good meal breeds a comradeship, a togetherness among the listeners, I have found, and such is just what is needed to end this stupid, sanguineous spate of dueling and raiding and open warfare between two groups who should be living in brotherly harmony, one with the other.

"And you can be of no little help, you and the cats, broadbeaming a wordless, featureless soothingness, just as you have demonstrated yourself capable of doing."

Gy blushed. "I learned to do it in gentling captured warhorses, Uncle Milo."

"It works in just that same way on people, too, as you clearly have learned, Gy," said Milo. "And if ever two-legged creatures needed gentling, it is this fine flock of hot-blooded fighting cocks that strut and crow about this camp . . . though I think that all the pride plumes have been singed off one of the loudest of them, this night. Let us hope his painful example will prove efficacious for the rest of the pack, Skahts and Linsees alike.

"Now, son-Gy," he said as he stood up swiftly, "Sacred Sun does not delay rising for any man, so it were best that we and all of the others seek our blankets. There is much to do upon the morrow, are we to bring back a meaningful supply of jerked meat, smoked fish and dried tubers to the clans."

But before he himself sought sleep, Milo squatted by the feverish, moaning body of young Rahjuh Skaht. With the ease of long experience, he entered the burned boy's mind, the subconscious below the chaotic jumble that the conscious mind was become. He there effected the release of the natural narcotics to end the pain. It was all that he could do; the body just must heal of itself. He then trudged off, leaving the boy to the ministrations of the pairs of Skaht youngsters who would watch over the patient and refresh the wet compresses covering his burns throughout the night hours, watching and sleeping in relays. It was only the way of the Horseclans to care for ill or injured kinfolk; it was how the Kindred had so long survived in a hostile environment. But there would have been no survival of the Sacred Ancestors to breed other generations of survivors, had it not been for a man called Milo Moray.

About the Author

ROBERT ADAMS lives in Seminole County, Florida. Like the characters in his books, he is partial to fencing and fancy swordplay, hunting and riding, good food and drink. At one time Robert could be found slaving over a hot forge making a new sword or busily reconstructing a historically accurate military costume, but, unfortunately, he no longer has time for this as he's far too busy writing.